THE STONE HAWK

Other books by Gwen Moffat:

Snare
Hard Road West
Over the Sea to Death
Miss Pink at the End of the World
Space Below My Feet

THE STONE HAWK

Gwen Moffat

St. Martin's Press
New York

Library of Congress Cataloging-in-Publication Data

Moffat, Gwen.
        The stone hawk / Gwen Moffat.
            p.   cm.
        ISBN 0-312-03434-2
        I. Title.
    PR6063.04S7   1989
    823'.914—dc20   89-34938
                                                                       CIP

First published in Great Britain by Macmillan London Limited.

First U.S. Edition
10 9 8 7 6 5 4 3 2 1

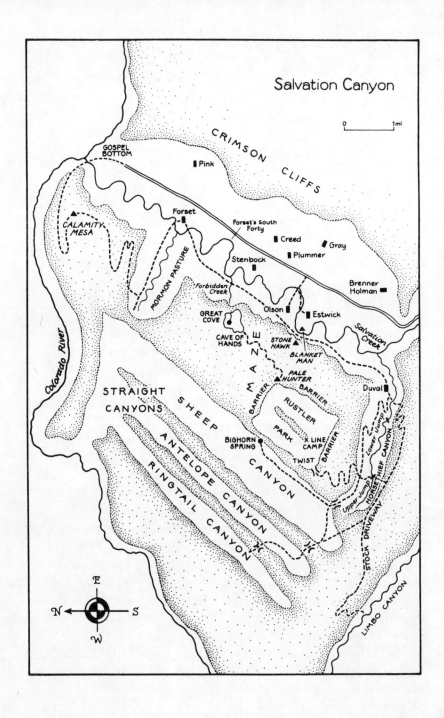

Salvation Canyon

Chapter 1

Where she stopped on the mountain road the traveller's vision was limited only by the curve of the earth – and most of the land looked flat. The ground was shadowless, without colour, dull under a low ceiling of cloud, but far to the west a pale lemon streak suggested that the sun was shining out there beyond the San Rafael Desert and the Dirty Devil canyons.

On closer inspection features could be distinguished that were not horizontal, or not completely. Long lines of cliffs might terminate in sharp prows, but these appeared diminutive above an expanse that could have been water reflecting the cloud. No forests were visible, no lakes or rivers, no roads.

The traveller walked back to her jeep and climbed into the driver's seat. As she reached for the ignition the world brightened, like a stage at the start of a performance.

The sun had dipped below the edge of the cloud and its light came flooding eastward. The land took on substance but, streaked and scalloped with shadows, it was even more alien than when it had been horizontal and dull. This was a plateau – but not a tableland; pink, black, orange, white: every rent and pockmark in that tortoiseshell landscape was a declivity. Canyon edges were delineated by the light and their depths were black as a black cat's fur. And then, turning her gaze to the long escarpments with their sharp prows, Melinda Pink (from the rural fastness of Cornwall, England) adjusted herself to the scale and decided, not without a thrill, that those headlands she had thought diminutive could be all of two thousand feet high.

She had not been prepared for this, but the lack of preparation had been deliberate. Miss Pink was a person who revelled in the initial impact of strange country. Years ago she had glanced at a coffee-table book on Utah's canyon country: a crazy red rock wilderness of sandstone pinnacles and reefs and plunging canyons. She had been in the Mojave Desert of California at the time and she had put the book down with the feeling that if she remembered those images, then one day she would gravitate to the reality: would walk those sandy washes, feel the rough red stone, see new birds and strange flowers.

She went to the Montana Rockies, returned to Cornwall, wrote gothic novels through wet raw winters and dismal summers – and she pined for the clear soft air of the West where you might see for a hundred miles. And when, in response to a nostalgic *cri de coeur*, she received a letter telling her of the writer's friend: a rancher in straitened circumstances who would be only too glad to rent her a cabin in a Utah canyon, those old images thrust themselves forward and she took the place unseen for a month.

Now, looking out over a space floored with stone that was nowhere level, in which, somewhere within view, must be her destination, she was awestruck. *That* was home for a month? What was it really like, outside the pages of a coffee-table book? She speculated and sighed and shook her head helplessly; there was only one way to find out. She switched on the ignition and eased down the gradient, her mind washing clear of surmise, the cool notes of a Mozart concerto a gentle and civilised comment on the elemental exuberance below.

With every hundred feet that she descended, the country dropped a veil, not coyly but with blatant carelessness. Miss Pink was reminded of other spires, other towers, of the Cioch (that great lizard's head on the Isle of Skye) all of which had remained unsuspected although in full view until one day the mist crept in behind the rock and threw the feature into prominence against its parent cliff. So her first impression of this land had been of a vast level; the second, of a dissected plateau. Now, with the slipping of the veils, the slow drift down the mountain became a descent into fantasy as buttes and mesas, spires and tusks and incredible cliffs rose like slow magic. From above she had seen only the crevasses; as she dropped a thousand feet, two thousand, she realised that, in the same way that crevasses are separated by *séracs*, so these canyons, many of them, were bounded by reefs some of which were so thin that holes had been eroded in the mighty walls.

She stopped and climbed down to stare upwards at one of these dizzy windows. At that moment a dark form detached itself from the lintel and plunged towards her. She lost sight of it against the rock but then, through the whisper of water close at hand, she heard a thin angry chattering and a scream. In the space above her head two shapes parted abruptly, one with a clumsy lurch, the other veering widely at high speed. A red-tailed hawk had come too close to the peregrine's eyrie.

She drove on silently. In the face of this land and all its promise – peregrines too – Mozart would be gilding the lily.

Miss Pink did not look the kind of person who used music as background. Her eyes, behind the latest in designer spectacles, were extremely sharp (although she could assume a blank expression with ease). She looked like a solid, elderly lady, affluent – with her big jeep, the expertly layered grey hair, the man's Rolex on her wrist – the modern traveller in Explorer trousers with bellows pockets, and a mulberry polo shirt. On the maps covering the passenger seat was an old but serviceable straw hat.

The road was running down a canyon with a full creek in the bottom, the banks lined with cottonwoods. The cloud cover was disintegrating and as she came round a corner and emerged from the trees she was blinded by the sun. But now, as the road continued to descend, the shadows lengthened, the sunlight climbed a wall to her right until suddenly she was in a defile so black under

9

both rock and trees that, panicking, she switched on her lights.

She crept round a tight bend, the rock stood back, the wooded creek sparkled away to the left, and she was looking down a wide canyon below ranks of golden spires that walled it on the west, their crenellated shadow reaching across pastures that glowed like emeralds, across clusters of trees where, a culminating fantasy, smoke climbed lazily from shingled roofs. She had reached Salvation Canyon.

She was surprised to feel relief. People lived in this wilderness; they built houses and worked the land, lit fires and cooked the evening meal. On her left cattle grazed in lush grass, on the right a notice was nailed to a post at the start of a track. JUNQUE AND WHAT-EVER, it announced shakily. Underneath and attached to the same post, a smooth piece of driftwood had been neatly lettered in black and red: PAINTINGS BY CREED.

At the end of the track was a low cabin. A small figure sat on the planks of the porch, immobile, watching the road. Miss Pink waved but got no response. She drove on, bound for the end of the road. When you reach the river, her landlord had said, you've gone too far. She wanted the Forset place and that was at the mouth of the second side canyon. The first was opposite the cabin with the notices: an obvious rift running back to a hinterland of jumbled cliffs. There was a ranch in the mouth of this canyon, dwarfed by shade trees. Then came the skyline of bristling spires in which she could see no break for miles.

She passed more cabins and, on the far side of the creek, a group of children on ponies stood in a field while one of their number tore round barrels, leaning inwards at an alarming angle. As she slowed, Miss Pink realised that some were waving. They were all waving. With so many children about, this was no dying community.

On her right, now, were three newish cabins, all big A-frames, set too close together to have much land attached. They looked like a sub-development. There was no land to speak of behind them either: steep rocky slopes running back

10

to end against the great escarpment that had walled the canyon all the way down the road. She passed more cows and a disproportionate number of horses. A stream entered the main creek on its far side and there was a cabin near the confluence but no canyon behind it, no break in the jagged wall. There were white goats in a paddock where a figure in a long skirt stared towards the road. Miss Pink waved again and the woman raised an arm uncertainly.

At length she saw what might be a break in the fretted reef: a wide side valley, still bounded by rock but running back far enough to be more than just an amphitheatre. The far wall was a mesa, flat-topped with a crumbling scarp above slopes that were dotted with juniper and stunted pinyon pines. Below the mesa was a cluster of ancient cottonwoods, a group of buildings and the inevitable corrals. A placard stood beside the ranch gate: a faded painting of a red and white bull below a caption: FORSET HEREFORDS. She turned in under the high cross-bar.

The house was set back a few hundred yards from the road: a structure of ageing wood in which could just be distinguished an original cabin. Other log rooms had been added at diverging angles, each with its shingled roof. A yellow Labrador stood on the porch and barked at the approaching jeep. A screen door opened and a large, thickset man clumped across the boards to welcome her.

Her first impression of John Forset was of familiarity. The thinning hair was cut as short as that of an old-fashioned military man, and he affected a small clipped moustache. He wore a mud-coloured shirt, a yellow cardigan with a hole in one elbow, and khaki slacks. Only the high-heeled riding boots marred the image of an English country gentleman caught before he had had a chance to change for dinner. She recalled that her friend had said he had served in England during the War.

She was ushered through an interior so dim that she was aware only of a passage between objects. She blundered against the dog. 'Allow me to go first,' Forset said. 'Get on, dog! This,' he explained, 'is the original cabin. We

11

just use it for junk. Should be cleared out and most of it burned.'

A large, light room showed through a doorway. Miss Pink stepped over its uneven sill and gasped in astonishment. She had a sense of large pieces of solid furniture but her eyes were drawn immediately to the view. One wall was mostly glass, and she looked diagonally across the shadowy valley to the regiment of pinnacles, their burnished summits presented like lances. She walked forward, entranced, and saw, through a second window at the side of the room, that the red escarpment to the east was quietly smouldering.

She became aware of silence and turned to find her host observing her almost smugly. 'I like watching people's reactions,' he said. 'I'll never regret the cost of that window – although I might have second thoughts if it shattered in an earth tremor. What would you like to drink?'

'A dry sherry,' she murmured absently, turning back as if mesmerised. 'And they complement each other,' she went on: 'the golden towers and the long red wall.'

'The Crimson Cliffs. Will California *fino* be acceptable?'

She smiled acceptance, reflecting that circumstances were conspiring to enchant her.

'And you will eat with us,' he said, as if reading her mind.

She remembered her manners then and relinquished the spectacle, but he placed her in a chair that turned her to the window again. He walked to a doorway and gave a shout. She heard a clatter of dishes and realised that part of the pleasure of this unique welcome had been a good smell: of sautéed meat and hot wine.

A woman appeared: red-faced from a stove but sparkling, a small, buxom person with damp curling hair, wearing jeans and an apron patterned with sunflowers.

'The chef,' Forset said, beaming, 'Dolly Creed. Our guest is dying for her sherry, Doll, and too polite to start. Drink up, girl, and get back to your kitchen.'

Miss Pink saw that he was embarrassed. Dolly Creed wiped a palm on her jeans and shook hands firmly. 'Did you have a good trip?' she asked, taking a glass from Forset,

12

sitting down and giving all her attention to the visitor.

'Creed?' Miss Pink repeated, ' "Paintings by Creed"? Did I pass your house?'

'I'm Creed,' Dolly admitted cheerfully, 'but that was Myrtle Holman's cabin; she just sells my stuff. I live in one of the hideous A-frames you passed afterwards.'

'They were economical,' Forset put in coldly, 'and they're convenient.'

'If you go for that sort of thing,' Dolly countered. 'They clash with the environment. And they'll never blend in, because they're the wrong shape.'

'You could have had Weasel. Then short-term tenants like Miss Pink here could have rented a nice modern place.'

'There's no light at Weasel.'

'Weasel Cabin?' Miss Pink ventured.

'Creek,' Forset told her. 'It's the old Mormon place to us, but since all the older cabins are Mormon, we distinguish yours by its creek.' He sniffed. 'Do I smell burning?'

Dolly went out, carrying her glass. 'A fine artist,' he murmured when she was out of hearing. 'That's hers.' He gestured to the wall behind Miss Pink, who turned and then stood up, the better to observe a picture of pinnacles with, in the foreground, a dusty little path running through a meadow starred with flowers. It was pretty but too close to chocolate-box art for her taste.

'How did she get that glow of reflected light on the walls?' she asked.

'She takes photographs and paints from the prints. Very clever. These are all hers.'

He meant those that were not photographs of bulls and horses. She walked round the room pausing at Dolly's paintings, which were mostly of the local sandstone country, but there was one small view of a great canyon, cloud-filled, with just the suspicion of a distant rim and, off-centre, the tip of a butte. Far, far below, glinted a loop of water.

'That's the best,' she said firmly.

'It's her favourite too. She wouldn't sell it to me until

she needed a new saddle. Then she had to let it go.'

'She must make a good living.' Miss Pink was aware that western saddles cost a small fortune.

'She does, but so does Myrtle Holman, who takes a commission. Doll sells mostly in town. We don't get many tourists down here. It's a dead-end road, and dirt at that. City folk don't like driving on dirt roads. A few river-runners come up in summer but you're not going to buy pictures when you're going down the river, and they don't get as far as the Holman place anyway. Usually they reach here, see the "Private" notices and turn back to the boats. Leave us to ourselves; that's how we like it – except for invited guests, of course,' he added quickly.

'There must be a number of young couples living here. I saw lots of children.'

'Ah, you came past the Olson place. Jo and Erik have ten kids. Poor Jo. I don't mean the kids, but she was so unfortunate with her menfolk. They say women gravitate towards the same kind of husband each time. Erik is . . .' He trailed off and looked puzzled.

'Can I dish up?' Dolly asked from the doorway.

It was not until Miss Pink had pronounced judgement on the *boeuf Stroganoff* and an excellent burgundy that Dolly asked curiously: 'You were saying Erik Olson was – what?'

'Ah, yes. Olson.' Forset put down his glass and looked up the valley. 'Careless?' he ventured.

'Accident-prone,' Dolly suggested.

'No, that's not it either. He's thoughtless. He's the kind of guy will be talking to you, and he'd walk round the back of a kicker when the flies were biting and slap it on the rump to emphasise a point. All Jo's husbands were like that.' His gaze had returned to Miss Pink. 'The first was killed when he flew his plane into a mountain in cloud, the second got himself shot— '

'He shot himself,' Dolly said firmly.

'That implies something different. He was climbing through a fence and his gun was propped against the wire and it slipped and went off.'

14

After a moment Miss Pink said: 'So all the children have different fathers?'

'There are four from the first,' Dolly said, 'two from the second, and all the little ones are Olson's.'

'Where do they go to school?'

'They don't. At least, Jo's educated all of them. She used to be a teacher. Must have been a good one. All those kids are bright as paint, and they've got beautiful manners. Not like some,' Dolly added darkly.

'Now, now.' It was a warning from Forset. 'Don't be racist.'

'*What?* Oh, I see. I didn't mean Birdie; I was thinking of Shawn.'

'Shawn has a lot— ' Forset began, and stopped. Dolly and he turned suddenly to their plates.

'Jo teaches all the valley children?' Miss Pink asked brightly.

'They kind of go along to classes,' Dolly said slowly. Suddenly she seemed to get a grip on the conversation. 'Birdie is Indian,' she said firmly. 'A little Ute girl who was adopted by the Estwicks: Sam and Paula; they have the place across the creek from the Olsons. There was a Ute hand working at Wind Whistle – the upper ranch – about seven years back, wasn't it, John?'

'He was married,' Forset said. Dolly glanced at him. 'And they left,' she said. 'Poor people, you know? Paula – the Estwicks adopted the baby. They didn't have any children of their own.'

'I see.' Miss Pink was affable, knowing there was more to it than that, but it was not her business. She went on smoothly: 'But the teacher won't have twelve children in class all at the same time. Is that right? Twelve children in the valley?'

'If you include teens,' Forset said, 'but Jo's three eldest are working, but then they all work. Even the smallest can do jobs around the ranch – except the baby, of course.'

'Full employment.'

'You could say that. We may not all be earning, but everyone's doing something, wouldn't you say?' This was

15

addressed to Dolly who did not respond immediately but twirled her empty glass. Forset replenished their drinks. 'There are nine households,' Dolly said at length, as if she had been calculating: 'two ranches, three homesteads and the four cabins. Obviously the ranchers work: John, and the Duval brothers at Wind Whistle. Of the homesteaders, the Olsons have got a couple of cows and a few calves, not enough to keep that huge family, of course. Erik works for John.'

'Seasonally,' Forset put in. 'I don't employ a man full-time.'

'The same applies to the Estwicks,' Dolly went on. 'They've got only a hundred acres or so and a few steers. Paula could run that place with one hand behind her back. Sam Estwick works for the Duvals. They take people into the back country: pack trips, hunting in the fall, that kind of thing, so there's more work there than here on John's place.'

'They're younger than me,' Forset said, as if she had accused him of malingering, 'and they lease all that land in the Straight Canyons. They can afford to run several hundred head.'

'And then there's the four cabins,' Dolly said, ignoring him. 'Myrtle Holman and her daughter and grandson in the top one; of the A-frames, one's owned by a retired biologist who's writing a book on the natural history of the area, and the others are still owned by John. I rent one and the other's let to a multi-millionaire who's dreaming up a scheme to build a resort and marina at Gospel Bottom where Salvation runs into the river.'

Miss Pink was startled. 'But aren't there cataracts— '

'He's got that worked out. There's going to be another dam, of course, and the river will back up, flood this whole canyon – among others – right back to Horsethief, even *up* Horsethief, behind Wind Whistle.'

'Don't take any notice,' Forset said comfortably. 'She pretends Plummer's got a forked tail and horns. She makes it up as she goes along; it's an ongoing war between her and Plummer, adds spice to everyday living.'

16

'To Glen Plummer,' Dolly said, 'the environment is the air conditioning and central heating in his house – and the temperature of a pool. He can put a value on scenery only because that's the point of having picture windows, but scenery would command a far higher price if you could change it when you got bored with it.'

Miss Pink smiled and changed the subject. 'Who keeps goats?'

'I forgot the Stenbocks,' Dolly said. 'How could one forget Lois and Art?' She giggled. 'They're self-sufficient, or trying to be. Living off the land – with goats, can you imagine? Why is it organic people always have to keep goats? They make a desert of any place you tether them. Goats made the Sahara; did you know that?' Miss Pink nodded. 'Wait until you meet them,' Dolly went on. 'They're city folk, from Minneapolis. Grown daughters working in LA, they don't come home much, can't blame them for that. It's not just that Art and Lois are trying to be self-sufficient; they're so intense about it.'

'They're doing their best, Doll.'

'Of course.' She was contrite. 'Forget it. You'll have to judge people yourself as you meet them.' She stood up and started to clear the table, returning from the kitchen with a platter of English water biscuits and a small Stilton. 'We have them mailed to us,' Forset said, seeing Miss Pink's surprise, 'from a place in the English Midlands, what's it called?'

'Hartington,' Dolly supplied. 'I was taken over the factory once and I've had Stiltons sent to me ever since. I forgot the wine, John.'

He went out and came back with a dark bottle. After she'd tasted the contents Miss Pink sighed luxuriously and said: 'I never thought that I would end a dinner in Utah with a ripe Stilton and a venerable port.'

'All credit to the chef,' Forset said. 'She educated me, even in wines. I was a beer and bourbon man before I met this girl.'

'Not so much of the girl,' Dolly protested. 'I'm forty-three and I love it. But thank you for the compliments.

I think, if you enjoy food, then you enjoy preparing it and watching people eat it. And if you like good food you've got to complement it with the proper wine, otherwise it's like elegant clothes and tacky jewellery and your hair in a mess.'

They drank brandy with Turkish coffee while the afterglow faded, and then Miss Pink was escorted across the road to the cabin on Weasel Creek. As she stopped the jeep Forset came back asking for her bags. Behind him light streamed from an open door and two small windows as if from a cabin in a fairy tale.

Her cases were deposited in a room that was lined with pine, where a large bed stood with the sheet turned down over a patchwork quilt. She smelled lavender. Dolly stood in the doorway reminding her that they were going to ride tomorrow, assuring herself that the guest had everything she could conceivably need, promising a lovely morning and that she would be there at ten, saying goodnight. The light in the living-room was switched off, the outer door closed. She heard the truck drive away.

She sat on the bed and kicked off her shoes. Through an inner door there was a glimpse of white porcelain: not just a shower but a bath too. It might be an old cabin but it certainly wasn't primitive. She bathed and got into bed. The reading lamp was positioned correctly on the wall and on the bedside table was a set of Chandler novels, some Hillerman, P. D. James and Ruth Rendell. She was too tired to start a new book. She switched out the light. The room was pitch-black and the silence was profound. Then, from above the cabin, curiously resonant among the rocks, came the long hooting call of a great horned owl.

Chapter 2

'We have a small problem,' Dolly said, 'a small Ute problem.'

She stood at the cabin door, her back to the light. Miss Pink was drying her breakfast dishes. Dolly sounded casual, only a trifle put out. 'Birdie,' she went on, 'the Indian child, is missing. There's nothing to worry about – ' as Miss Pink looked concerned, ' – it's not the first time. The worst that can happen is she'll get off her pony and go to sleep and the pony will wander home. She's too small to walk far.'

'How old did you say she was?'

'Six.'

'You mean, she goes riding alone, in this country, at six years old?'

Dolly shrugged and looked round the cabin. 'I've brought lunch so you don't have to prepare anything. It's a gorgeous morning. We're not going to change our plans. Birdie will have gone up Horsethief Canyon and that's what I intended anyway, take you into Rustler Park. And Birdie will be headed that way. She did that last time.'

'Why, what's the attraction there?'

'There's an old cave, a ruin or something . . . This valley's full of Indian ruins. I guess Birdie's old enough to start look-ing for her roots.'

'Aren't her people worried?'

'Paula's always worried about Birdie, and Sam's in trouble because he's supposed to keep the child's pony in a locked paddock. The idea is she's too small to go off without the pony. And then she goes and jumps it over the rails – bare-back! I ask you: she's not going to come to much harm on the trail if she can do that, is she? Sam will be thinking

19

that way too, so I guess he's not bothered. Come on, let's go before the sun gets too hot. You drive to John's place; I'll follow.'

A handsome, mouse-coloured horse was tied to a rail outside the cabin. Dolly handed Miss Pink a pair of saddle bags. 'Put anything you want to take in those. Bring binoculars, if you have any; they could come in useful.'

'I always carry them,' Miss Pink said shortly, not liking this, thinking that the situation held sinister undertones, trying to stifle the thought with the reminder that a child who could jump her pony over rails bareback could not be incompetent on a trail.

At the ranch they found Forset saddling a muscular yellow horse which eyed the newcomers with interest. Miss Pink tied her bags behind the saddle and adjusted the leathers. She looked round and spied a section of tree trunk, solid as a rock. Using it as a mounting block, she climbed on, settled herself and started to walk the yellow horse in a circle. Dolly and Forset watched critically.

'He may do a little buck on the grass,' Forset said. 'He hasn't been out recently. Just keep his head up and that'll be the end of it.' He turned to Dolly. 'You're going into Rustler. Then what?'

'Either Rustler or the Straight Canyons, I thought, but if we see Birdie's tracks going up Horsethief into the Straights, we should go that way. We can go up Rustler another time.'

'She won't go into the Straights. She knows it's in the Barrier.'

'Is it?'

'It has to be. Someone would have found it otherwise. Never mind Birdie; I want to know where you're going to be.'

Dolly sighed. 'There are two of us, John. Tell you what we'll do: at the Y below the Twist, we'll build a cairn in the middle of whichever trail we take. How's that?'

'All right as far as it goes, but if you go up Horsethief and into the Straight Canyons, how are we to know which one of those you're in?'

'You mean, if we don't come back by dark? If we'd *both* fallen under our horses and been so seriously injured neither of us could get back? Come *on*, John; you're as bad as Paula Estwick.'

She was mounted now. He looked up at her dumbly: an elderly greying man wearing his heart on his sleeve, forgetting that a third person was present. Miss Pink turned her horse and started to walk away. Suddenly Dolly was beside her and both horses sprang towards open ground. For a moment the women had their hands full. Miss Pink's mount sketched a buck before she had him under control and then they turned and waved to Forset who was watching anxiously.

'He's getting senile,' Dolly said. 'He thinks I'm one of his daughters.' She grinned tightly as her gelding danced. 'Maybe he's worried about old Yaller there.'

Not as much as I am, Miss Pink thought. She had no time for the view, not even to notice their direction. She was waiting for more bucks. They came to the creek and plunged through, scattering diamonds in the sun. Their jeans were drenched. As they came up the far bank Dolly shouted: 'O.K.?' on a rising inflection which Miss Pink recognised with a sinking heart. 'Keep behind me,' Dolly shouted, and they were off.

The yellow horse moved like a dream and in a moment her qualms evaporated and she was enjoying herself, remembering just in time to stay on the trail where the mousey rump ahead effectively blocked Yaller's attempts to break into a gallop. Dolly was going at the brisk lope of a range rider and Miss Pink admired the control she had over her mount when another animal was pounding on its heels.

After half a mile they came to a loop of the creek and slowed to a walk. The trail ran along the bank, in places eroded by flash floods. Suddenly the ground crumbled under the yellow horse and his hind quarters went down. Scrambling with his front feet he clawed his way back like a dog, emerged on the bank and tried to take off as he felt the grass under his feet.

21

'Hold him,' Dolly called – softly so as not to exacerbate matters.

Miss Pink did so. Restrained on the spot, the yellow bucked, bucked higher, his rider clutching the horn. Then Dolly walked her horse deliberately past his nose and he fell into place behind, mild as a lamb.

'Now we can settle down,' Dolly said over her shoulder. 'How do you like him?'

'He's great fun,' Miss Pink said. 'Smooth as silk – most of the time. But an appalling name – Yaller.'

Dolly dropped back and walked beside her. 'John is devoid of imagination. This one's Mouse.'

'I thought that was your horse.'

'John gave it to me.' Miss Pink was silent. 'You might have noticed,' Dolly said delicately, 'that John's taken a shine to me. His wife died years ago, and his girls live in the East and he's lonely.'

'He's also in love.'

'Is it all that noticeable?'

'Perhaps I'm more observant than most people.'

'Yes, well— ' Dolly was defiant, as if the question had been asked. 'I'm not going to marry him. I value my independence.'

'We all do.'

Dolly shot her a glance. 'You saw how protective he was. I couldn't stand that. At the cabin I can stay out all night, visit with friends in Grand Junction, wherever. How could I lead that kind of life with John? Old men are terribly possessive. I like things as they are. I've got my horse and my home and a studio; I've got enough money for good food and nice clothes and pay the vet's bills, and I've got my freedom. What more could I want?'

'You never married?'

'Ladies like me don't marry; they have relationships.'

'And children. You never wanted them?'

'No, I didn't.' She turned innocent eyes on her companion. 'And you? You never married?'

'*Touché!*' Miss Pink smiled. After a moment she said:

22

'I'm not all that different from you; I write romantic novels where you paint, and perhaps there were fewer – relationships – but, I agree, one does cherish one's independence. Of course, being able to earn a comfortable living puts one in a position to choose.'

'A lot of women marry just to be supported. They're kept women.'

'An old concept.'

'It's true, though.'

Conversation lapsed. They had come to another loop of the creek which meandered all the way down this level section of the valley. Now they were approaching that side stream which Miss Pink had noticed last night, and across from the confluence stood the cabin with the goats that belonged to the organic Stenbocks. Miss Pink looked right, up the course of the tributary, and saw rock rising in massive benches to a shadowy cliff that must be showing a false summit, for its crown of spires was hidden from this point; they were too close underneath. About a hundred feet above them, above a black stain on the slickrock, the cliff was gouged: scooped out like an enormous cove in a sea coast. The walls of this cove, what they could see of them, were several hundred feet in height and overhung gently.

'What an intimidating place,' Miss Pink observed. 'Can you get into it?'

'Climbers might, with ropes, but I wouldn't advise it. There must be a spring, you can see the tops of trees, and this stream has to come from there. It will go underground for a way. The black stain down the rock is just a bit of seepage. But a spring means rodents, so that big bay will be crawling with snakes. Why are you interested?'

'It's fascinating to think that we're looking at a place where no one's ever been.'

'I doubt that. The Ancient Ones will have been in there. They've been everywhere. A lot of their ruins are inaccessible without ropes. The Indians used ladders to reach them.'

23

'You mean the Anasazi Indians, like the ones who built the cliff houses at Mesa Verde?'

'All over the South-West. Mesa Verde, places like that, are just the best examples. The people who lived here weren't nearly so sophisticated. Their art is good, though. Superb sometimes.'

They stared up at the impending walls. 'What is Birdie looking for?' Miss Pink asked quietly.

'It's just a legend. She's heard a rumour, that's all. You know how kids embroider things.'

'A ruin? Or something else?'

'There's a story about a cave. Of course there are caves all over the place. Look around you.' She was right; the cliff walls were pocked with caves, large and small.

'But this cave is special,' Miss Pink pressed.

'They call it the Cave of Hands. It's only a story.'

'What is the story? Real hands?'

'Oh no! Nothing like that. Just a cave with handprints, you know? They often signed their pictures with a handprint, the Ancient Ones, but this cave is just hands, nothing else. I mean, that's the story.'

'And no one knows where it is?'

Dolly turned to the trail. Miss Pink fell in beside her. 'It's like the stories about lost gold mines,' the younger woman continued. 'Someone found the Cave of Hands and told someone else where it was and then died. The second man went to find it and never came back so no one knows where he went. That kind of thing. You ask me, someone made the whole thing up to attract the tourists except the tourists never caught on. I don't believe the place exists at all.'

'John said it had to be in the Barrier.'

'Because everyone's been all the other places: Mormons, miners, ranchers. And no one's been in the Barrier or the Maze except probably Indians. So that's where Birdie thinks it is. I suppose the kids think it's there and she got it from them. But she's living in a fantasy world! She's only a little girl; she can't *reason*.' Dolly's voice dropped. 'She's not a secure child,' she muttered. 'She can't be, with her background. I suppose it's not long since she understood Sam wasn't her father, that she's Indian. And she's looking for traces of other Indians. It's ironical when you think about it. It's the Pueblo Indians down south in New Mexico that have the Anasazi blood, not Utes. If the cave exists someone ought to take her there, let her see it. She might be quieter then.'

Miss Pink made to respond but Mouse broke into a trot and Yaller followed. As they advanced, the rock behind quickly blocked the cove from view. The formations above them now were different from the elongated spires; these were squat towers in shades of red with pale caps like solidified dough. In places the caps overhung as if they had been petrified the moment before they started to drip. Here and there an outer tower had subsided, like a high-rise on poor foundations, and the cap had slid off to shatter at its foot.

The pastures ended at a point where the towers came close to the creek. The trail was overhung with cottonwoods. They could hear children calling in the distance. They were passing the Olson place. On the other side of the water the bank rose high and rocky. A butte appeared with a strange triangular rock on its summit.

'That's the Blanket Man,' Dolly said.

'Do all the features have names?'

'The unusual ones. I named some of them. Look, that's the Stone Hawk.'

Above on their right, aloof from the towers, was a grey image like a perched bird, its head sunk between its shoulders as if it were watching the valley. It must have been fifty feet high.

'I didn't notice that last night,' Miss Pink said.

'It wouldn't show up against the cliff. You see it best from Rustler. If you stand under a column called the Pale Hunter at the side of Rustler, and you get Stone Hawk in line with the Blanket Man, there's supposed to be a way down to the valley through the Maze. Rustler's just above us: a mile away perhaps, but there's the Barrier and the Maze between. The

25

Barrier is the needles and the Maze is these old towers. When you go round, as we're going to do, it's nine or ten miles to Rustler.'

'And is there a short-cut?'

'John says there isn't, and he was born here. Or if there is, no one's found it, so far as I know. It's played down anyway; no one wants the kids in the Maze, looking for a way through and getting lost. I've flown over it; John gave me a trip in a plane my last birthday. It's terrifying to look down on. The towers have what are called joints all the way round them but they're not always continuous. If you tried to get through you wouldn't be able to walk in a straight line for more than a few yards.'

'In mazes you can leave threads, string . . . You could build cairns.'

'It's not that simple. Rustler's a few hundred feet higher than this point, so any route would be descending. Imagine jumping down to a lower level and then finding you've got to retreat because the next jump is about fifty feet – and then finding you can't get back. Or you've forgotten the way back. Or someone's kicked away a cairn by accident!' Dolly shuddered.

'But no one has been lost there – that you know of?' Miss Pink's smile was replaced by an expression of horror.

Dolly shook her head vehemently. 'Birdie would never leave her pony – anyway, she's got enough Indian blood in her not to attempt to get through the Maze on foot. When they found her the other times – once in Rustler, asleep under a juniper with the pony tied to the tree, the other time in the Twist – each time they heard the pony first. It neighed. Let's move on. We're too close to the Estwicks' place and I can't stand Paula in hysterics. Or anyone else for that matter.'

After a mile or so the trees ended at a wire gate and beyond was a flowery meadow between the rocks and the creek. Dolly closed the gate and they cantered towards buildings in the distance. At the far end of the meadow the Duval brothers were trying to cut a bull out of a herd. Dolly went to help them and, with the approach of another rider, the bull turned meekly into a lane that ended in a corral.

The Duval men did not look like brothers. Bob was dark and intense and he regarded Miss Pink seriously, even critically – or was he, she wondered, resenting the interruption and thinking of whatever they were about to do with the bull? Alex Duval, on the other hand, was a big bluff man, a jolly fellow, beaming at her, crushing her fingers in a powerful grip, naïvely expressing his surprise that an English lady should be mounted on old Yaller: 'You didn't come off when he bucked?'

Nothing was said of Birdie until Dolly remarked that they were probably going into Rustler, to see if the child were at the old line camp.

'That's where she'll be,' Alex said, smiling: 'Fast asleep in the shade with that ol' pony standing guard; there or somewheres in the Twist.'

His brother threw him a glance, then studied the bull in the corral. 'She'll come to no harm,' he said tightly. 'Nothing to hurt her in the valley.'

'No one'd hurt a little girl,' Alex said, varying it slightly, his smile fading to be replaced by a frown.

'She'll be thirsty.' Bob's tone was suddenly loud, his eyes jumping in the shadow of his hat brim. 'She'll be wanting home. We won't keep you.'

'That was rather a curt dismissal,' Miss Pink said as they rode away.

'Bob's like that.' Dolly was casual. 'Terribly intense about everything. And of course: two ladies interrupting men at work – with a bull!' She hooted with laughter.

'They're very different. You'd never take them for brothers.'

'You think not? Bob's the elder, and Alex is a bit – naïve. Not very worldly, you know? I think he's illiterate, so that could imply he's simple – but harmless. He wouldn't hurt a fly.'

'That was my impression.'

Beyond Wind Whistle ranch they left the main valley and

turned up that canyon, called Horsethief, which Miss Pink had noticed the previous evening. 'This is magnificent,' she announced with sudden fervour. 'To be entering a canyon which a few hours ago represented the Unknown. I feel like a pioneer.'

Dolly was closing the last gate. Miss Pink held Mouse's reins and stared up the swath of cottonwoods in the bottom to the rock that formed the headwall. Dolly relieved her of the reins. 'This is where it gets a bit hairy,' she said. 'Keep in my track. I never asked: you don't mind heights?'

The canyon was steep-sided and, upstream of the gate, water fell over a band of rock – the Lower Jump, Dolly called it. The trail doubled back on itself. After a long gradient there was a hairpin and the path continued, gently rising, graded for horses, the exposure increasing.

Miss Pink was disturbed when she thought of Birdie above these drops. She found herself thinking: but the child is an Indian; she may have some ingrained sense of danger like an animal. She shook her head. 'Do you see any tracks?' she called, herself seeing only trampled dust.

'There's a pony ahead of us,' Dolly shouted. 'The Duvals have been up here recently, or someone, but the small prints are the latest.' She rounded a couple of hairpins, gave Yaller room to complete the top turn, and stopped for a breather. They studied the slopes ahead.

'Do we go up that rock?' Miss Pink was trying to sound casual.

'It's all right, the horses are used to it. That's where the trail splits: at the slickrock above the Upper Jump. You take a right and go through the Twist into Rustler Park, or continue up Horsethief and out into the Straight Canyons. Why, there's someone coming down the slickrock.'

'Birdie?'

'No, her pony's a pinto and this is dull. It must be Sarah Gray. She rides a blue roan.' She fumbled in her saddle bags and produced a pair of binoculars. 'It is Sarah,' she said, focusing. 'She must have gone up ahead of Birdie.'

'Could these prints be hers?'

'No, her horse is too big. This is Jerome Gray's girl, the retired biologist I told you is writing a book. Sarah's seventeen and very laid-back. Jerome must have been quite old when she was born; that could explain it: elderly parents. Sarah's almost too cool; she was grown up already when she was a teenager. Like Birdie . . . Now why did I say that?' She looked up the canyon and thought about it. 'They're not a bit alike. Birdie's impulsive – but the child's taken a shine to Sarah. There's the parentage: Birdie's – and Frankie is Sarah's stepmother. Her own mother died when she was quite small so Frankie raised her. They hit it off, though; you'll see for yourself.' She started to move then checked. 'Funny thing,' she went on. 'We're not ordinary folk in this canyon, and you'd expect sparks to fly more than they do.' She grinned and Mouse moved up the trail. Miss Pink caught something about 'the Olsons'.

'What was that?'

'I said maybe the Olsons keep us sane. They're normal.'

'Who isn't?'

But this was too sharp a question for such a lovely day. Dolly interpreted it as rhetorical and made no response.

The girl on the blue roan was waiting for them below the slickrock, horse and rider immobile against the shining sky, the abyss plunging beneath them. Statuesque and watchful, they fitted their environment, even their colours blending with the rock: the horse's grey coat, the girl's faded shirt and jeans, her drab hat. She was slim and tanned with long russet hair. Pale eyes were shadowed by the hat brim. There were bulky packs behind her saddle.

'No sign of her?' Dolly asked, and made the introductions.

Sarah smiled and said: 'No sign of who?'

'Birdie. She's gone again. Disappeared this morning. Where were you?'

'I've been in Ringtail for two days trying to get pictures of sheep for Dad's book. You're going to Rustler?'

'If you were in the Straights and saw no sign of her, then she has to be in Rustler. Her tracks are here. You've overlaid them now but we were following them to this point.'

29

'Right. I'll come with you.' The roan turned neatly and they fell in behind, the girl automatically assuming the lead.

The trail ran into bedrock and forked at a large cairn. They took the right fork which started to climb and now the way was marked by the rudimentary cairns which hikers call ducks: one stone placed on another at salient points. The rock was soft and rough and the only sounds were the muffled clop of hoofs and the creak of leather. They began to feel the power of the sun reflected by rock which had been exposed to the heat since early morning.

They came out on a brow and saw the next duck on a lip above. They were mounting a system of rounded terraces that rose, one above the other, to a rank of pinnacles in which there seemed to be no break large enough for a cat to slip through. The terraces, although horizontal, were not always continuous. Some ended abruptly above a precipice, others were blocked by the outer edge of buttresses. In places the riders would approach a short but impassable wall to swing sideways along its foot until a line of weakness allowed them to turn the obstacle. They scrambled up shallow gullies and climbed bulges with a screech of nails. They did not dismount but they rode with loose reins, allowing the horses to pick their way. The ledges were not bare. Juniper and small pinyons had established themselves in cracks, and here and there a clump of Indian paintbrush flamed scarlet against the sun.

They reached the fissured wall that formed the base of the pinnacles, and turned left along a platform where patches of sand were marked by tracks. 'You see?' Dolly called to Sarah, and the girl nodded. 'She came by here,' she called back. Miss Pink noticed that she did not say: 'She is here.'

'Is there no other way out?' she asked.

Sarah turned to regard her levelly but it was Dolly who answered: 'No, no other way.'

Deep chimneys rose above them, inviting for a distance: pleasant back-and-foot work for old climbers, and then, fifty feet up, the way would be blocked by a monstrous wedged boulder. Or a rough crack, with splendid holds, fined down to a line which, defying convention, would angle across a wall to a sheet of ochre rubbish like flaking plaster. This was one place where no one would ever want to climb, but a spectacular place for all that, and more so as one penetrated its mysteries.

Miss Pink had a sudden hawk's-eye vision of their party traversing this ledge under the titanic wall with its jagged skyline. The terrace was strewn with rock like breadcrumbs and the junipers were bonsai trees, the three riders dwarfed and all but lost under the rock. She was askance at their temerity in coming here. She heard a squeak and saw a chipmunk perched on a boulder, scolding them, its tail jerking spasmodically with every cry.

The chipmunk was not awed by the scale; the boundaries of its world were probably no further than it could see. Lulled by their steady progress, she reflected on her situation relative to that of a small rodent and concluded that she preferred to be human. She could, with application, reduce the scale to manageable proportions; the chipmunk was totally at the mercy of snake or buzzard: tangible dangers which could never be reduced. Prey animals must spend all their short lives listening for the soft passage of a body crossing sand, or the brush of wind through pinyons in the terrible penultimate moment before the strike.

A clump of cactus caught her eye, the blooms a spray of saffron cups. Yes, it was good to be human on a fine morning in Utah, with wars and violence far away, in another country.

Mouse turned at right angles; Sarah on the roan had vanished. Panic seized her. Where— ? Fallen? There was no commotion. Yaller swung round a rock as big as a cabin and a few yards away a grey rump was a pale blob in the gloom of a mighty portal. Still she could not see Sarah. The horses' hoofs were silent in the sand. Walls rose on either side, near enough to touch, sometimes both at the same time. She had to be careful not to scrape her knees. The shadowed rock

31

soared until it caught the sun blindingly. This, then, was the Twist. A canyon wren suddenly burst into song, the notes descending to a gurgle. Mouse turned again and she saw his muscles bunch. He heaved and was on a higher level. Dolly shouted something and Miss Pink grabbed the horn a moment before Yaller gave a lurching spring up a bank.

On they went, turning, twisting, until they came to a level defile still between walls but now they could see sunshine on ground ahead, and grass in a frieze against the light.

At first sight Rustler Park was a gently sloping meadow surrounded by rock, with an isolated reef towards the centre. On three sides were the pinnacles, on the fourth was a wall, not very high, perhaps a hundred feet, a wall that was a plinth for towers and buttes in fantastic shapes with the light showing through in the most unexpected places. 'Incredible!' breathed Miss Pink and turned with relief to ordinary grass, clumps of sage, wildflowers.

'We'll try the line camp,' Sarah said, and they moved out towards the reef.

It was a large park, over a mile square, and it was not at all level once they were crossing it. There were old water courses, quite deep, into which they disappeared for minutes at a time. A person might stay hidden in this place even if he were mounted. They climbed a bank and paused. Dolly swore softly. 'There's no pony about,' she said. 'It would have whinnied. And our horses are showing no interest.'

'It's hot,' Sarah pointed out. 'She'd be round the other side, in the shade.'

They came to the reef at a point where a corral had been built against the rock. The rails were broken now and a low cabin was in no better shape, sagging forlornly, its roof collapsed. Sarah looked down through the beams without dismounting. There was a sound from the interior; they all heard it: unmistakable, like a big grasshopper clattering as it took off. The roan jumped and tensed, its eyes glaring.

'Well, she wouldn't be there,' Dolly said grimly, 'but the pony's tracks are here.'

They moved towards the end of the reef. Miss Pink remarked that there must be rattlesnakes everywhere.

'There are,' Dolly assured her. 'Normally they get out of your way. It's only in enclosed places they're dangerous, when they're cornered. But no one in their senses would go in a ruin, particularly that one.'

'That snake's years old,' Sarah said conversationally. 'It was there when Dad brought me up here the first time. I was twelve then.'

'You can distinguish them?' Miss Pink asked in amazement.

'Of course. They're all marked differently.'

'She can't distinguish all of them,' Dolly said with a trace of irony. 'Just the ones she knows.'

Sarah said nothing. They came round the point of the reef and there was a screaming neigh from the shadows. The other horses nickered and snorted; there was a jangle of bits and, from Dolly: 'The little monkey!'

A small figure was sitting up in a drift of lupins, rubbing its eyes. Miss Pink saw an unexpectedly pale face above a grimy T-shirt with Mickey Mouse across the front. The skewbald pony, tied to a pinyon, had slewed to face them. It had turned wisely; had it gone in the opposite direction it would have trampled the child.

Sarah dismounted, took a flask from her saddle bag and knelt in front of Birdie, watching her drink. The child took rather longer over it than seemed necessary, even if she were dehydrated. At length she lowered the flask and regarded Sarah warily.

'O.K.?' the girl asked.

There was a nod and then: 'Is Jo mad at me?'

Sarah shrugged. '*I* don't go off without I tell someone where I'm going.'

'They wouldn't have let me go. He locked the gate. I'm going to kill 'im some day.'

Sarah raised her eyebrows. 'That's baby talk. It's what the littluns say.'

The eyes were defiant but the lower lip trembled. The

watchers were forgotten. 'Where's my dad?' Birdie asked.

'I don't know where my mom is either.' Sarah sounded eminently reasonable. 'I changed moms, same as you changed dads.'

'They didn't let me choose.'

For a moment Sarah's shoulders slumped, then she stood up and went to lift the child to her feet, but Birdie hurled herself into the big girl's arms, sobbing wildly. Dolly shook her head at Miss Pink who, for something to do, dismounted, untied the pinto, collected the roan's reins and stood waiting until the sobs subsided. Shaken by the occasional hiccup, Birdie stood red-faced and miserable while Sarah wiped her eyes. Suddenly she thrust the older girl away. 'You show me that cave,' she demanded. 'Now!'

'You have to wait.'

'I won't.'

'So what makes you different from everybody else?'

'The others know.'

'They know about it. They haven't seen it. You know the story: they're not old enough.'

'You're telling lies.'

'So you don't believe me. You break my heart. I'm going home.'

'Shit,' Birdie said, and kicked the sand. 'Didn't you bring no Snickers?'

Sarah looked round, her eyes eloquent. Dolly nodded grimly, reached behind her and produced a candy bar. She tossed it over. Birdie unwrapped it in silence, studying Miss Pink.

'Who's she?'

'A friend of Dolly's.'

'I don't like her.'

'And Indians are supposed to be polite folk,' Sarah said.

'She's on Forset's horse.'

'Not everyone has their own pony,' Miss Pink said. 'You gotta ride well enough first.'

Dolly stared at her. Birdie thought about this and asked: 'Did you come off him yet?'

34

'Not so far.'

'Huh. Maybe old Forset will sell him to you, offer him enough.'

Dolly snorted. 'Come on,' she muttered. 'We've done our bit, and we're certainly not needed here.'

'We're on our way,' Sarah said, acknowledging the break-up of the party, taking the reins from Miss Pink. 'Thanks for the candy.'

She lifted Birdie on to the pinto's back, mounted, and the two trotted away through the flowers. Dolly gave a deep sigh. 'Let's get out of here; this place gives me the creeps with that rattler round the corner. We'll go over and have lunch under the Pale Hunter.'

They moved across the park to a slim-waisted tower of light rock that stood on the boundary and marked what appeared to be a breach in the Barrier. They tied the horses in the shade and removed themselves to a distance in order to escape the flies. Dolly arranged lunch on napkins on the ground: chicken, rolls, the Stilton in foil but somewhat the worse for the heat, cans of beer, pears. 'So what did you think of that?' she asked, not looking at Miss Pink.

'Birdie? That she's not a full-blood.'

'That's not what I meant.' Miss Pink was silent. 'I wouldn't have thought you'd notice.' Dolly sat back on her heels and stared at the food like an anxious hostess. Miss Pink was not deceived.

'I'm uncertain whether you're being naïve or trying to cover up,' she said. It was Dolly's turn to be silent. 'Look,' Miss Pink went on, 'I'm proposing to stay here for a month, and on my first day you present me with a situation which is obvious to any person of normal intelligence. Here's a child who is only half-Indian, but since you maintain that she's wholly Ute then there's a secret which you – and no doubt others – know but don't discuss with strangers. Birdie, you say, is an Indian child adopted by the Estwicks.' Dolly was expressionless. 'It's not an uncommon situation,' Miss Pink went on. 'The husband has an affair and the wife agrees to adopt the child. Only with Birdie it's obvious because of her colour. Now do you want me to conform and put on blinkers? If so, I'll forget the whole thing, which will be easy because it's not my business – but don't insult me by inferring that I'm too dim to know when a child has a white parent.'

Dolly popped a can of beer and proffered it. 'Sorry. It was a last-ditch effort on my part to bluff it out. Neighbourhood loyalty and all that. You're right about her parentage, except that the one who, as you so delicately put it, "had an affair" wasn't Sam, but Paula. She's Birdie's real mother, and the father *was* a Ute working for the Duvals like I said last night. Paula and Sam married after Birdie was born. When Paula got pregnant she was living alone with her old dad and she went away for a year or so, came back with the baby and the usual story of marrying a guy and he ran off and left her with the kid. Said he had Mexican blood, which accounted for Birdie's dark colouring. I mean, it's darker than white, isn't it? When Paula's dad died she and Sam got married. He was just a cowhand and glad of a home and a woman to look after him. Am I being bitchy?'

'How much does Birdie know?'

'She has to know Sam's not her father. You heard her ask Sarah where her dad was. She'll have got the story from Jo's kids, but they wouldn't tease her about it. That tribe is so mixed up with all the different fathers that I don't expect the younger ones give it a thought that she's not Sam's child.'

'What's Birdie's mother like?'

'Big, plain – typical ranch wife. She was brought up Mormon by the old man and, although she lapsed after he died, she's hung on to some of the bad habits, like no coffee or drink, so Sam would have a hard time of it but that he visits with the neighbours, particularly . . . Well, he has to go out for his drink,' she ended lamely.

'Is Paula a good mother?'

'Sort of . . . No, she isn't, not the way you mean. She swings between being over-protective and permissive. She just doesn't know how to cope. But Birdie would be a difficult child for any woman to raise. She drives me up the wall.' Dolly thought about that and went on: 'Jo has a very loving relationship with her, though; you heard her ask if Jo was mad, not a word about her mother – and you saw how she was with Sarah. She can be sweet. I feel sorry for her although she's so damn rude – but, six years old, a half-breed and a bastard: poor little kid. Trouble with Paula is: she feels guilty; six years ago she committed a sin – perhaps the only one of its kind – and there's Birdie to remind her of it for the rest of her life. If she was Jo's baby it would be no different to her from having a baby by a Mexican or a Swede. And Sarah! She'd be fascinated to see how the cross-breeding'd turn out. Sarah's a scientist's daughter to the core. Me, if I was Birdie's mother, what I'd see is fine bones and bad manners, but Paula – hell, all she sees is sin.'

'How do the other children treat her?'

'Carefully. She behaves better when she's with them because, I suppose, in her mind Jo belongs to them. But she likes to be cuddled by Jo and then she'll stare hard at the others as if she's won a point. I've seen it happen, and the little Olsons look away and get very busy doing something else. It's obvious that she needs people to be demonstrative and if she can't get it from her own mom she'll come to the old earth mother. Jo mothers everyone, including her men.'

'How does Birdie relate to other Indians?'

'Now that's odd. You know we adopt the culture we grow up in, irrespective of parentage? Birdie behaves like an Anglo child as regards Indians. Jo takes the kids to town in the pick-up and Paula lets her take Birdie. She acts just like the others: ignores adult Indians and stares at their children coldly. But she's fascinated by the Anasazi, no doubt about that. And it's not surprising. Jo tells them stories about the Ancient Ones, and then there are all the ruins. It's the fashion to cultivate the first native Americans; they were too long ago to have any vices. And their houses are beautiful, the way they blend with the rock. It's difficult keeping the children out of them.'

'Why shouldn't – oh, rattlers.'

'That, and where they're built: in the weirdest places.'

Miss Pink looked down the slope below the Pale Hunter and into the stony wilderness they called the Maze.

'I was thinking more of cliffs,' Dolly said. 'They wouldn't build houses here; they had to be close to water. No one would ever live in the Maze.'

Miss Pink wiped her greasy fingers on a napkin and stood up. She took a few steps to the edge. 'You line the Stone Hawk with the Blanket Man?'

Dolly came and stood beside her. 'That's right; Blanket Man is almost hidden by the Hawk, but look at what's this side of them!'

The ground fell gradually towards the hunched stone bird, more distinctive from here than it had been from below. It must have been a mile away but in the translucent air it looked only a third of the distance. Immediately below them there was an earthy gully, and the towers started at the foot of it: squarish formations, perhaps eighty feet in height, each crowned by its thick white cap. 'So close,' Miss Pink murmured, 'it looks as if you might jump from one to the other.'

'I'm sure you can: downwards.'

'Let's go a little way: just a few yards. We'll build cairns.'

'You're a spunky lady.' Dolly was amused. 'O.K., but I'm not going more than a hundred yards. After that you're on your own.'

They gathered the remains of the picnic and stowed them in the saddle bags. They moved the horses until they were in deeper shade. Dolly picked up a dead branch and they started down, Miss Pink leading. 'Here,' Dolly said at the foot of the slope, 'take this.'

Miss Pink took the branch and hit the rock experimentally. 'They ought to hear us coming anyway,' she said loudly. 'Trouble is, down here, it's rather difficult for them to get out of our way. They might feel cornered.'

'We're going to go slow, building cairns.'

'There *is* a cairn.'

They stood and stared at a neat pyramid at the mouth of the slit between the first towers. It had not been visible from above. 'That's wild,' Dolly breathed.

They moved forward, forgetting the noise they should be making to drive the rattlesnakes away. They looked down at the cairn, they peered into the dark joint; their gaze travelled sideways. 'No!' Dolly gasped. A few yards away, at right angles, was a diminutive duck.

They walked to it, found it stood outside another joint at the end of which was a cairn in a ray of sunshine. They moved down the joint carefully, their eyes scarcely having time to adjust to the gloom before they came to the cairn and saw that it was at the intersection of three ways. The wall of the tower on the right overlapped. They looked, and saw the next cairn along the joint on the left.

'They're built where you turn,' Miss Pink said.

'Yes, but who built them? I never dreamed there was a trail here.'

'You didn't look.'

'I never came down the first slope. I've passed the Pale Hunter dozens of times but there's no way I'd come down into the Maze on foot – until today. I'd sooner have swum the Colorado.'

'But this trail is well marked.'

'There are no tracks. Didn't you notice? There's not one footprint ahead of us.'

'You're right. And the sand is wavy. No one's been here since the last rain. When was that?'

'The rain took the last of the snow. That would be in February. You're not going on . . . ' Miss Pink made to move forward.

'Why not? We've got the cairns to guide us back.'

'As long as – ' Dolly looked round and shivered, ' – as long as they're the only cairns.'

'You think there's more than one trail?'

'We don't know there *is* a trail. All we know is there are cairns. They don't have to be the only ones; we could follow the wrong line back.'

Miss Pink studied the other's face. 'We'll put a duck beside each cairn.'

They penetrated deeper into the Maze, placing ducks beside the cairns as they went. Above them the needles that surrounded the park sank below the level of the towers until they were lost from view. Now, but for the sun, they would not have known in which direction they were going. They worked their way along the bottom of the joints, occasionally sliding down a slope, sometimes forced to sidle between constricting walls. Despite the slit of sky overhead it was like being in the bowels of a stone earth. Sometimes the walls almost met above them. It was a relief to emerge in a kind of well, shadowed at the bottom but with lank grass at the foot of an ash sapling, its crown a sunlit diadem of spring foliage.

They looked round for the next cairn but there was none. There were four joints leading from the well: that by which they had come and three others. They scouted separately but neither went beyond a corner from which they could look back to the clearing. They found no more cairns. They returned to the ash tree.

'I can only think,' Dolly said, 'that someone started to explore and this is as far as he got.'

'Yes.' Miss Pink didn't sound convinced.

Dolly glanced at her and went on, with a touch of defiance: 'Well, that's that. We'd better get back. Can't leave the horses long in the sun.'

Miss Pink refrained from pointing out that the horses were in the shade. She looked thoughtfully at the entrance to a joint that Dolly was supposed to have explored. 'Wait a minute,' she said, moving away.

'You're on your own,' Dolly called, trying to sound amused but with a shrillness behind the words. Miss Pink smiled and nodded reassurance. Dolly's eyes were wide. 'Only a moment,' Miss Pink pleaded, and walked into the joint.

Halfway along, a passage went off to the left, the main joint continuing. She stooped, placed two stones with a slab on top and she had a Welsh cromlech: something that could not be confused with a marker placed by someone else. She walked up the side passage to discover, on the right, a sloping gully leading to a heap of jammed boulders. Behind the boulders there was a hole with the light showing through.

It was quite a large hole, big enough to allow the passage of an adult. She emerged on top of the boulders – which shifted a little under her weight but not alarmingly – and she saw that a few yards away the left wall leaned back, and there were pockets – natural holds – in the rock.

The angle was easy and the holds were nicely placed. She climbed about twenty feet to a crack which ran up to a pale band of rock. She had found a break in one of those dough-like caps that crowned the towers.

She stepped out on the summit and looked around, and was overwhelmed by panic. She did not know how long she was confused, probably only for a few moments. When she did manage to get a grip on herself she realised that the basic cause of this disorientation was the light, which was different: emanating from the wrong place; the sun was behind her when she had expected it to be on her right. Worse, she had thought to step out on the summit of the tower to find the Stone Hawk close at hand and the Crimson Cliffs visible on the other side of the valley. What she did see was a great wall looming above the tops of trees and no Stone Hawk, no Blanket Man, not one feature that she could recognise.

There were the towers, certainly: rising behind her and level on both sides. But in front, this side of the trees, there were only one or two towers, somewhat lower than the one on which she stood. She had come to the outer edge of the Maze and the reason why everything seemed to be askew, even the sun, was that she was facing not south-east but north-east. During their progress inside the labyrinth their general direction had changed by ninety degrees. If they had been observing the sun more carefully they would have realised it. Now she was not looking across the valley but down it, towards the Colorado, although that vista was obstructed by the looming wall. She was above the great cove, that wooded depression set high in the stone barrier that was supposed to be inaccessible except to the Anasazi.

The Anasazi. At one point, near the foot of the wall, she could see the start of an overhang, a soft bulge, shadowed but softly gleaming with reflected light. There seemed to be marks on the rock below the bulge but the edge of the next tower cut the view, even through binoculars.

She moved forward and looked down on the next summit which was only marginally lower and so close that a jump would be no more than two or three feet, but downwards. The move could not be reversed. Even if one could spring upwards, there was nothing on the smooth and convex cap to grab hold of, and below – she felt sick – below, the joint could be eighty feet deep. The top of the next tower was remarkably tempting but it was as bare as the one on which she stood. There was not even a scatter of stones to indicate that a cairn had once stood here.

'Melinda! For God's sake! Melinda! Miss *Pink!*' The shout climbed to a despairing shriek.

'I'm coming back. Right now!'

She knocked down her cromlech-cairn and met Dolly in the joint before the clearing, the woman's face pale in the gloom.

'I was terrified! Where were you?'

'Just looking. I'm ready to go back now.'

'You were up somewhere. I heard you.' Miss Pink raised an eyebrow. 'Well, that's how it sounded,' Dolly said sulkily. 'It must have been the echo. You shouldn't go off on your own. You don't know what could happen: sprain your ankle, anything. It's dangerous.'

'Who would be likely to come here?'

Dolly chose to misunderstand this. 'I don't mean people. I mean getting lost – or bitten. There are scorpions besides rattlers. What are you doing? Why are you knocking down the cairns?'

Miss Pink was not knocking them down but carefully dismantling the ducks which they had placed themselves.

'Because,' she said, 'if the Cave of Hands is in the Maze and someone is looking for it, but is keeping quiet, it's good manners not to advertise that we've been here.'

Dolly was astonished. 'You're thinking of Birdie?'

'No, she wouldn't build cairns. This is an adult, but secretive. It would be – neighbourly – to keep quiet, don't you think? We haven't been here; we just had a picnic in Rustler and rode out again.'

'You're suggesting someone thinks he'll make money out of it if he finds the cave, that there'll be a ruin or a tomb and artefacts: pots, weapons, that kind of stuff? Turquoise?'

Miss Pink had not been thinking along those lines. She would be hard put to it to say how her mind had been working. In eliminating the evidence of their presence she could be demonstrating a tidy nature rather than prudence. 'Our tracks are here all the same,' she pointed out.

'They'll be washed out in the first storm, and who cares anyway?' The earth slope appeared ahead, and tall flowers below the Pale Hunter. Dolly was suddenly cheerful now that they were back on familiar ground. 'He doesn't have to worry about anyone discovering his secret; there were no cairns after the little ash tree, unless you saw any when you wandered off on your own. Did you?'

Miss Pink stumbled and paused to catch her breath. She looked back into the Maze, blandly innocent under the sun, the Stone Hawk once again in line with Blanket Man. 'No,' she said. 'I didn't see anything familiar at all.'

Chapter 3

'What's this mark?' Dolly asked suspiciously, staring at a painting of Rainbow Bridge. 'It looks like soot.'

Myrtle Holman peered through her ornate spectacles. 'That's shadow, deep shade. I love this picture; it has an aura of magic about it.' Her tone changed. 'You should put a higher price on it. A hundred dollars would make it more valuable.'

Dolly licked a finger and touched the black smudge. 'It *is* soot.' She showed her dirty finger to Miss Pink who nodded agreement and turned away to encounter the stare of a small boy standing in the doorway of the room, watching them.

The Holman store (Junque and What-ever) was an extension of the main cabin. Light entered by way of one small window and the open door. It revealed shelves crammed with rusty gin traps and unidentifiable bits of cracked harness, broken pots, smeary glass bottles, and a rank of books with tired jackets. There were two chairs, their backs carved so elaborately that it was a safe bet raw edges would be revealed if the pieces were up-ended.

The largest piece of 'junque' was a glass display cabinet which served as a counter. Its shelves were cluttered with cheap silver and blue plastic jewellery simulating turquoise: belt buckles, bangles, rings and pendants, with polished pebbles and broken crystals and a few badly made kachina dolls. The legend on a belt buckle read: 'I will give up my gun when they pry my cold dead fingers from it' above a moulding of a smoking gun. 'That was my late husband's,' Myrtle had informed Miss Pink proudly, seeing the other's interest.

One side of the display cabinet had lost its glass which had been replaced by a sheet of plywood. A square of dusty black velvet lay on the flat surface.

Myrtle stepped back from the painting of Rainbow Bridge and tripped over to the counter on her spiked heels. She touched her lacquered blue rinse and said brightly: 'I forgot. I cleaned and everything had to be re-hung. Maybe I touched it then. Shawn will get a clean cloth, won't you, sweetie?'

The boy's eyes moved slowly from her to Dolly. Miss Pink's lips compressed. He was perhaps ten years old: a country boy, and yet that lack of expression was streetwise. 'Do you have television here?' she asked curiously. His gaze was transferred to her and now it was calculating; he was taking her measure. Without a word he turned and disappeared.

'We can't get T.V.,' Dolly said, 'but Maxine's got one of those sets that will take videos and she belongs to a library. Shawn is an addict, but I doubt he could be corrupted by anything he's likely to see, and that includes hard porn.' Her tone was casual, conversational. Miss Pink was astonished but Myrtle listened politely as if Dolly were discussing her painting. 'So what did your little grandson do?' she asked sweetly. 'Put his hand up the stove pipe and wipe it on my picture?'

Myrtle fingered the gold chains at her throat with scarlet talons. 'He's a child, Dolly— '

'Why do you let him in here?' Dolly started to lose control. 'Can't you keep the place locked? You wouldn't let a dog in, shit all over the floor, but that little bugger can— '

Shawn slipped in and placed a rag on the counter. He did not look at Dolly.

'You smeared my picture!' she said furiously.

'Now you don't know that,' Myrtle protested. 'He's only a little boy and you got no proof— '

'That's no little boy,' Dolly said with withering contempt.

'Is there anything else I can do for you right now?' Shawn asked his grandmother in a child's voice.

Myrtle looked flustered. 'Go ask Mommy if she needs any help with the supper.'

'I'll chop some sticks.' The tone was ingratiating but the expression remained blank.

'Such a helpful kid,' Dolly threw at his back as he left the room. 'I don't owe you anything, Myrtle.' The tone was loaded.

The old woman looked suddenly defeated. She must have been in her late seventies and was so thin as to appear anorexic. The sharp features and the big glasses with their ridiculous 'jewelled' chains, her fierce make-up and outrageous eyelashes made her look like some exotic bird in a fashionable fairy tale. She wore a peach-pink dress with coloured chiffon scarves, the waist cinched by a wide gold belt. Half a century ago she might have been in the chorus of a third-rate musical and she had never lost the art of presenting herself. Before the interested regard of Miss Pink she fidgeted self-consciously. Picking up the rag she made to approach the picture.

'No!' Dolly cried. 'Don't touch it! I'll clean it myself. I'd take it now but I'm riding. I'm going home and get my car and come straight back. I'll take all my stuff. We're square, you and me; well, not exactly,' she amended viciously.

Miss Pink looked away from Myrtle's stricken face and saw, through the doorway, the back view of Yaller and Mouse standing patiently at a rail. At that moment something occurred which for an instant she could not identify. There was a movement in the air, a quick sharp flash that seemed to terminate on Yaller's big rump, and she heard something fall to the ground. All hell broke loose. The horse squealed and kicked, Mouse lashed out in retaliation, Miss Pink plunged through the doorway and saw a screen door closing further along the porch. She strode down the boards and yanked the screen open. Behind her Dolly ran to the horses.

In the middle of the cabin a woman had caught the boy

and held him, his head pressed against her stomach. She was a startlingly beautiful woman, not thin like her mother, but fragile all the same. Her hair was piled carelessly on top of her head, lifted and caught there with Spanish combs. Flaxen tendrils had escaped to curl against the slender neck. She stared at the visitor with eyes the colour of violets, then smiled like an angel.

'You have to be Miss Pink. Hi!'

'He kicked me!' Shawn gasped. 'I only petted him and he kicked me!' He tried to rub his leg but his mother held him too tightly.

'I've told you,' she said patiently. 'You don't go near the big horses. They can be vicious. And you're too small for them to see you anyway; you could be a fly touching them. Poor little boy. But nothing's broken; you can stand properly. Show Mommy.'

'He can move fast too,' Miss Pink said grimly. 'He threw a stone at the horse and was in here like greased lightning.'

The lovely eyes narrowed. Maxine Brenner released her grip on her son and he moved carefully to one side, out of reach. His mother said gently: 'I don't think you see too well.'

Miss Pink became aware of a sweet cloying smell. 'I see well enough— ' she began.

Dolly's voice came from behind her. There was a hiss in it. 'What did he do, throw something? A rock?'

Shawn faded into the shadows like a mouse. His mother stepped back and closed a door. She swayed as she turned to face them and put a hand on the door jamb to steady herself. In that position she resembled a beautiful animal defending its young, but the eyes were vacuous. She was breathing hard and the sweet smell seemed to fill the room.

'Why don't we all sit down and have something to calm our nerves?' she asked, subsiding in a chair and staring at Dolly. 'I've never been able to understand this thing you have against kids,' she went on mildly. 'It's not natural in a woman, even middle-aged.'

47

Dolly muttered an obscenity and turned, then stopped short. 'You've got a customer,' she said.

A pick-up was turning in off the road. 'Sam needs a drink,' Dolly went on nastily. 'Has to be that; there's nothing else on offer.'

'Christ!' Maxine stared down the track. 'I can do without *him*.'

Sam Estwick was a tall, spare man in his late thirties. He had a brown hatchet face, cool eyes and a drooping moustache. He wore a greasy cap which he did not remove as he stepped into the cabin. He looked round as if he belonged there, nodding to the company, his eyes resting longer on Maxine.

'Oh, it's you,' she said rudely, focusing on him. 'This is a neighbour, Sam Estwick,' she told Miss Pink. 'He lives in the canyon and his wife won't let him drink so he comes here. And that makes me popular, as you might expect.'

'Listen, Sam.' Dolly was urgent, ignoring Maxine, as everyone was doing. 'Shawn threw a rock at the horses. Can't *you* do something?'

He shrugged. 'He's not my boy.'

Dolly opened her mouth then exhaled audibly. She tried again. 'So what would you do if it was your horse?'

'I'd beat him.' He grinned. 'It was your horse. You beat him.'

'Over my dead body,' Maxine said. She had found an empty glass and was staring at it vacantly. Now she waved it. 'Beer's in the fridge, Sam. Get me one while you're there. Sorry – Miss Pink, what'll you have?'

'Nothing for me, thank you.'

'We're on our way,' Dolly said. 'I'll be back shortly. He put soot on one of my paintings too,' she told Estwick, 'but you wouldn't be interested.'

Maxine was regarding her pointedly. 'You're letting yourself go, Dolly,' she said, as if she had given the matter considerable thought. 'You're putting on weight and your pants are too tight. How about we go to Denver, buy some new clothes, have our hair fixed nice – a facial perhaps?'

48

Dolly took a breath but Miss Pink was at her elbow. 'Let's go,' she urged, manoeuvring the younger woman towards the door. Estwick followed them out of the cabin. 'Is that kosher?' he asked. 'He really did throw a rock at the horses?'

Dolly glared at him. Miss Pink said: 'I saw it.'

'The bugger! He's been on at me to get him a pony for months because Birdie's got one and all the other kids ride. He can ride himself – but I'd trust him with a pony only as long as he was in my sights. He's never touched my animal, mind. He knows what would happen.'

'Over Maxine's dead body,' Dolly said sweetly.

'Yeah, well— ' He looked away. 'The kid needs a father.'

'You can't be that, Sam, but you might try acting as a substitute.'

'No one can control that kid. And the old lady encourages him. She suggested she'd buy him a pony if I found one cheap. He's got her eating out of his hand, his mother too for that matter. All I can say is: don't bring an animal up here – ' his lips stretched, ' – and if you come in a car, park where you can keep an eye on it.'

Miss Pink's jaw dropped. Dolly said: 'He means it. We got a budding psychopath on our hands.' They rode away. 'And small wonder,' she went on, when they were out of earshot, picking up the conversation where she had left it. 'What can you expect with an alcoholic for a mother, and that raddled old witch for a grandma? All the same, he's a runt: he should have been drowned at birth.'

Miss Pink said: 'Estwick didn't mention Birdie's coming back.'

'And the part we played in it. He might not know about us. Maybe Sarah didn't say; she hasn't got much time for Paula. Anyway, Sam's used to Birdie going off and he probably thinks it's a great joke, her jumping her pony out of the paddock. That makes Birdie one up on Paula.' Dolly glanced sideways at Miss Pink. 'I shouldn't think that's a smooth marriage; everything's public in a place like this, and Paula has to know where Sam is at the moment, and what he's doing. It won't make it any easier for her that. Maxine is bored to tears by Sam; more than that, she wants him out of her hair. Maxine's set her sights on Glen Plummer.'

'The millionaire?'

'Who else? Maxine's broke. I know she's lived on food stamps in the past and – tell you the truth – that's why I let Myrtle go on selling my paintings after I started selling well in town and didn't need Myrtle any longer. I felt sorry for them, you know? And Maxine hasn't always been mean. It's only lately she feels I'm treading on her toes and she's gotten real nasty. O.K., I know I'm overweight and my hair's in a mess but that's not the kind of thing you make remarks about in public. 'Course, she was drunk – and I guess I'd let Myrtle keep the pictures, but not with that little bastard fouling them.' Dolly's voice was rising.

'How are you treading on Maxine's toes?'

'Oh, that. Why, Glen Plummer comes over to my place now and then, but he's the kind of guy will visit with any woman who'll listen to him. He says he's bored with all that money and no goals. His wife died last year, of hepatitis, and he's not over it yet. Maxine's full of sympathy and since he likes a drink himself I'd never be surprised if they drove off to Vegas one weekend and came back married. She could manipulate him that far – but she gets mean when she remembers I might steal him from under her nose. As for Sam Estwick: he's in the way; she's afraid he'll drive Glen off.' She was thoughtful. 'I wonder if she sounds off in front of Shawn. If she did, that could be why he mussed up my picture. They're very close, those two – and that could account for a lot. She didn't wean him until he was three years old. At least, that's her story. I'm not sure Maxine hasn't a rather peculiar mind in addition to every-thing else.' Dolly's attention was not on the road and the horses loitered. Mouse tripped. She was alert immediately, glanced at her watch and said: 'I want those pictures where I know they're safe: in my house. Can we go faster? I must get the car and rescue them before young Shawn decides to

50

get his own back because I spoke my mind back there.'

But the ground was giving up the stored heat of the day and Miss Pink had no desire for speed. 'You go on at your own pace,' she said. 'I shall walk and enjoy being lazy.'

'Right. I'll see you at John's – or somewhere. There's no chance of missing each other in this canyon.'

She cantered ahead. Miss Pink checked Yaller's eagerness to follow suit and when they were ambling peaceably in the dust again she saw that they were overtaking Lois Stenbock and a large white goat. Observing Miss Pink's approach the woman waited: a thickset figure in a tiered skirt of mauve cotton and a green T-shirt with the head of a jaguar on the front. She looked harassed but not self-conscious, even when the goat jerked her backwards as it made a dive for some weeds.

'Quite a handful you have there,' Miss Pink said pleasantly. 'I'm John Forset's new tenant: Melinda Pink. I passed last evening.'

'I'm pleased to meet you,' Lois said. 'This animal dragged her tether and I've been chasing her up the road. Don't ever keep goats; they're untrainable, except they'll always come for food. Their milk's good, though; it's free of tuberculosis. Come down to the house and try some. My husband wants to meet you.'

Evidently Lois said what she thought and without following through, the implication here being that she had no interest in the visitor. Miss Pink's lips twitched with amusement as she dismounted to stroll slowly down the track. At the end a man was splitting logs in the yard. As they approached he took a mighty swing at a log, the blade glanced off, chipped the chopping block and there was a resounding clang of steel on stone. Miss Pink winced. The man was wearing sneakers and he could have chopped off half his foot.

Lois called: 'I've brought our new neighbour to see you, Art. Here, take Snowball, and drive the peg in real hard this time. You've got to use the sledge; she'll pull the

51

peg out if you just push it home with your hand. No, wait; say "Hello" first.'

Flustered, dropping the axe, wiping his hands down his jeans, he gave Miss Pink a limp handshake.

'I've been hoping you'd come by,' he told her, his eyes wide and ingenuous. He was a lanky man with thinning grey hair and a grizzled beard. carefully trimmed to a point.

'He's writing a book,' Lois said with a proprietorial air. 'He hopes you can give him some pointers.'

Miss Pink smiled, sighed inwardly, and went to tie Yaller to a rail. Stenbock pulled the goat round a corner and his wife took the visitor inside.

The cabin was dim but airy, screens on door and windows keeping insects at bay, and there were many of these on a warm afternoon. As her eyes became accustomed to the gloom Miss Pink made out a sofa covered with flouncy chintz and scattered with small, hard cushions, easy chairs to match, a large, solid table, scrubbed pale and with a bowl of eggs to one side, an oval stove in the centre of the room and another with a square surface in an alcove hung with copper pans and a battery of kitchen implements. The wooden walls were covered with posters: mountains, islands, a marsh with egrets, a baleful wolf, a sleepy puma licking its paw.

Lois came from an inner room carrying a jug and glasses. Miss Pink sat down and tasted the milk, which was cold and very good. She admired the posters, the stoves, and the cosiness of the cabin, and was given a run-down on the Mormons of Salvation Canyon who had settled here in the nineteenth century, having had such a strenuous time working their way through the country north of the river that, once across the Colorado, they decided to go no further. The intention had been to colonise the empty region further south, but by the time they reached what they were to call Gospel Bottom their cattle were failing, they had lost two mules drowned in the river crossing – and a woman went into labour on the south shore. They looked around and the men decided that they could not do better than settle here.

Stenbock came in with his hat full of eggs. 'That little

red chicken,' he told his wife. 'I found her nest under the old plough back of the apricot trees.' He was transferring the eggs to the bowl. Lois watched him absently. 'While they were exploring,' she went on, 'a boy rode up Calamity Mesa on a mule and it slipped and rolled down the slope, taking him with it. That's why it's called Calamity. Should you be mixing those eggs, Art? How long's she been using that nest?'

'Why, there's six eggs, so I guess around a week.' The couple regarded each other dubiously. Lois looked cross. 'Now they're all mixed up.'

'No, I know which were the new ones, but some of them will still be fresh.'

'Don't *touch* them, just leave them.' They argued, handling the eggs, the visitor forgotten.

Miss Pink sipped her milk. A tortoiseshell cat came to the screen door and mewed. Still talking, Stenbock opened the screen, closed it, opened it again for three kittens to come bouncing in like furry balls. He checked and stared through the mesh.

'Isn't that Forset's horse? Were you out with Dolly? I saw her go by.'

'We were looking for the little girl: Birdie.'

The Stenbocks exchanged glances. The woman's lips were compressed to a thin line but her husband looked curiously helpless.

'Has she turned up yet?' Lois asked tightly.

Miss Pink observed them with interest as she recounted the details of finding Birdie in Rustler Park. They listened with all expression carefully smoothed away. She found herself wanting to arouse some kind of reaction in them. 'It's a reflection on the atmosphere in this valley,' she began, realising that in choosing her words she was sounding pompous, 'or on the inhabitants, that no one seems the least concerned about the child's safety, except her mother, or so I'm told.' She paused.

'There's a lot of hysteria in this country about the safety of children,' Lois said.

'In urban areas it's justified.' Miss Pink was firm. 'Not hysteria, but concern. It's not out of place in many rural areas either.'

The man's eyes gleamed. Lois said, as if Miss Pink had not spoken, 'I don't hold with teaching children to distrust strangers. What kind of adults are they going to grow into? Frightened parents have paranoid children. I know Art doesn't agree with me on this but I raised our two girls without fear or prejudice and now they're afraid of nothing. And of nobody.'

Miss Pink glanced at Stenbock for his contribution but he appeared merely attentive as if he were listening to someone else's debate. She said: 'Fear is not a bad thing.'

'Respect,' Lois contradicted, 'not fear.'

'We could be skirting the same ground.' Miss Pink was equable. 'I still find it amazing that a small girl can run loose anywhere without people worrying even a little.'

'Except her mother,' Stenbock reminded her, adding, at last, his own criticism, indirect though it was: 'And our girls are now in Los Angeles, nursing. I'm only thankful they're sharing an apartment.' He stared at his wife who sniffed and said angrily: 'People are like animals; if you show fear they'll attack. Ruth and Katherine are more than capable— '

A telephone rang, the sound alien in this cabin with its woodstoves, the goat's milk, the eggs. Lois rose with a swirl of skirts and went to a sideboard.

'Why, it's for you,' she said in surprise, holding the receiver for the visitor: 'It's Frankie Gray,' she added in a stage whisper. 'She must have seen you come down the track.'

In a pleasant, cultured voice Frankie Gray introduced herself, mentioned the meeting with Sarah that morning, and asked Miss Pink to come and eat with them. Miss Pink, who held that a certain etiquette should attend dinner invitations – some advance warning – declined politely, citing the need to bathe and unpack. Mrs Gray, however, was persistent, and she was forced to compromise, agreeing to come up later, around nine.

She turned back to the room. Stenbock had disappeared, Lois was shaking eggs to see if they were addled. 'You must come and eat supper with us when you're settled,' she said pointedly. 'Art has to milk now and we won't keep you any longer if you're going up to the Grays. I'll be in town tomorrow and I'll go to the library, see if they've got any of your books.'

Miss Pink saw that she was being given to understand that a favour was being conferred on her: she warranted study. They went outside where Yaller, annoyed at the interruptions to the homeward journey, was pawing the dust.

'Would you hold his head?' Miss Pink asked.

Lois was suddenly diffident. 'What do I do?'

'Just grip the bridle firmly – here.'

Yaller rolled his eyes. 'I'll call Art,' the woman said, wanting nothing to do with it, turning with a flare of skirts under the horse's nose. Miss Pink muttered as he jumped and flattened his ears. There was nothing to do now but wait for Stenbock. He came and held the bridle.

'Are you going to be all right?' he asked anxiously as she mounted from the chopping block and before he released Yaller's head.

'I'm heavy enough to hold him down,' she responded grimly, and managed to do so over the last two miles to the Forset ranch, trotting at a good clip along the verge and sending the sandpipers screaming down the creek when the road came close to the water.

Chapter 4

From the outside the A-frame was raw and lacking in character. There was a balcony at half-height with breeze-block walls below and yellow pine above, except that most of the western wall that opened on the balcony was of glass. The steeply pitched roof lent a cramped air to the structure, dispelled as soon as one approached the main door, which was at the side. Now it could be seen that the accommodation was extensive, stretching back with rooms on two levels. The living-room boasted a mezzanine.

Sarah, in white bib overalls and a black shirt, had met her at the door and taken her to the main room. Fore-warned, remembering the lure of Forset's picture window, Miss Pink ignored the glass wall and concentrated on the people present.

Frankie Gray, despite a hospitable welcome, gave an impression of restraint. She was in her fifties, big-boned, with a solidity that suggested exercise and rigid dieting, nevertheless she was clearly not an outdoor type. In this harsh climate she had retained the delicate skin of a girl, and her fine silky hair had been layered and tinted by an expert. She wore a blouson and slacks in pale blue linen with a navy shirt. On anyone else it would have made the wearer appear massive but on Frankie it was chic.

Her husband, Jerome, was an old man but well preserved. He had the kind of pouchy mobile face, not uncommon among American academics, that is reminiscent of an elderly turtle. From behind large spectacles he observed Miss Pink as if she were a new species, while greeting her in a gravelly Eastern accent and with elaborate courtesy.

Dolly Creed, in designer denim, stood at a small bar with a stranger who turned out to be the tenant of the third A-frame: Glen Plummer. He was oddly proportioned. Basically a tall man, broad-shouldered with narrow flanks, he had developed a pendulous paunch which, far from making any effort to disguise, he accentuated with a close-fitting shirt decorated with mauve flowers on a white ground. It was hard to relate his taste in clothes with the astuteness required to make millions. No doubt, thought Miss Pink charitably, the old robber barons had their blind spots too.

Apart from his dress Plummer was intriguing if not prepossessing. His hair grew low on his forehead and had been blow-waved to the extent that he looked furry. He had heavy brows, spreading nostrils and a prognathous jaw, the whole effect being Neanderthal. When he informed Miss Pink that he had been looking forward to meeting her, his voice was surprisingly soft. Exchanging small-talk she looked past him at the view, which was similar to that from Forset's ranch except that from here they looked directly across the valley at the needles, now a silhouette against the light. Plummer was talking about a Hasselblad. Her gaze came back from the skyline to the long pool below the balcony where the needles were inverted in the water. Out of the corner of her eye she caught sight of the bulge of his stomach and was irritated.

'You use a Hasselblad, Mr Plummer?'

'I always buy the best.'

She could think of nothing to say to this and he seemed to find her silence disturbing. 'With a Leica,' he went on, 'you pay for the name.'

'And what is your field of interest?'

He was disconcerted. 'How do you mean?'

'In photography. You don't use a Hasselblad for snap-shots.'

'Oh, I don't know. I'm bored with photography now. It held my interest for a while but I can't remember the last time I used a camera. D'you know anyone wants to buy a Hasselblad? Same with everything: I buy a power boat for

57

racing, sell it next month. Skiing: go up to Tahoe, buy the complete outfit, never use it after a coupla weekends. My garages are full of toys: water skis, trail bikes, racing cars, you name it. I got no motivation.'

'What's your work?' Finesse was not called for with Mr Plummer.

He beamed. 'I buy and sell. I'm an entrepreneur. I promote, I finance, I get schemes off the ground, sometimes I manage them. Getting the right calibre of employee these days is impossible. The labour turnover in my companies you wouldn't believe.'

'Office staff?'

'Everyone. Senior executives, clerks, truckers, you train 'em . . . why, I had to learn myself how to operate the computers, then you train people to take over, soon as they're proficient they're off: working up the road for better wages than I'll pay 'em.'

'Where is your business located?'

'Which one?' He was enjoying himself. 'I've got so many I have to count them; let's see, there's the condo in Santa Fé but that should be sold this weekend. The consortium that was after it was holding out for us to knock off half a million. I'm not bothered. If they do back off, there are other people anxious enough to buy. It's a bargain at two million.'

'You're selling a condominium in Santa Fé for two million dollars?'

'It's in a select neighbourhood.'

'It's cheap,' Dolly said from behind Miss Pink. 'You're being taken for a ride.'

They started to argue. Frankie Gray approached and suggested they move out on the balcony to enjoy the evening. There she seated herself beside Miss Pink and said calmly: 'I was rescuing you. Dolly and Glen will now argue themselves hoarse over money. She wants to divert some of his millions towards the environment. So far she hasn't succeeded. I don't think Glen is greatly drawn to the environment somehow. And how are you liking Salvation Canyon?'

'Enchanting.' Miss Pink made to continue but stopped.

'You'd qualify that?'

'Not to retract. I wouldn't say that rattlesnakes and childish pranks are enchanting, but they have drama. I don't imagine life could ever be dull here.'

'Some people find it so.'

'But they don't live here. If you choose to stay— ' She faltered and looked away from her hostess's smart suit.

'I choose.' Frankie smiled, guessing what was in the other's mind. 'Because I live in the sticks is no reason to go about in an Indian skirt and sneakers. But I love the canyon; I wouldn't want to live anywhere else. I enjoy our trips; we like to go to London for a week or so in the fall, and sometimes I go with Jerome when he attends a conference in a place I'm fond of: Paris or Rome or Vienna, but I can't wait to get home. People *en masse* bore me very quickly.'

Sarah came and sat on the foot of her stepmother's *chaise longue*. 'Frankie's got no interests outside of salons and shows,' she said.

'Cooking is no interest?'

'I meant when you're abroad. You don't care for skiing and you're not interested in horses. When we go to another country,' Sarah told Miss Pink, 'we split up like atoms. My dad's at a conference, Frankie's shopping, I'm at Olympia or Badminton or St Moritz.'

'You go to conferences too,' Frankie said.

'I go to some of the lectures, those I can follow, but most of them are too specialised for me. I'm no academic.'

'Are you thinking of a career?' Miss Pink asked.

'It's a difficult question. At the moment I'm doing the illustrations for a book my father's writing on natural history. It's quite demanding. I was in the Straight Canyons for two days trying to get pictures of bighorn sheep. I used three rolls of film and I haven't got anything that's even passable.'

'Are you sure?' Frankie asked, concerned. 'What does Jerome think?'

'We haven't troubled to print any. We can see what they're like from the negatives. I'll just have to go back. It doesn't matter. I mentioned it to demonstrate the trials of an illustrator. I *like* spending days in the canyons trying to get the definitive picture of a bighorn ram.'

'I wonder if Birdie might grow up like that,' Frankie mused.

'Of course she won't.' Sarah was surprised. 'She doesn't have the background.'

'You can't mean—'

'No, I don't mean her birth; that could work to her advantage. The genes don't matter so much as the environment however, isn't that so?' Sarah turned to Miss Pink.

'Nurture not nature?' she hazarded and saw that Jerome had approached and was listening attentively.

'Sarah has been coming in to the field with me since she could walk,' he told her.

'Anyway, Birdie is all emotion and mysticism,' Sarah pointed out. 'She'll be into Tolkien and Richard Adams in a few years.'

Her parents laughed. Everyone was on the balcony now and Dolly said, mystified: 'What's wrong with Tolkien?'

'I was just saying Birdie's the type will lap him up.'

'You're right – providing she settles down enough to learn to read. What did Paula have to say when you brought her home?'

'I didn't go to the house. I left Birdie at the road-end. I asked her if she'd be all right and she said Paula wouldn't whip her because if she did she – Birdie – would run away again.'

'She'll run in any event,' Frankie said. 'Paula must learn to accept that.'

'Could you?' Miss Pink asked. 'If she were your child?'

Frankie said: 'She rides as if she'd been born on the back of a horse, and Sarah says her pony is very steady. What could happen to her?' She had turned to her husband but he addressed his reply to Miss Pink.

'These country children know all the dangers,' he told

her. 'They absorb them instinctively, like animals; you never hear of a ranch child being bitten by a rattler— '

'Yes, you do,' Sarah contradicted, 'but they're subnormal, or at least, they're kids without any fear . . . There was that boy in the Nebo valley last year, only six, and he was hunting snakes in an old barn. Same age as Birdie but a lower level of intelligence. He could be spared.'

Miss Pink pricked up her ears but Jerome was saying: 'How intelligent is she?'

'She's shrewd. She may be more than that; it's early yet to tell.' She regarded her father. 'Doesn't this running away – three times now – remind you of something?'

He nodded. 'Suicide? Contrived attempts at it: *cris de coeur*. You think she's sending out messages?'

Plummer burst in, wide-eyed: 'You don't think she's going to commit suicide?'

Dolly patted his arm soothingly. 'No, dear. The similarity is just in sending messages. Birdie is trying to call our attention to the fact that she doesn't have a father.'

'So if she's doing it consciously: attracting attention,' Sarah resumed, 'that suggests a high level of intelligence for her age.'

'It'll be interesting to see how it develops,' Jerome said.

Sarah looked thoughtful. 'Badly, would be my guess – unless Paula sees the light and adopts a more reasonable attitude.' She exchanged a long look with her father.

'It's not worth it,' he said. 'I think we should leave well alone, let Birdie take her chance. After all, she's got the Olsons across the river, it's not as if there were no one to befriend her. How does she play?'

'She's wild, but not violent. It's all talk, this stuff about killing people— '

'Who does she say she's going to kill?' Plummer interrupted. He was the odd man out in this company but the others were patient with him. Miss Pink realised with some amusement that, with the exception of herself, the party was composed of the occupants of the new cabins. There was no one from the other side of the road, but Plummer, she

61

thought, did not really belong on this side. She concluded he had been invited as a partner for Dolly.

'Where other children sulk,' Sarah was telling him, 'Birdie says she's going to kill people. But like I said, it's only talk – unlike Shawn, for instance, who says nothing and behaves violently.'

'Guess what!' Dolly exclaimed. 'He threw a rock at Miss Pink's horse!'

Everyone looked shocked and clamoured for an explanation. Dolly obliged them: 'And that's not all,' she went on, and related how she had found her painting daubed with soot. 'Of course, that's why he threw the rock, because I was bawling him out. So that finishes me with the whole family, because obviously Myrtle and Maxine will have nothing to do with me after I sounded off about Shawn.'

'I think Shawn has more problems than Birdie,' Jerome said.

'And for the same cause,' Frankie put in: 'A broken home. No father in either case.' She looked at her step-daughter fondly.

'It doesn't always follow,' the girl said. 'Look at the Olsons. Six of them don't have natural fathers and see how they've turned out.'

'Yes, but they've got Jo.'

'Where would we be without earth mothers?' Dolly asked, and everyone smiled indulgently except Glen Plummer who looked as if he were trying to discover the joke.

Chapter 5

Jo Olson looked no more like an earth mother than did Miss Pink. She was plain and dumpy, with long hair of an indeterminate shade caught back in a clasp of plastic beads. She wore a blue work shirt, jeans, sneakers, and the type of granny spectacles that had been the rage a few years ago. She was sitting in a rocking chair on the porch of the Olson cabin, two kittens and a naked baby on her lap, surrounded by six more of her children. The younger ones had observed Miss Pink's approach, had gone to meet her at the road-end and accompanied her like a guard of honour to the cabin. Of course, it was a formal visit, a necessary one. The Olsons were the only family in Salvation Canyon that she had not met and, although intrigued by the occasion, she had had qualms about meeting them. She was not always at her ease with children but now, seated in the shade of the eaves, she felt as if she were participating in a kind of entertainment.

'No school,' Jo was saying in answer to her question. 'It's Saturday.'

Debbie, a child of five with a blond pony-tail, in slacks much too large for her and a purple velveteen blouse, had been regarding the visitor intently. 'Did you forget it was Saturday?' she asked.

'I did,' Miss Pink confessed. 'How do you remember?'

'Because we have school Monday through Friday. Saturday and Sunday we work.'

'She means weekends we do the farmwork we don't have time for other days.' The speaker was a beauty in a western shirt and a man's tweed cap. She was darning a sock with great care. 'The littluns mostly play weekday evenings,' she added.

'There's the milking evenings,' a small boy pointed out. He was as blond as his little sister, and as serious, concerned now that the visitor should not think of them as idle. 'But we don't have lessons Saturday and Sunday; that's the difference.'

'Who says what jobs you shall do?' Miss Pink asked.

Jo rocked back and forth, kittens and baby comatose on her big thighs. She smiled serenely at her brood and let them do the talking.

'Mom says what has to be done,' the blond boy said.

'We tell her first,' a six-year-old reminded him. She must come between him and the solemn five-year-old. Miss Pink had been told all their names – and those of the absent trio who were doing odd jobs for neighbours – and had forgotten most of them, although, after ten minutes in their company, she was sorting them by their appearance. The four youngest were obviously all from the same father, fair and blue-eyed: the boy of eight, his young sisters and the baby. These were the Olson children.

There was a dark, thin pair of twins, boy and girl, perhaps ten years old, who did not say much, and there was the girl, Jen, in the becoming cap, who was also dark, and the only real beauty among them. She was about fifteen, very different in appearance from the little Olsons, but they were all united by their manner, and their manners. They were very still children but it was a stillness charged with vitality and intelligence. They were attentive. Even the small girl, Debbie, perhaps she more than her siblings, listened, considered and pronounced. Now she said, summing up carefully: 'We tell Mom what has to be done, if she doesn't know, and she says who's to do it.'

'Like now,' Jo said, coming to life. 'How about some milk, Rob, Laurel?' The twins stood up and went into the cabin.

'Do you have goats or cows?' Miss Pink asked.

'Cows,' Jo said. 'They're more economical, providing you've got the land.'

64

'We've got four milkers,' Debbie said. 'I make the butter.' There was a concerted movement, a turning of heads. 'I help make it,' she amended.

'And we've got five steers and a coupla calves,' her brother said, 'and we'll have another calf any time.'

'You better go and look at Lucy,' Jo told him, and he got up and jogged round the corner of the cabin.

'I'm not watching,' Debbie said firmly. She came and stood at Miss Pink's knee, leaning forward confidentially. 'I don't like it when they fall out; I'm afraid they'll break their necks.'

'I never heard of one breaking its neck,' Miss Pink said, responding in kind.

'You didn't? You're quite sure? Well, maybe I'll watch next time.'

An Australian collie approached the porch, a kitten dangling limply from its jaws. Behind it came a distraught cat, mewing. The dog walked up the steps and deposited the kitten on the baby's naked stomach. Jo stroked it absently. It opened a tiny mouth and yawned. The cat rubbed itself against the rocking chair.

'Shelly, see to this lot,' Jo said.

The girl removed the damp kitten and put it on the boards. The cat picked it up by the scruff and turned away. Shelly followed with the other kittens, accompanied by the collie.

'That cat goes to be spayed,' Jo said, handing the baby to the oldest girl. 'We've saturated the neighbourhood with her kittens. Everybody's cat's descended from her.'

'The Grays don't have a cat,' Debbie pointed out.

Jo went indoors.'You can try Mr Gray,' Jen said. 'See if you can convince him to take a good hunting kitten. He likes you.'

'The Brenners don't have a cat neither,' the child mused.

'No, I won't take a kitten to the Brenners.'

'Why was the collie carrying the kitten?' Miss Pink asked.

Debbie turned to her, obviously pleased at her self-imposed role of mentor: 'What happened is that Bluey lost her pups – she only had two and they died – so she takes

Tabitha's kittens instead. She's got – what?' She appealed to her big sister.

'Post-natal depression.'

Debbie nodded solemnly. 'That's what she's got.'

People emerged from the cabin with milk and mugs and a platter of chocolate-chip cookies. 'We'll have to weed those beans before it gets too hot,' Jo said. 'Why, here's Birdie.' A small figure was crossing the bridge over the creek.

'They still got her pony locked up,' the boy twin said in disgust.

In a sudden silence Jen exchanged looks with her mother. The boy who had gone to inspect the cow came back. 'She's just grazing,' he told Jo. 'No sign yet. She'll be a while— ' His gaze followed that of the others. 'No pony,' he said flatly.

Jen said: 'She can ride the sorrel.'

'He's too big for her. It'll have to be Buster. After we done the weeding, eh, Mom? She can't ride without we're there, can she? S'pose she took off?'

'No sweat,' Jo said comfortably. 'Birdie will help with the weeding.'

Shelly returned empty-handed. 'I've shut that bitch in the tack-room,' she said. 'Let the cat suckle 'em for a while in peace. Mom, Bluey ought to have more pups . . . oh, here's Birdie.' It was a flat statement of fact but then she shot her mother a look of enquiry. Jo smiled reassuringly. She doesn't need to say anything, Miss Pink thought; they know how to behave.

Birdie was wearing a clean shirt and denims and her dark curls were damp from a recent shampoo. As she approached she surveyed the company without expression, climbed the steps, walked deliberately to Jo and leaned against her thighs. Jo encircled her with a large arm. Birdie regarded Miss Pink. 'Hi!' she said.

'Hi!' It was the first time Miss Pink had made such a response, but the situation was unique. She felt she had to be careful.

'They put my horse in the stable,' Birdie said. 'Where *she* can see if I takes him out.'

Miss Pink was saved from comment by Jen. 'You asked for it,' she said equably. 'You shouldn't have run off.'

Birdie looked up at Jo and pressed closer. 'You go an' talk to her,' she pleaded.

Debbie tapped Miss Pink's knee to gain her attention. 'How old were you when you started to ride?'

She thought about it. 'I don't remember being on a pony before I was nine.'

'I started when I was three. Birdie was riding before she could walk properly.'

Emotions flitted across Birdie's tough little face: surprise – quickly suppressed, an assumption of arrogance – then suddenly all feeling was gone, the eyes widened and turned stony. A child on a bicycle was crossing the Olsons' pasture: Shawn Brenner.

'We've got a full crew of field-hands this morning,' Jo observed.

Again there was an odd silence, full of unspoken thoughts. Miss Pink did not like it and she expressed a wish to see the garden. Debbie said it was a mess but she would show her all the same, meanwhile Shawn arrived, dropped his bicycle on the ground and came to the porch, his face as blank as Birdie's.

'Can I help in the garden?' he asked Jo.

'We're not riding till after dinner,' Debbie told him.

He ignored her and kept his eyes on Jo. Birdie squirmed closer to the woman and sucked her thumb.

'We'll find a job for you,' Jo said.

Debbie turned to Miss Pink and spoke in a very grown-up voice. 'I want you to meet my dad.'

'I would like to.'

'After dinner? I'll take you. Mom, Miss Pink wants to meet Dad. I can take her after dinner.' It was a statement, not a question.

Jo hesitated. 'I'll go along,' Jen said.

'Yes,' Jo told the little girl. 'I guess you can do that.'

Miss Pink saw that Debbie had neatly engineered what was almost certainly an 'adult' expedition, and that Jen had taken it upon herself to supervise the trip. She saw that Birdie and Shawn were staring at each other. Birdie looked up at Jo. 'I want to go with them.'

Shawn tensed, hanging on the response.

'The others are going to have a rodeo,' Jo said.

'Oh, no!' It was a wail from Birdie, then: 'I'm going 'ome, get my horse. I'll kill anyone tries to stop me.'

Shawn's jaw dropped. Suddenly he was just a disappointed little boy. Jo said calmly: 'There'll be horses for everybody. You can only compete one or two at a time.'

'But Tommy's best!' Birdie cried. 'I can beat everyone.'

A look of fury showed in Shawn's eyes, and was gone. Jo said to Birdie: 'Maybe if your mom knows we're having a rodeo, if you promise not to run, we'll see if we can go get Tommy.'

Birdie's face softened. She pushed her head into the big breasts, while behind her Shawn turned and stared across the creek to the Crimson Cliffs. His hands were thrust deep in his pockets and even through the stuff of his jeans it was obvious that his fists were tightly clenched.

'You certainly lead exciting lives,' Miss Pink observed. 'How many girls of your age would have a choice of competing in a rodeo or exploring a canyon on a Saturday afternoon?'

They were riding abreast up the track behind the Forset ranch, Debbie bareback on a small black pony, Jen on a sorrel. The little girl gave the observation serious thought.

'My pony needs exercise,' she said at length. 'And I can't do a lot of the things the others do in a rodeo. I can't rope without a saddle. Anyways, I'm too small to rope.'

Jen rode silently, staring at her horse's ears. Miss Pink was reminded of the girl's mother, who let the little ones do the talking. 'What can you do?' she asked Debbie.

The child took a deep breath and glanced at her sister. 'Not very much,' she confessed. 'I can try but it don't get me nowheres.'

' "Doesn't",' Jen murmured. ' "Doesn't get me any-where." '

'So what does Birdie do at a rodeo?' Miss Pink asked.

'Well, she's got a saddle,' Debbie conceded quickly, 'so she can do lots of things I can't. 'Sides, she's six, and there's only one of her. She's spoiled.' It would appear that sometimes she repeated other people's words.

'And Shawn?'

There was no answer. Miss Pink glanced sideways but the child was well below her level, and the cute little cowboy hat obscured her face.

'Shawn wouldn't want to be left out of anything,' Jen supplied drily, 'but he's not all that good at the trick stuff. He hasn't ridden as much as the rest of us.'

Debbie asked politely: 'When Mr Forset said Dad was "up the top" did he mean the top of the canyon or the top of the mesa?'

'The canyon. There's no fence on the mesa, 'cept at the bottom of the talus.'

'That's what I thought he meant. I think we ought to let them out a bit.'

The pony broke into a springy lope. The big horses ignored it and continued to amble in the rear.

'Are you ever bothered about her becoming an infant prodigy?' Miss Pink asked, aware that the tense was wrong. Debbie was a prodigy.

Jen laughed. 'She's a caution, isn't she? We try not to encourage her and if she starts to show off we squash her flat. And no one spoils her – I mean the neighbours don't.' She considered that. 'People who might try to spoil her – or who could take offence at some of the things she says – them, she hasn't got time for.'

Miss Pink murmured a response, thinking of Myrtle and Maxine, of Paula Estwick. 'I haven't met Paula,' she said. 'I've met Sam Estwick but not his wife.'

Jen sketched a nod but made no comment. Debbie came back, jogging, riding like an Indian.

'How old do you have to be to get a saddle?' Miss Pink asked as the pony ranged alongside.

'When I'm old enough for a horse as'll fit a big saddle.

Small kids always ride bareback; there's no money for little saddles. Mom says it was the same with shoes until sneakers came along. Kids had to go barefoot 'cause they grew out of shoes too quick.' Solemn eyes were turned up to Miss Pink. 'I wouldn't like that; think of all the prickly pear and stuff! 'Course, it wouldn't never have happened in our family, everything's handed down.'

'I was wondering where you got the pretty blouse.'

'This old thing? It was Tracy's. Mom said it made her look like an old movie star, so she gave it to me and Jen made it over. Did you meet Tracy yet?'

'No. Let's see: seven of you today – so I haven't met three: the three eldest.'

'I'm the third eldest,' Jen said. 'Tracy's eighteen and Sandy's seventeen. They were working for the Grays this morning; they run a maid service. Mike, he's thirteen, he's up at the Duvals', pulling fence.'

'This fence is in poor shape,' Debbie said critically. 'Dad's got his work cut out. He ought to be up in this old canyon full-time, just mending fence.'

'Mr Forset can't afford to pay him full-time.'

Debbie sighed. 'It's not fair. Everyone's poor these days.'

'Not much money,' Jen corrected. 'We're not poor.'

'So how come Mr Plummer's got so much money he don't know what to do with it? He could give some to Mr Forset.'

'It doesn't work that way.'

'Why not? Why can't he— '

'Be your age, Debbie. It's economics, and I'm not a teacher. You want to know, ask Mom, get her to explain so's you'll understand.'

But Debbie had lost interest. They were coming to the end of the flat land that they called Mormon Pasture and the canyon walls were closing in. This was a box canyon with no way out at the headwall; only about a quarter-mile from the end, a trail left the track they were following to climb the talus below the cliffs of Calamity Mesa. In response to her query they told Miss Pink that the trail came out on top of Calamity and a ride across the plateau to the north rim would give them a view of the Colorado. They were standing at the fork in the track when a man on a mule came down from the direction of the headwall. Debbie shouted delighted greetings and Miss Pink turned her horse to meet Erik Olson.

The initial impression was sombre: a man in dark clothing on a dark mule. Even his hat and chaps were black, his shirt grey, but when he went to wipe the sweat from his forehead he exposed hair as pale as Debbie's, and light Scandinavian eyes. He acknowledged Miss Pink's presence gravely, accepted a bag of cookies from his daughter and attended to her chatter. 'Calamity,' he repeated, with speculation. 'Did you ask if Miss Pink'd feel happy on that trail riding a strange horse?'

'He's not strange to her. She took him up Rustler yesterday.' Debbie turned, her eyes anxious. 'You're quite happy on this old trail, aren't you, ma'am?'

'That old trail,' Jen said. 'It goes up.'

Debbie was mouthing: *please!* 'This horse is very sure-footed,' Miss Pink told Olson.'I think we can cope.'

He nodded, evidently satisfied. 'So what time d'you expect to be down?' he asked Jen.

'Long before dark.'

'Right, I'll be watching for you. I'm packing it in and going home; I need to fix that old chicken-house in the orchard before a skunk gets in after them young chicks. You take care now.' He looked hard at Debbie. 'Remember?'

She nodded vehemently. 'Yessir!'

She explained the emphasis to Miss Pink as they started up the trail. 'Dad says accidents are always the rider's fault. Whatever happens: if your horse goes over the edge, or puts his foot in a hole, or gets bit by a rattler, it's your fault 'cause you're cleverer than the horse.'

'It's like, anticipating events,' Jen put in. 'There are exceptions, I guess, but that's the general rule.'

'A good one to live by in this country,' Miss Pink said, thinking of the cliffs above.

71

In fact they looked more imposing than they turned out to be, and from underneath the ledges had not been visible. Unlike the Twist below Rustler Park, this trail was open and there was no slickrock. For several hundred feet it slanted diagonally upwards to the foot of the cliffs where there was a gully so wide that the path could zigzag without putting undue strain on the horses. In any case, as Jen remarked cheerfully, the exercise was good for them; they had all grown too fat on spring grass.

Miss Pink was bothered about the heat. The sun beat full into the gully and the air was stifling. Far to the south-west, beyond the big mountains, clouds were piling up ominously, their tops like silvered cauliflowers.

They came over the lip of the gully and halted. A thousand feet below the green pastures gleamed, in striking contrast to the rosy screes. The slanting route had brought them way out to the east so that they had an uninterrupted view up Salvation Creek to the narrows. Three miles away, a bright yellow speck in the pinyons could be part of an A-frame, while from close below their perch came the whine of a chainsaw. 'Sounds like fall,' Jen said: 'Mr Forset cutting logs.' Miss Pink could distinguish her jeep standing outside the ranch house, full in the sun. The sun was glaring. She glanced to her right and saw a monstrous anvil-shape, smudgy white and shadowless, looming above the mountains.

'That's nice,' Jen said. 'We may get some rain.'

'We don't want to be on top in a storm,' Miss Pink pointed out.

'Race you to the Stone Man!' The black pony leapt away.

'No!' Jen shouted. Debbie slowed and came round to wait for them. 'No racing,' Jen told her. 'This isn't the home pasture – just remember that, miss. We take it steady to the rim; you keep with us.'

For over a mile they jogged across the high tableland towards a tall cairn which evidently marked the highest point of a mesa that otherwise looked level. As they drew nearer Miss Pink saw that, a mile or two beyond, an escarpment curved gently across their line. They could see about a thousand feet of rock but its base was blocked from sight by the near rim of the mesa. They came to the cairn and below their feet an abyss gaped like a wound in the crust of the earth.

The cliffs opposite dropped to talus that ran down to the lip of a lower cliff and then plunged, smooth as a diver, into the brown ribbon that was the Colorado. There were pale specks on the surface of the water and, once the horses were standing quietly, the riders could hear the whisper of the cataracts.

Swallows, their backs iridescent in purple and emerald, flicked along the rim, a hawk screamed; far below an eagle floated in the sunshine.

Thunder muttered behind them and wonder was superseded by alarm. 'Come on,' Jen called and, to Miss Pink's surprise, the girl set off westward along the rim. The mouth of Salvation Creek lay below to the east.

She was somewhat reassured when she caught sight of a trail below the cliffs. She did not mind rain, just so long as they were not on a high point when the storm struck. She glanced round at Debbie, thinking that the child should be in the middle, an older and more experienced person bringing up the rear, as would be the case if they were on foot, then Yaller stumbled, she grasped the horn – and thought grimly that the order was correct; the least able rider was in the middle.

Jen stopped and waited. Miss Pink came up and saw that they were at the top of the trail. She saw too that going down, with the drop visible and yawning all the way, was going to be a very different matter from an ascent over easy gradients when all the attention was directed upwards and the drop was hidden, except on the hairpins, and then one did not have to look. She wanted to ask: 'Will Debbie be all right?' and she looked back at the child who smiled and said: 'Just let Yaller see where he's going; he won't fall.'

'Thank you,' she said acidly, and followed Jen's sorrel over the edge.

The clouds came up and the thunder rolled. The sorrel

stepped out in a hurry and Yaller followed, the black pony sometimes trotting to keep up. Occasionally, at a steepening, there were zigzags, which the horses skittered round impatiently, kicking stones over the edge. Halfway down, lightning flashed and the thunder followed like an explosion. The animals jerked their heads but they did not falter. From behind Miss Pink came a cry of delight: 'Wow! That was close!' The others said nothing.

They were not far above the river when lightning struck again, but this time, when the thunder exploded and should have rolled away in echoing waves through the mighty canyon, the crashes continued and grew louder, *bumping*.

Jen stopped and looked back, panic in her eyes. 'Wait,' Miss Pink ordered. 'Try to locate it.'

'There it is!' Debbie yelled, pointing.

Rocks were bounding down the talus on the other side of the river, rocks so large that even a mile away they were easily distinguishable. Debbie was saying: 'They won't— They can't— '

'We're safe here.' Miss Pink was trying to keep her voice steady. 'They're going to make a big splash, though.'

Jen was silent. Miss Pink thought: we must get out of here; we're sitting ducks if the lightning strikes the rim on this side.

The leading rocks leapt the edge of the lower cliff. For a moment they saw great shapes against the sky and heard the rending tear of their passage through the air. Miss Pink thought of chipmunks and hawks, of the wind through pinions, then the rocks hit the river and the gorge was filled with a liquid roaring, and the sound of a huge volume of water falling back on water from a height.

Subsidiary falls came chattering in the wake of the titans and even when it was all over they could hear faint trickles and eerie bumps as the unstable slopes shed poised stones that had been left behind.

By that time the riders had reached a grassy bench by the river where they broke into a steady lope. As they approached the mouth of Salvation Creek, hidden in thickets

74

of willow, they saw a wall of rain advancing down the home canyon. They turned up Gospel Bottom and the black pony went streaking ahead, the horses following at a hand gallop. They met the rain and in a moment were drenched. 'See you!' Miss Pink shouted as they reached the Forset road-end and Yaller swerved without breaking stride.

She pulled up in the yard where Forset was waiting, gleaming in a slicker. 'Nice drop of rain,' he said. 'Don't bother about that – ' as she went to undo the cinch, ' – I'll see to him. You go home, have a bath and get into some dry clothes. Come down for a drink after you've eaten. I'm going to run up to Estwick's. Birdie's gone again.'

'In this weather!'

'She'll take no harm from a drop of rain. Trouble is, the pinto's come home. So Paula's a bit bothered. She's always worried, but this time could be different, the pony coming back. Thought I'd go up, have a look round.'

'I'll come too, just as soon as I've changed.'

Chapter 6

Paula Estwick appeared ungainly and sexless, slumped on a kitchen chair in the dark cabin. Her hair was clubbed short and she wore clothes which looked as if they belonged to her husband, from the Big Mack shirt to the worn boots. With her reputation for hysteria it was surprising to discover her that Saturday evening so still as to appear cataleptic.

Jo Olson came to the door as Miss Pink drew up outside the cabin. 'She won't move, or even speak,' she whispered. 'What would you do?'

The evening was gloomy after the rain and the lights were switched on in the cabin. The door was open for a breath of air, but for all that the interior was stuffy. There was a smell of fried meat, but if Paula had prepared supper, someone had cleared away. The stove was alight and she sat beside it, staring at nothing. Her eyes did not focus as Miss Pink entered. Jo looked a question, received a nod, and she performed introductions as if the situation were normal. Paula's face did not change. Miss Pink sat down as far from the stove as possible.

'Tell me what happened,' she said loudly, looking at Jo, who hesitated, then collected herself.

'I'd gone up to the Duvals' to collect Sandy and Tracy in the truck,' she said. 'They were baking at Wind Whistle—'

'The Duvals don't cook?'

Jo was startled by such an interruption but she got the point after a moment: Paula might be aroused by domestic trivia. 'They don't have the time,' she went on. 'The girls do them a big bake every few weeks, freeze most of the stuff . . .' She sighed, unable to keep it up. 'She was there in our

76

meadow when I started out ... Birdie ... ' There was a flicker of movement from the side of the stove. 'I shouted to the kids that they should pack up, there was a big storm coming, and then I went on to Wind Whistle. I visited with Bob Duval for a while and when we came home the rain had started. The kids were in the barn. They said Birdie went home when they left the meadow.'

'Did she reach home?'

Jo was silent and they looked towards Paula who made no sign that she had heard. A log shifted in the stove. A cricket chirped in a corner.

'How far is it from the field where they were playing to here?' Miss Pink asked.

'About half a mile.' Jo was looking miserable.

'Show me.'

They went outside and moved away from the door. 'It's that that's bothering the menfolk,' Jo explained, drawing Miss Pink still further away. 'It's such a short distance but the quickest route, on a pony, is to cross the creek.' She gestured vaguely in the direction of the Olson place but creek and cabin were hidden by the dense growth of willows and cottonwoods. 'The creek's running high since the storm,' she went on, 'so they're searching way down the banks.'

'But the level of the creek was low before the storm.'

'Yes, but if she didn't come straight home? I mean, Birdie, she's always going missing ... But the pinto's here. He stayed with her when she was— ' She could not go on, could not utter the word 'alive'.

'We must go back to Paula,' Miss Pink said.

They returned to the hot kitchen. They made tea and they talked. Frankie Gray arrived, bringing a bottle of brandy and some shot glasses. They accepted the brandy gratefully and still there was no sign from Paula. Darkness had fallen. Miss Pink went outside and, by the light of a torch, walked round the buildings trying to see something of the searchers but it was impossible. The Estwick place was an enclave of cleared land surrounded by trees.

She felt a breath of air and looked up to see the first stars showing through a break in the clouds. When she looked down she saw that lights were approaching from the direction of the creek. She went to meet them. It was John Forset and Estwick and they had found nothing.

Estwick went towards the cabin. Miss Pink asked Forset: 'Is there no sign of any kind? Couldn't you trace the pony's tracks backwards, to try to discover where it had left her?'

'We tried, but all the tracks were washed out by that hard rain, time we came to start looking. And there are dozens of places where horses go down the banks to drink out of the creek. It would have been impossible to find where she crossed this afternoon.'

'But John, the creek was low when she left the other children. The storm hadn't started. If the pony stumbled in the water she might have come off but she couldn't have been drowned.'

'No? S'pose her head hit a rock?' She was silent. 'Then the storm came,' he went on, 'and the flood washed the body downstream. We have to search the banks clear to the river. After that, of course, it's hopeless.'

Then they were both silent, thinking that there was little hope anyway, even if Birdie had not reached the Colorado.

They searched throughout the night. The women managed to move Paula into a more comfortable chair and they brought a mattress from a bedroom so that one person could doze while the other stayed awake beside the listless mother. She looked more relaxed now and had closed her eyes. The watchers felt a certain relief at that but it lasted no longer than the first doze. On waking there was only dread.

At seven o'clock Jo's two oldest girls, Tracy and Sandy, brought food down in a pick-up and cooked breakfast. Sarah was now sharing the watch with Miss Pink. They had just started to eat when a truck drove into the yard. Paula seemed to be asleep and she did not stir. Miss Pink went outside to find Erik Olson standing by the open door of the truck, evidently waiting. John Forset came round the rear of the vehicle and she saw by his face that something had happened. His eyes were those of an exhausted old man.

'We found her,' he said. She glanced in the back of the truck and he guessed the thought. 'No, we left – it – where we found it.' She stared at him. 'There are – wounds,' he said.

After she had absorbed the initial impact of the shock and understood what he was trying to tell her – that the child had been raped – she said she would see the body. He refused to allow it. She said: 'There are a number of men in this community. If one of them is responsible then it's imperative that the right man is arrested. This state has capital punishment. However good the local police are, no one's infallible.' She held his eye. 'It's not the first time I've seen a murdered child.'

Evidently he knew that already. He showed no surprise, and her argument had good sense behind it. 'I'll show you,' he said. 'But you're barking up the wrong tree if you think it was someone in this valley. There's nobody, *nobody*, here would have done what's been done to that child. It's a maniac's work, a monster. No one could keep a nature like that hidden all these years in a little place like this. We know everything that goes on— '

She edged him towards the truck. 'All the more reason why an innocent man shouldn't be suspected.'

'The police are hopeless.' He stood immovable by the passenger door. 'They can't find a thief in Nebo; they can't find a lost *horse*!' His voice cracked.

'I'll drive.' She was behind the wheel. 'Get in, John; let's do something before the police arrive. There's not much time.'

He got in. 'It could have been a river-runner,' he said. 'Or a tourist – a motorist from out of state. Now, why did I say that? Could have been a man from Nebo; there was a fellow last winter, shot his wife in cold blood . . . and there was that hippie— '

'*John!*'

'What?'

'I asked how far? On whose land did you find the body?'

'Eh? Oh, mine, I s'pose. Of course it's my land; we came out of the gate in the South Forty, just up here, where the creek comes close to the road. Don't drive in; you'll get mired. Leave the pick-up on the shoulder.'

As she got down and started across the grass she made a deliberate effort to change gear, to eliminate emotion. There was a time when she had considered a career in medicine, and decades later realised that had she become a surgeon she might well have gravitated to forensic work. Here was yet another acid test and she must forget about beauty and small children on ponies, must concentrate in advance – trying to forestall the shock – on blood and a corpse.

There was no blood because she had been in the water too long. They had lifted the body out of the creek and laid it on the bank face upwards. The eyes were open. She appeared to be wearing the same clothes she had worn yesterday morning: the white T-shirt, the jeans and sneakers.

'Is this how you found her?' Miss Pink asked.

'No.' He was staring dully at the body. 'It was snagged in those willows there and the pants were kind of dragging from the ankles. Someone pulled them up.'

'Who found her?'

'Erik Olson. The others don't know yet.'

She was stooping but she glanced up at that. He looked back blankly and she thought that she must get him home soon and find Dolly; she would look after him. She bent back to her task and drew in her breath as she lifted the damp shirt and saw the wounds like small mouths on the livid flesh. She heard him move away. She looked at the rest of the body, forewarned now and cold. She joined Forset.

'Are there wounds on the back?' she asked.

'Not knife wounds. The back of the skull is crushed in.'

She stiffened. She went back and lifted the head. The skull was soft and yielding to her fingers. She stood up and looked round, hearing voices. Jerome Gray and Sarah were crossing the meadow towards them. Supported by numbers, Forset came back and the four of them stood above the body in silence, as if they were at a graveside. After a while Jerome asked: 'Did she die from the wounds or did she drown?' He spoke softly as if to himself.

'I think the blow to the head would have been fatal,' Miss Pink said. 'Probably the knife wounds all occurred after death. There is no bruising.'

'Why should she be knifed after she was dead?' Sarah asked, and Miss Pink remembered with a shock that the girl was only seventeen.

'To cover evidence of rape.'

'Rape would be obvious in a child of six.' Sarah's voice was like ice.

'The genitalia are lacerated.'

The water chuckled past the willows, its sound laced by the trilling of blackbirds. 'Come along now,' Jerome touched his daughter's elbow. 'There are things to be done.' He hesitated and turned to Miss Pink. 'Shouldn't we leave some kind of guard here?'

'I'll stay,' Sarah said. 'I'll wait by our car. You can give Dad a lift.'

'I called the police,' he said, as they came to Forset's pick-up. 'Frankie said probably no one else had thought of it.'

Miss Pink got in behind the wheel. The men stood irresolute on the road, waiting for guidance. Sarah leaned against her father's Mercedes and regarded the skyline of the Barrier. She had an air of being apart from them, aloof. Observing her, Miss Pink said absently: 'Paula has to be told. Does Sam know yet?'

'I don't know where he is,' Forset said.

She looked at them sharply and saw two badly shocked old gentlemen. There was nothing to be done for Birdie now. The immediate concern was to try to mitigate the repercussions of her violent end on the community. She turned the truck and called to Sarah: 'We're going to your house. If anyone comes to take your place, you follow us. We'll see you there.'

Her tone alerted the men and they climbed into the truck. She drove to the Grays' cabin, vaguely aware of some anomaly about the distribution of her companions. She went slowly and no one protested, the others too preoccupied with their concerns to notice that the vehicle was crawling. If these two had to be nursed like children, if only temporarily, how could she have left a young girl on guard beside a murder victim? She pondered this in amazement and with a sense of guilt, then remembered that it was Sarah who had suggested the arrangement. Back there in the meadow she had been in charge. Of course, thought Miss Pink, a seventeen-year-old would not be aware of the full implications.

Frankie was not at home, and the cabin was empty, the living room full of sunshine reflected from the pool. Seeing that Jerome had automatically assumed the role of host in his own house, she allowed him to start brewing coffee while she went to the telephone to discover what was happening elsewhere.

Beside the phone was a card with the numbers of everyone in the canyon. She called Dolly's cabin but there was no reply. She tried the Olson number. Jen answered and said that her mother was at the Estwick place. The girl's voice was strained.

'Is your father home?' Miss Pink asked. Erik Olson came on the line. 'It sounds as if you've told them,' she said.

'They had to know some time.'

'I'm not criticising. It's just that we need to know the situation in the other houses.' She explained where she was and who was with her. Had Paula been told? Did Sam Estwick know the body had been found?

'I don't know as anyone's looked for him,' Olson said in astonishment, as if he had forgotten Estwick's existence. 'I don't even remember where he went. Ask John Forset; he'll know.'

'So Paula hasn't been told – you didn't tell her when you came to the cabin at breakfast time, when I drove off with John?'

'No, ma'am. I told Sarah and she said to leave Paula sleeping, not to wake her. Then Jo come down to sit with Paula and I come up to our place. I remember now: Sam and Mr Plummer and Art Stenbock, they all went downstream below Forset's place, working their way down to the river. That's where you'll find 'em, down to Gospel Bottom. Do you want me to do anything?'

'Leave it a while. We'll talk about it here. The best thing you can do is stay with your children . . . Then we know where you are – if we need you.' She bit her lip; what *was* she saying?

'Stay with the children?' There was a long pause on the line. 'I'll be around,' he said with transparent casualness.

She put down the receiver slowly and turned to encounter Forset's eyes. 'It wasn't one of us,' he said firmly, offering her brandy.

'What I was thinking was that the children need an adult there to keep them on the right track. They could invent fantasies – nightmares, become terrified, fly right off the handle. There's no saying what they might do. The father's presence will control them. That was all I was implying.' She was being garrulous.

'It didn't sound like that.'

'I'm too shaken to pick my words. Thank you, John.' She took the brandy. Jerome came over with a tray of coffee mugs. She dialled the Estwick place. Dolly answered.

Miss Pink said without preamble: 'Just say yes or no if it's difficult. Is she awake?'

'Yes, but— '

'Does she know?'

'Yes.'

'Hysteria?'

'No. I can talk, Melinda; she's in the bedroom and the door's shut. Jo's with her. I don't think she took it in when Jo told her. She said she'd always expected the worst, every time Birdie went off, she'd picture her lying dead. She went through hell every time, she said, she knew it would happen eventually. She says it's her judgement. I told you, didn't I?

83

All the concern's for herself, not for Birdie. She said: "Now it's all over," and she sat there and I thought: Christ, she's off again, but after a while she got up and said she'd go and lie down a while. Jo went with her.'

'Dolly, you must make some excuse and look in on them.'

'They're all right; I can hear them talking – both of them.'

Miss Pink relaxed a little. 'Well, at least she's been told. Now there's Sam.'

'Yes. Poor Sam.'

'Who would be the best person to break it to him, d'you think?'

'Why, Jo. I could go in and spell her . . . Here's Frankie, just pulled into the yard. Jo could go and find Sam now.'

But Jo never had to perform that onerous task. She started down the canyon and at the gate into Forset's South Forty she saw several cars, among them Estwick's. There was no one in them but there were people on the bank of the creek. After a short time Sarah came across the meadow followed by Estwick, Art Stenbock, and Glen Plummer. Sarah and Jo went to the Grays' cabin, leaving Stenbock by the body. When Miss Pink was told this she frowned but she made no comment. Sarah was drinking coffee that her father had laced with brandy.

'How did Sam take it?' he asked. They had all been wondering that.

Sarah sipped her drink and seemed to be studying the design on the mug. 'He went mad,' she said flatly. Her lips stretched in what might have been a smile in different circumstances. 'There was no question of not disturbing the body –' she stared at her father, ' – of guarding it so that the killer couldn't come back and remove something that pointed to him. Sam picked her up, and hugged her tight, and rearranged the clothing; he felt the skull and he saw the wounds— '

'All of them?' Miss Pink was aghast. 'Does he know— '

'I didn't tell him. What difference does it make? He can't do more than kill the man, which he's going to do – when, if he finds the one responsible.'

Jerome nodded. 'That would be the best solution. And done right away, in hot blood, still in shock, he'd get off. Every normal person would be behind him, but, in that kind of mood, will he get the right man?'

The question dropped like a stone in a well. No one answered it and no one met his neighbour's eyes until Miss Pink noticed that Jo was looking, not at her, but through her. She recalled that when they met Olson yesterday he had been going home to fix his chicken-house.

'You were up to Wind Whistle,' Forset said suddenly, barked rather, and glared at Jo.

'Erik was fixing the chicken-house,' she said, shaken.

He didn't pursue that. 'You visited with the Duvals.'

'With Bob. Alex was—' She stopped. Miss Pink was watching Forset and saw him shake his head fractionally.

'He was there,' Jo said, but she was overridden by Sarah: 'Alex was with Mike Olson, up Horsethief, pulling fence.'

'That's what I was going to say,' Jo said.

'Ah.' Forset seemed to subside, his face, momentarily agitated, was that of an old man again, tired but relaxed. 'Some bum,' he muttered. 'A river-runner.'

Miss Pink said: 'Jo, could I ask you to give me a lift? I left my car at the Estwicks'.'

Forset stared at her. 'I can't think where everybody is,' he complained, 'let alone their cars. It's Sunday morning, for God's sake!'

'It's the shock, John.' Jerome seemed to have recovered his equilibrium. 'Spend the day with us. Here, let me give you a refill—'

'I shall be asleep.'

'You can sleep in the guest room.'

'No, no. I have to go back, see to the animals.'

'I'll come with you, John,' Sarah said.

'John's taken it badly,' Miss Pink remarked as they drove down the track. Jo murmured inaudibly. 'But Sarah!' Miss Pink exclaimed. 'She's behaving as if it hadn't happened, totally without fear: volunteering to stay by the body, going off alone with John . . . '

'You're not suggesting she's in danger from John?'

'Someone is dangerous.' There was a long pause, then Miss Pink continued: 'There are eight men in this canyon. Jerome Gray is surely too old to be considered. If you don't think it was John, and one assumes you're certain it wasn't Erik – and the Duval brothers are out because they have alibis, that leaves Glen Plummer and Art Stenbock. Apart from Sam Estwick, that is. I wonder how those two reacted when they saw the body.'

'Plummer threw up, and Art looked devastated. Sarah told me. But I agree with John: it was no one we know. That's impossible.'

'I wish you were right. But if there was a river-runner or a strange motorist, even a hiker, even a tramp, he had to be seen by someone – surely? In any event, I'm afraid the police aren't going to agree with you.'

Jo said nothing. She turned off the road and started down the Estwicks' track. Miss Pink studied her surroundings. On the far side of the canyon the Stone Hawk was gilded with light against the needles but after a few yards the pick-up was in the trees. She twisted in her seat. 'A vehicle couldn't come down here without running the risk of being seen. The start of the track is overlooked by the Grays' cabin. It was a gloomy evening certainly, but a car would have had its lights on.'

'Not necessarily. And how do you know it happened here? She could have gone down the creek for some reason. With Birdie you never knew where she might go, or why.'

'There are gates on the bank of the creek. It's all pasture land. Birdie wasn't big enough to open these wire gates, and she would have had to, because of the pony.'

'Maybe she came to a gate, couldn't open it, tied the pony, and it got loose.'

Jo was talking out of character. Gone was the placid earth mother of yesterday morning; this was a desperate woman clutching at straws, one who was suffering from shock, and possessed by the compulsion to shift the site of the attack further away from her own home.

'The trouble is,' Miss Pink mused, 'with the conditions prevailing, and no doubt everyone busy with closing windows, securing things, covering up against the approaching storm, no one would have noticed what other people were doing – at a distance and in poor visibility. I don't expect your youngsters watched Birdie leave.'

Jo did not respond to that. She brought the truck to a stop in the Estwicks' yard, which seemed cluttered with vehicles. Frankie appeared in the cabin doorway, came over and looked in the driver's window, seeing Miss Pink. 'We're going to have trouble with Sam,' she said. 'He came home, loaded his rifle, and then – thank God – he couldn't think of where to go.' She grimaced. 'Seven men, seven directions – which one should he take?' Her eyes were anguished.

Miss Pink said: 'There'll be a medical man arriving shortly. He's bound to have tranquillisers.'

'That will do for a time; then what – oh!' A black and white police car was nosing into the yard.

Miss Pink felt her bowels lurch as if the police had come for her. She turned back to the others, saw the terror in their eyes and knew that the guilt was real if vicarious. Someone else had seen the police car pass, or would see it shortly, and that person had heard the wind in the hunter's pinions. Her attitude hardened. She knew that her companions were terrified for their menfolk, and not because they thought their husbands were monsters but because they knew they were not. Suddenly, personally involved, she realised the full impact of one argument against capital punishment: that *they* might get the wrong man.

'Where is the father?' And that tone was a threat in itself.

She watched Frankie turn and observe the speaker and the approach of his partner. They were both overweight: clean khaki shirts strained over fat. She was mesmerised by the guns on their hips.

Frankie said: 'You are— ' but the patrician pose slipped as Sam Estwick emerged from the barn, curry comb and

87

brush in his hands. He stood in the sunshine observing the tableau about the cars.

Jo got out of the truck. 'You're Clint Schaffer,' she said pleasantly to the younger of the two officers. 'You were at school with my two eldest. I'm Mrs Olson.' She held out her hand and he was forced to take it. The other man watched tight-lipped. 'Not a good time to meet again,' Jo went on, including the partner, 'and you'll be wanting – information? How can we help?'

It was wasted effort. Estwick asked with undisguised menace: 'So where are you going to start?'

Miss Pink sighed and met Frankie's eyes. The police looked as if they were carved out of wood.

'Where is the deceased?' asked the second man, and Miss Pink winced. Estwick stared, puzzled despite the circumstances. She said: 'If you go back to the road and drive down the canyon for about two miles, you'll come on a parked car. Mr. Stenbock is waiting there. He will show you.'

The young Schaffer gaped at her accent. The other man asked rudely: 'Who are you?'

'My name is Pink. And what are you called?'

'Morgan. Who's in there?' He nodded at the cabin. 'The mother?'

'Mrs Estwick is severely shocked,' Frankie said. 'We've sent for a doctor.'

Estwick said: 'You did?' He moved towards the cabin, the police close behind him. 'Oh, no!' Jo whispered, and the women followed, obstructed by the bulk of the men.

Paula was sitting at a table in the kitchen. Dolly stood beside her, waiting; she would have observed the encounter in the yard. Estwick entered, crowded by the police. It seemed to cost Paula a physical effort to raise her eyes. She looked so exhausted, so drained of emotion, that she had acquired a serenity seldom seen except in death. She blinked slowly, staring at her husband.

'You?' she asked, with a kind of wonder. 'Why?'

And while they were all considering the question, the slender thread of control snapped.

'*Why?*' It was an explosion of rage, not a question, but she still possessed some reason. 'You could have got it from the whore,' she shouted. 'Not good enough? You wanted *innocence*— ' She was on her feet, cups rolling across the table spilling liquids, everyone's eyes drawn to her groping hands, a carving knife by the bread ... Dolly was clinging to her arms, buffeted and gasping, and the other women plunged past the police to block her from Estwick and push her through a doorway into a bedroom.

'Here, wait— ' shouted Morgan.

'Go to hell!' Frankie hurled at him, and Miss Pink had one glimpse of Estwick, standing limply, all the aggression and hatred gone, before Frankie slammed the door and they applied themselves to the job of soothing Paula.

In no time she was retracting. With four women to restrain her physically she could do no harm, neither to others nor to herself. As she regained normality she seemed surprised to find so many people in the room. They had put her on a bed (as the most convenient position to keep her immobilised) and now they allowed her to sit up. Frankie made tea and brought cups to the bedroom.

'They've gone,' she told the others. 'All of them.'

'Did they take Sam?' Paula whispered.

'I don't know.'

'Because of what I said. I didn't mean it.'

'So why did you say those things?' Jo asked.

'Because of Maxine Brenner, of course.' Paula sounded surprised.

Frankie asked helplessly: 'What's Maxine got to do with Birdie?'

'Nothing.' Paula was listless, calm and eminently reasonable. 'I were taking it out on him for going to her, drinking and whoring with her for months now, and him with a child needed a father's guidance. So – you see?' She looked round their circle, her eyes coming to rest on Miss Pink. '*You* understand,' she said.

'You were punishing him for going to Maxine,' Miss

Pink said carefully, 'so you accused him of the worst thing possible.'

'They put it in my mind,' Paula said. 'If they'd arrested him – if the police thinks he did it, that give me the idea, see. Now I realise how wrong it was. You stand by your man whatever.'

'*What!*' Frankie gasped, but Miss Pink took her elbow and they retreated to the kitchen. 'I thought she was retracting,' Frankie whispered angrily, 'but she does think he did it! They can't have arrested him solely on her accusation, surely?'

'I think they've probably taken him with them because they had to see the body and couldn't very well leave him here. Of course, he will be a suspect.'

'Bloody ghouls.' Frankie had heard only the first part of this. 'I suppose we can expect swarms of them now.' She started to pick up the cups that Paula had knocked over. Miss Pink fetched a cloth to wipe the table. She became aware that Frankie was staring at her. 'I was going to ask you,' the woman said, 'whether you thought Sam could have done it, and then I realised, remembered, that if he didn't, it has to be someone else and really, there's no one even remotely unlikeable in this canyon; I can't believe that there's anyone so depraved . . . D'you see what I'm getting at? This doesn't affect just Sam, but everyone. Here we've been concentrating on protecting him against hysterical accusations by his wife, and there are seven other guys out there, equally in need of protection. Take that back. Six. My sweet Jerome just isn't in this at all. So – who? The man we know least is Glen Plummer but – a rapist and a killer, *him*? Rubbish. Why don't you say something?' Miss Pink was looking at the carving knife on the table. Frankie said tightly: 'He wouldn't have brought it *back*.' Deliberately she picked it up, looked round fiercely, saw the knife rack and placed it in the slot which seemed made for it.

'I was thinking,' Miss Pink said equably, 'that someone else might have brought it back.'

'My God, fingerprints. Now I've smudged them.'

'Don't worry. He would have wiped them off.'

'So what happens now?'

'I don't like that pair,' Miss Pink said quietly. 'The police. I don't mean personally, but they're just uniformed men, ciphers; everything's done by rote. Detectives will be here shortly but the first impact is what counts, and those men are going to report that the wife accused the husband – and it's a fact that a close relative often is the murderer. What makes this worse for Sam is that he's only a stepfather.' She walked to the door.

'What are you going to do?'

'I'm going to try to find out who saw her last.'

Chapter 7

Miss Pink walked out of the cabin but she did not go to her car. Instead she went to the small barn from which Estwick had appeared when the police arrived. Inside there was stabling for horses and stalls for cows. A ladder went up to a trap door and the hay loft. The pinto was standing in a stall and he turned when her form blocked out the light. She spoke quietly and ran her hands over him but she learned nothing. The animal was unmarked and his shoes were firm. She emerged from the barn, passed through a gate at the far side of the corrals and found herself in a pasture shaded by cottonwoods: more open woodland than meadow. A group of steers stood somnolent in the shade, swishing their tails.

A path meandered through the long grass, its dust caked and unmarked. The storm had washed out all prints except, set as if in concrete, the track of a skunk which must have been made since the rain. The path brought her to the creek, sinister below its green canopy of foliage, to a fence and an open gate. At this point there was a ford and the banks were marked by cattle. The level of the creek had dropped considerably since the storm. She rolled up her jeans and waded to the other side, the water reaching to just above her knees. On the far bank the path turned and followed the creek downstream. She came to another fence and a small wooden gate, just wide enough for a horse to pass. There was a low latch that would be within reach of a six-year-old child. The sand was indented here but the heavy rain had obscured all outlines.

The path continued along the creek bank to the field

where the children had held their impromptu rodeo; through tree trunks on her left she could see the oil drums they used in their barrel racing.

'What did Birdie do when you left the meadow?'

Five other children had been playing with Birdie and four of them were on the front porch with Miss Pink. Some of the others were there too; Tracy, a brilliant redhead, was in the rocking chair with the baby on her lap. Erik Olson was seated on the porch steps. He had raised no objection to Miss Pink's asking questions. 'There's no way you can stop them talking,' he had said. 'I've not tried. You talk sensible to them, you might be able to find out something. This matter's got to be cleared up one way or another.'

Predictably it was Debbie who took it upon herself to introduce Mike – the lad who had been away at Wind Whistle yesterday morning – although it was not she who raised the subject that must have been preoccupying the older children. But if Debbie seemed less concerned than they, she was subdued, as were all of them, and seemingly dumbfounded when Miss Pink asked that first simple question about Birdie's movements. Debbie, of course, had not been there; she had been on Calamity Mesa, so in this context she would not have anything to say. She sat on the step below her father, her hands in her lap, and stared at the track that led to the road.

Shelly, the sister closest to her in age (and Birdie's age, reflected Miss Pink), said: 'I didn't see; I was trying to untie Buster, he'd pulled his knot tight, and he's frightened of lightning, and I couldn't undo the knot— '

'I went to help her,' said Steve, the small Olson boy. 'I never knew Birdie left. I didn't see her go.'

'She went home,' Laurel said. She was the girl twin. 'She said her mom was gone to town.' She stopped suddenly.

'And?' Miss Pink prompted.

'Well,' Debbie said in a remote voice, 'her dad was on his own so Birdie'd go home. She liked her dad.'

Miss Pink drew in her breath and caught Olson's eye. For

93

a moment neither could look away. She heard Debbie say something else and forced her mind back to the present.

'What's that got to do with anything?' came the angry voice of Robin, the boy twin.

Debbie looked sullen. 'I don't know what you mean.'

'What did you say, Debbie?' Miss Pink asked, but for once the child would not respond.

'She asked if Shawn went with Birdie,' Robin said.

'Oh.' Miss Pink was startled. 'And did he?'

'No.' Shelly stared at the visitor. 'How could he? He couldn't cross the creek. He was on his bike.'

'Shawn always went home by the track,' Laurel explained. 'Birdie went home across the creek if she had her pony. She did yesterday. I saw her go into the trees.'

'Going towards the gate upstream?'

'Of course. She had to, to reach home. There's no other way.'

'Would Shawn have left at the same time?' Miss Pink wondered.

They thought about this. 'Do you mean exactly?' Robin asked, frowning, trying to remember. 'Mom hollered to us to go home 'cause of the storm and we started to break it up . . . '

'Shawn went right away,' Shelly said. 'He's afraid of thunder and he had a long ways to go to get home.'

'So that means he left before Birdie?'

No one agreed with this or contradicted it. She opened her mouth to ask another question, then checked. She did not want to suggest that Shawn had seen a stranger, to put the idea of homicidal strangers in their heads, but was that any worse than the alternative, a homicidal neighbour? In any event her caution was superfluous. The thirteen-year-old Mike spoke for the first time: 'Shawn could have seen a strange car,' he said. 'Or a rider, or a hiker.'

Miss Pink regarded him: a redhead like his eldest sister, snub-nosed and attractive. 'When did you come home from Wind Whistle?' she asked. 'Did you see anything: a car? Did you pass Shawn?'

'I didn't come down the road. I was riding so I came home by the trail this side of the creek.'

'You can get glimpses of the road from that trail. I was on it yesterday. Did you notice any cars?'

'Not that I recall – and certainly no strange cars; I'd remember if I had.'

'He wouldn't have seen anyone,' Olson said quickly. 'He came home not long after three; he was helping me with a chicken-house out back.'

Mike glanced at his stepfather. The lad looked puzzled. 'Yeah, that's right,' he said, scuffing his boot on the boards.

Debbie said wistfully: 'When's Mom coming home?'

Sandy jumped up. She was another pretty girl, although less brilliant than her older sister. 'I'm going to make zucchini bread,' she exclaimed. 'Debbie, you come and help. You too, Shelly.'

Miss Pink went back to the Estwick cabin. She found Dolly in the kitchen, drying dishes. 'Where were you?' the younger woman asked, making it sound like an accusation.

'At the Olson place. How is she?' Nodding towards the bedroom.

'She's sleeping. Jo's in there. Frankie's gone home; she wanted to be with Jerome. And I have to go down to John. Would you stay here?'

'Sarah's with John,' Miss Pink said absently. 'Give me half an hour. I'm going to talk to Shawn.'

'What's he got to do with anything?' Dolly's tone was petulant. Everyone was upset.

'He could have seen a strange car.'

'I envy you, putting your trust in strange cars.'

There was nothing to say to that. 'Tell Jo the children are all right. The older ones are holding the fort. And Erik, of course.'

'Of course.' The tone was sardonic.

Miss Pink sighed and went out to her car.

As she emerged from the trees around the homestead, three vehicles were going fast down the road, raising a cloud of dust. The leading car slowed at the road-end, evidently as someone noticed the jeep, but it picked up speed again. Thinking that this convoy would contain the doctor and other forensic experts, she remembered the existence of the press, and the probability of their imminent arrival, and groaned inwardly.

'He can't tell you anything,' Maxine said. 'We haven't told him the details – and we're not going to. He's only ten. Did you forget that?' She stood on the porch: beautiful, poised and stone-cold sober. 'All he knows,' she went on, 'is that Birdie had an accident in the storm. He thinks she drowned in a flash flood.'

'How did you learn what happened?'

'Erik Olson told me this morning. Shawn had called to ask the children were they riding today, and Erik asked to speak to me. I didn't tell Shawn of course, but my mother knows. She's a tough old lady; I guess you come to accept horror as you get older. Me, it makes me want to throw up, what he did.' Shawn appeared and put his arm round her slim hips. 'Sweetie, I'm talking to Miss Pink.'

He looked up at her with the eyes of a frightened little boy. 'He's been like this since he came in yesterday,' Maxine said, smoothing his hair. She dropped down beside him. 'What happened, baby? Tell Mommy.'

He drew back against the door jamb and stared across the valley, his eyes glazed. He shivered.

'What did you see?' Miss Pink asked.

Maxine turned astonished eyes on her, then on her son. Myrtle came along the porch from her store. 'What happened?' she asked. 'Good morning, ma'am. What did Shawn see?'

'Nothing,' he shouted. 'I never saw nothing!' His lower lip trembled and he made a tentative move towards his mother.

'Of course he didn't!' She pulled him to her, and now she looked even more bewildered than he did. 'What could he have seen? What're you talking about?'

'A strange car,' Miss Pink said in surprise. 'I came here to ask if Shawn saw any strange cars, or people about – such as a man on a horse whom he didn't know, or hikers – if he saw anyone like that when he came home last night.'

He had twisted in his mother's arms and was regarding Miss Pink, quite still now and his eyes suddenly intelligent, then, without obvious transition, his face was stony again. 'I never saw nothing,' he said dully.

'You mustn't badger him,' Myrtle chided. 'You can see how badly shocked he is.'

She drove to Weasel Creek, bathed and dressed in clean clothes, and it was not until she was sitting in the shade drinking coffee and contemplating the Crimson Cliffs that she remembered she had agreed to spell Dolly. She thought about this. For some time she had been vaguely aware that cars were passing her road-end and had felt relief that she was no part of this busyness. If she returned to the Estwick place she would be drawn in again. She compromised. She got up, meaning to telephone and find out if Dolly was waiting for her, but from her living-room window she recognised a white car that was turning down Forset's track. She climbed into the jeep and followed.

'I'm not surprised you forgot,' Dolly said, meeting her in the yard. 'You must be worn out after last night. No sweat. The doctor's given Paula a sedative and Sam's with her.'

'*Sam* is with her?'

'He can cope. He refused to take any tranquillisers himself, said he'd got to go see to his cattle. That's a laugh; he's got about three steers. But if he's still thinking of going after the killer, he's got no more idea who it is than anyone else. Anyway, the place is swarming with police and no doubt they'll be watching to see he doesn't leave the place armed.'

'But— ' Miss Pink was nonplussed. 'After Paula's outburst in front of those uniformed men, I thought— '

'You're behind the times. Some plainclothes men arrived and they're a lot different than those fat guys. Everyone knows it was just shock and hysteria with Paula. Hi, Sarah – '

as the girl appeared on the porch. 'What did you do with John?' The tone was brittle.

'He's resting. What happened up the road?'

Dolly shrugged. 'They didn't take me into their confidence, but there are people on the banks of the creek so I guess they're looking for the place where he – where she was put in the water.'

'And the weapon,' Miss Pink said. 'They'll be searching for that, unless— '

'Unless what?' Dolly asked sharply.

'Unless it's been washed and replaced.'

'So – the police won't know that. They'll still be looking.'

Sarah regarded them thoughtfully, then turned her attention to the valley. The creek was hidden by the near swell of a pasture and only the tops of distant cottonwoods were visible.

'What's going on here?' Forset's voice came from the shadows. 'Come in, ladies; don't stand in the yard.'

They went into the living-room. After the last twenty-four hours Miss Pink felt a sense of shock that the view should be the same. Only the light was different. Forset brought beer and glasses, sat down and studied her face. 'You've had a lot of experience with murder,' he stated heavily.

'Some.'

'What's your opinion of this – outrage?'

She had been afraid of this. 'You have to keep an open mind at the start— ' she began.

'Is it Estwick?'

'John!' Dolly was appalled.

He turned on her. 'Paula accused him – and isn't the first suspect always a member of the family?'

'If the spouse is a victim,' Miss Pink agreed. 'But this is different.' Unhappily she reflected that the difference made it worse, not better for Sam.

Dolly asked quietly: 'John, you want it to be Sam?'

He glowered at her. 'It's what the police think.'

The older women studied his face, trying to read his mind. All Sarah's attention seemed to be on the view.

'And you, miss,' he turned on the girl with a joviality that deceived no one: 'You've been very quiet; what do you think?'

Dolly's eyebrows rose. Miss Pink thought of Sarah's age and was deeply puzzled.

Sarah said: 'I think it had to be a stranger, some kind of drifter who came down here, looking for work perhaps, and could have been hanging around the Estwick place just when Birdie showed up. Afterwards, of course, he'd get back to the main road as fast as possible, hitch a ride with the first truck. He'll be over the state-line by now. He may never be found.'

'You got it all worked out,' Dolly said.

The others were silent. She had set them thinking. After a while Miss Pink asked: 'Would you get that kind of person in these parts? Is it possible?'

Forset nodded. 'It happens occasionally: people who have opted out, no car, no money; they'll work a few days, sometimes for a whole season, sleep in a barn, and then they move on again. They're not normal, of course, but harmless: reclusive, solitary men without family ties. And then there are men who take to the wild, live in caves or shelters, poach deer and steal the odd calf, break into cabins for flour and sugar and tobacco. They're more of a problem. Sometimes they're vicious.'

Sarah said: 'There's a theory that it's better to try to integrate mental patients in the community than keep them shut up in hospitals all their lives. Truth is, cutbacks in health care mean we can't afford to keep people in institutions; there are too many of them.'

'The same in Britain,' Miss Pink said. 'It's meant to be applied only to people who show no tendency towards violence, but there are always some who will slip through the net.' She returned their looks of dawning comprehension. 'The theory has some comfort,' she told Sarah, 'but if you're right, and he's pushed on, he has to be found, because children are at risk in other communities.'

'He could live off the land,' Forset pointed out. 'Keep away from people until the furore dies down.'

'If he keeps hidden,' Dolly said. 'And if he comes into a town, the police should pick him up. That is, if *they're* convinced the killer is a hobo.'

'You've made us feel better, young woman.' Forset stood up and, indeed, he looked quite happy. 'Another beer, ladies?' Dolly was staring at him. 'It's not pleasant to think that one of your friends is a monster,' he told her, evidently thinking his change of mood needed explanation. 'In fact, it's incredible. I mean, *who*? Of the seven others, six – leave out Jerome, of course – there's Sam, Art Stenbock, Plummer, Erik, the Duvals . . . it's madness. They'd have to be mad, and I ask you, I'm asking you: which one of those men is that mad?'

'Dolly said you went to the Brenners to ask Shawn something.' Sarah had followed Miss Pink out to her jeep. 'He left the other children about the same time as Birdie. Did he see anyone on the road?'

'It's peculiar; he's hiding something, I'm sure of that. He's a frightened little boy and he's protesting too much – that he saw nothing.' She regarded Sarah thoughtfully. 'Someone should make him talk; if he did see something, or someone, he's in danger all the time he keeps it to himself. He hasn't told his mother; she's more bewildered than he is. As for Myrtle, she maintains he's in shock. I think he's lost; he doesn't know what to do.'

'You think he saw a strange car, or a hobo?'

'He would have been in a position to – or would he? If Birdie was attacked on the way home, around the vicinity of the creek, say, her attacker would have to be there, in position, around the time she left the field, in which case Shawn couldn't have seen him because by the time the boy reached the road the man would have been already concealed by the Estwick woods.'

'Where was Sam?' Sarah was unexpectedly vehement. 'If you rule out Sam as the killer,' she explained, 'why didn't he see something?' She answered her own question. 'Either he was at the ranch and Birdie was attacked on the way home,

100

or he was away from the buildings, fencing, something like that, and she was killed when she reached home. Because she saw a bum stealing something? And Sam would have no alibi,' she murmured.

Miss Pink was not listening. 'If he reckoned he couldn't get home in time,' she mused, 'if there'd already been a peal of thunder, a bad one, as he was approaching the Estwicks' road-end, would he have raced down to their place for shelter? I think he would.'

'Who are you talking about?'

'Shawn, of course. Shelly Olson said he was afraid of thunder.'

'Is he? I didn't know that.'

'That's when he could have seen someone.'

'So why didn't Sam as well?'

Chapter 8

Estwick had seen nothing, because, just before the storm struck, he was burying the putrid carcass of a deer which he had found rotting on the bank of the creek upstream of his house. The police accompanied him to the spot and Schaffer and Morgan dug until they uncovered a hoof and a fearful stench, when they were told to fill the hole in again. Estwick, watching, had shown neither amusement nor interest. Miss Pink heard this account from Frankie Gray who, by late Sunday afternoon, seemed to know a great deal that had happened in the community since the discovery of the body.

'The telephone's a great help,' she explained. 'People don't want to go far from their houses, but they're bursting to talk.'

'Everyone is?' Miss Pink asked. They were sitting beside the pool, in the shade of a *ramada* made of cactus ribs. Jerome had been lounging with his eyes closed. Now he opened them and regarded his wife intently.

'No,' Frankie admitted. 'I was talking loosely. You force me to concentrate on my terminology. People were not bursting to talk when they answered the phone; just the opposite, they were wary and suspicious. Their first thought would be that this was the police on the line. However, after I'd gossiped for a space: "How are you? Are the children upset? Have the police been to you?" they opened up. Then they talked. But – everyone?' She glanced at Jerome. 'Not everyone.'

'Did you call Lois?' he asked. 'She must have been devastated: all her theories of trusting strangers blown sky-high.'

'I didn't get to speak to her. Art answered and I couldn't say much to him because he saw the body. I asked after Lois. He said she was all right. He was one of those who didn't want to talk. He sounded very subdued.'

'Where was he yesterday afternoon?'

Miss Pink, who had been watching a lizard stalking a grasshopper, turned to Frankie in surprise. 'You didn't ask him?'

'Of course I did. The police will. He was cleaning the flues in their cookstove just before the storm.'

'So if you asked him that, presumably you asked him how he could prove it?'

'No, he told me.'

'Oh, come on!' Jerome protested.

'Really. He said he'd chosen to do it then because it was a filthy job and Lois climbs up the wall if he cleans flues when she's home, but she'd gone to Nebo with Paula. She was delighted when she got back and found her stove drew properly.'

'He gave you a lot of extraneous information,' Jerome said drily.

'He was establishing his alibi. He bathed in the creek afterwards.'

'What!' Miss Pink sat up and the lizard skittered across the tiles.

'He was dirty, covered with soot.'

'Yes, he would be.' She exchanged glances with Jerome who looked across the pool in the direction of the Stenbocks' cabin, hidden by the tops of pinyon pines. 'He'd be over a mile from the Estwicks' place,' he mused, 'and the Olson cabin in between.'

'So Lois went to town with Paula,' Miss Pink murmured. 'And Jo was at the Duvals', incidentally giving them – well, giving Bob Duval – an alibi. Alex was "pulling fence". What's that, Jerome?'

'Dragging down the old fence, preparatory to putting up a new one. Where was Alex doing that?'

'I've forgotten, if I ever knew. Wherever he was, he

103

has no alibi. He had been with young Mike – Olson?'

'Warman, actually,' Frankie supplied. 'It's immaterial; we call them all Olson, they don't seem to mind. So Mike was with Alex. No one told me that.'

'Mike went home early and helped Erik mend a hen-house.' Miss Pink avoided their eyes, recalling Mike's ambivalent attitude when his stepfather said he came home at three. She said, looking over the pinyons: 'Mike and Erik alibi each other.'

'And I can't alibi my old man here because I was asleep.' Frankie smiled wryly. 'Do you realise how ridiculous all this is?'

'The police will be taking it seriously enough. It's better that we should too, then we won't be shocked when they start asking the kind of questions they ask of suspects.'

Jerome had relaxed in his chair again. 'Thank God I'm in the clear; I don't think they could seriously suspect me.'

Frankie's eyes widened. 'I was not asleep,' she said firmly.

'You'll tell the truth, my dear; you couldn't lie to save anyone's skin. You were asleep.'

Miss Pink found the exchange touching and smiled indulgently before she remembered the object of the conversation. 'They'll go to Plummer, a man living alone. He must have been in touch with you, Frankie.'

'My dear, he came here. What else could he do? After seeing the body he went home and bathed and had a drink and then he started thinking, and realised that his own position was awkward, to say the least. He tried to get hold of Dolly but he couldn't get a reply because she – and I – were everywhere this morning except in our own houses. For some reason he wouldn't talk to Jerome—'

'I was a suspect.'

'But as soon as I came home (he must have been watching for me to come down the canyon) he was here. By that time he was pretty incoherent. We poured black coffee down him and got him sober, more or less.'

'Did he say anything reasonable?'

'He told me that late yesterday afternoon he was asleep, in

104

his bedroom – it was pretty enervating in the canyon before the storm – and the first he heard of anything untoward was Art Stenbock calling him and asking if he'd go out and help look for Birdie.'

They were silent, Miss Pink calculating.

'That's everybody,' Frankie said, watching her. 'Alex Duval was fencing, Bob Duval was talking to Jo just before the storm; Art was cleaning flues, Glen was asleep, Jerome was right where he is at this moment – and John Forset was rushing round his buildings trying to stop things blowing away before the gusts.'

'Those are not facts,' Miss Pink demurred. 'Apart from Bob Duval, who's alibied by Tracy and Sandy as well as by Jo – they were at Wind Whistle too – and apart from Erik who must be alibied by countless Olsons, the whereabouts of the rest of them are not known. We only know what they say.'

'Six men have no alibis,' Jerome explained to his wife.

'Five.'

'No, my dear. I'm innocent but I don't have an alibi.'

Frankie stood up. 'I'm going to fix us a meal. You'll stay, Melinda? Shall I call Glen, sweetie? We can't leave him to eat alone tonight.' Jerome was silent. 'I won't call him,' she said easily. 'Where can Sarah be? She's been gone ages.'

Jerome sat up slowly. 'Where did she go?'

'I don't know. I saw her riding down the track and I called to her but evidently she didn't hear me.'

'She may have gone to the Brenners,' Miss Pink said, and told them of her conviction that Shawn was concealing something.

'Shawn's like Birdie – like she was,' Frankie said. 'Both introverts, and unpredictable.'

Jerome disagreed. 'Unpredictable, yes, and I'm not sure what you mean by introverts in this context, but Birdie was a wild little creature; like a young animal, Sarah says: instinctive, impulsive . . . You could say Shawn is the same superficially: instant gratification, but that boy has nothing of the animal about him.' He held Miss Pink's eye. 'I've met him occasionally, and stopped and spoken to him, as one does with all the children. He's extremely polite and soft-spoken and very, very careful.' He turned to his wife. 'He's the antithesis of Birdie, who was suspicious of everyone she didn't take a shine to – and she let you know it; she wore her heart on her sleeve. But I'm not surprised that Shawn's concealing something; he conceals everything.'

'The behaviour expert,' Frankie said fondly, and bent and kissed him on top of his head. 'Sun's over the yardarm, sweetie – ah, I hear a horse!'

It was galloping. A *frisson* ran through them; people who care for their horses come home slowly. Through the pines they caught a flash of the blue roan, then the hoofbeats dropped to a walk and Sarah appeared at the gap between the cabin and the pool. She did not dismount.

'The police could be headed this way,' she told them.

'That's all right.' Jerome made a show of reassurance. 'Did you talk to them yet?'

'Sort of, but I don't know anything, so I couldn't help them.'

'Well, that's true,' Frankie said. 'You don't know anything – do you?'

'Did Shawn talk?' Miss Pink asked, alert for the sound of an engine.

'He clammed up on me.'

'You've been gone ages,' Frankie said. 'Where else were you?'

'Just around. With the police. This horse is steaming; I have to go. They'll be here any minute.' She clattered away to the stable behind the house. Frankie frowned, watching her go, then stiffened as a car was heard coming up the track. 'Drinks, sweetie?' she asked brightly, then to Miss Pink: 'Can you hold the fort?'

The Grays went indoors. Miss Pink looked down at her clean slacks and reflected that, although she was not dressed for cocktails and dinner, at least she had not slept in these clothes. She got up from her *chaise longue* and took an upright chair. Reclining, she felt at a disadvantage.

The engine was switched off and the evening was still. Down in the pinyons a bird sang a snatch of song. Distinctly she heard twigs scrape and caught sight of something spotted slip through a patch of sunlight. Voices approached. 'I'll be right out,' Frankie was saying, appearing with two strange men. 'You must be parched in this heat. Come and meet our guest. Melinda, these are Lieutenants Pugh and Sprague. Miss Pink is from England. You'll have to excuse me for a moment.' She bustled away.

'Do sit down,' Miss Pink said. 'Pugh? Your people came from Wales?'

'Why, yes, ma'am.' He was slight and dark with the sharp features of the Celt. His companion was plump and genial. They wore white shirts with collars and she suspected that when they started out this morning they were wearing ties.

'How did you know I was Welsh?' Pugh asked.

'Pugh is a common name in Wales.'

Lieutenant Sprague cleared his throat. 'You're staying here, ma'am?'

'I have a cabin farther down the canyon.'

He looked out over the pool, which was large and clean and indicative of wealth. Sarah came from the stable, smelly and unchanged, collapsed in a chair and stared at the detectives incuriously. Miss Pink knew that she was acting the role of a typical girl of her age. The men were not unaffected and Sprague's hand went to his throat and hovered there as if he had meant to loosen a tie. He said: 'We're asking everyone where they were yesterday afternoon.' Sarah looked bored.

'I was riding,' Miss Pink said, and gave them an account of the ride up to the point when the rain started.

'So you saw no one before the storm?' Sprague pressed.

She considered. 'When we were on top we looked down on the Forset place.' She indicated Calamity Mesa which was the obvious feature from where they sat. 'John Forset was cutting wood. And he was waiting for me when I got back. I was on one of his horses. Otherwise, no; we didn't see anyone else – apart from Erik Olson.' She had told them already that they had met Debbie's father in Mormon Pasture.

'What did you do after you returned the horse?'

'I went home, changed, and drove to the Estwicks' cabin. Mr Forset had told me that Birdie was missing.'

'How would he know that?'

'Her mother had been telephoning people.' Miss Pink looked at Sarah.

'Her mother got hysterical,' the girl explained. 'Birdie was always going missing – you know that already, but this time, with the pony coming back and all, we thought the kid had come off, was lying unconscious somewhere.'

'She was too young to be riding alone,' Sprague said.

Sarah stared at him. 'She didn't come to grief on a horse!' she said with contempt. He flushed.

Pugh said quickly: 'So her mother came back from town, found the child missing, and no husband around, and raised the alarm. Now why was that? The kid had been missing already this week; she should have been used to it.'

'The pony,' Sprague put in.

'Ah, yes; the pony was tied up in the stable.'

Sarah stared at him, then blinked slowly. Miss Pink repeated: 'It was tied?'

'Yes, ma'am, the bridle had been taken off and someone had removed the saddle. Did she do that?'

'Why look at me?' Sarah said. 'I wasn't there.'

'Where were you, miss?'

'Over there.' She gestured to the far side of the valley.

'Doing what?'

'Taking photographs.'

'In the dark?' By late afternoon the west side of the valley was deep in shadow.

'I had a flash.'

'What were you photographing?' Pugh asked politely.

'Rattlers.'

In the ensuing silence Jerome came along the tiles carrying a tray. 'My dear,' he addressed his daughter, 'bring some soda and more glasses.'

'Your daughter says she was photographing rattlesnakes yesterday!' Sprague exclaimed.

'No doubt.' Jerome was making room for the tray on an iron table, transferring magazines and books to chairs, talking as he moved: 'She's not satisfied with what she has. Rattlers are difficult animals to photograph. You want them threatening, but when you're looking through a view finder, you can't judge if they're coming closer. You need two people really. Tio Pepe, Melinda?'

When he had served her he pressed whisky on the guests but they asked for lemonade. Sarah, who had returned with a tray, put it on the tiles and went back without a word. They were silent until she arrived with a jug and glasses.

'Did you see anyone in your travels?' Pugh asked her.

'Not to notice,' she said airily. 'I wasn't interested in people.'

'How did you come home?'

'Across the fields.'

Frankie appeared. 'That's that,' she said cheerfully. 'You'll stay and eat with us?'

They declined. Miss Pink wondered if they had deduced that the Gray family, unwittingly or not, were working to make sure their visitors were not at their ease. She said brightly: 'Are you working on the assumption that someone other than Birdie unsaddled the pony?'

It was Sprague who answered. 'I hefted that saddle and I don't believe a six-year-old child could have got it on a buck.'

'A buck?'

'They put saddles on sawbucks,' Pugh said.

'You mean, low, like that?' Frankie indicated the height of a sawhorse. 'Couldn't she?'

No one answered her.

'So the question is,' Sprague went on, 'was she killed before she reached home and the pony came home alone – or was led – and was unsaddled by the killer, or had she managed to unsaddle it herself – or been helped by someone – and then he killed her? Estwick says he never even knew

109

the pony was home until his wife told him.' Sprague's gaze rested thoughtfully on Jerome. 'Estwick was drenched,' he said absently.

'What is that supposed to mean?' Frankie asked, and Jerome made a small movement of protest.

Sprague smiled at her: a little triumph, he had riled her. 'There could have been a lot of blood so the killer'd need to wash it off, and at some time he was by the water because he put the body in the creek. He would have waded in fully clothed to wash off the blood. A man coming home wet would be suspect except that yesterday afternoon, early evening, everyone was drenched. Almost everyone. And Sam Estwick says he washed in the creek anyway after burying a deer carcass. Stenbock cleaned a stove and he washed the soot off in the creek – and there are his clothes, still wet and stained with soot. Alex Duval was out in the rain; even you were, ma'am.' He looked at Miss Pink.

'We've been to everybody,' Pugh said, and waited.

After a moment the Grays and Miss Pink realised that this remark held special significance. It was Jerome who asked stiffly for an explanation: 'And are you any nearer to learning the identity of the culprit?'

'Oh, yes,' Sprague said. 'Nearer than when we came. Of course, we don't have the autopsy report yet, but we should get that tomorrow.'

'The storm hindered us,' Pugh told them, 'washing out traces, but it gave us a break too. If it hadn't been for the storm Shawn Brenner wouldn't have gone down to the Estwicks' instead of going straight home.'

Reactions to this were only partially gratifying, and none was revealing. Miss Pink and Frankie were astonished, Jerome and Sarah inscrutable.

'Shawn talked to you,' Miss Pink said flatly.

'Yes. We understand that several people tried to make him talk today.' Sprague bared his teeth in a grin that was not amused. 'Perhaps we brought a little more pressure to bear than the neighbours could. And we got him away from his mother.'

110

'You couldn't interview him without her being present,' Jerome said quickly.

'We weren't interviewing him,' Pugh said. 'We were just talking to him.'

'And the mother wasn't that much interested anyways,' Sprague pointed out.

'She was drunk,' Sarah said, then, as disapproving eyes were turned on her: 'Well, I was there too.'

'And he wouldn't talk to you?' Sprague spoke as if to a child, indulgently. His tone changed. 'Shawn saw a man carrying something towards the creek.'

'Who?' Frankie asked.

'He couldn't see. It was gloomy and the man was just going into the trees. The boy looked in the stable and saw the pony. He went to the house, found it empty, and then he realised that what the man was carrying had been limp, with feet hanging down, he said. He ran away and went home.'

Jerome said heavily, 'It's fortunate for him that he talked. But he couldn't identify the man?'

Sprague shook his head. Pugh stood up and went away round the side of the house. As they waited for the next thing to happen Miss Pink realised that at some point the balance had changed, that however ill at ease the detectives had been, now they were in control of the situation.

Pugh returned and placed a transparent plastic bag on the table. Inside was a knife with a broad pointed blade about six inches long and a handle that looked as if it were made of black plastic.

'Did any of you see this before?' Sprague asked.

They stared at it until Jerome said: 'Everyone has hunting knives; this one has nothing remarkable about it. Where was it found?'

'In the creek,' Pugh said. 'About a coupla hundred yards from the Estwick place. We didn't find it early on because the creek was muddy but as the level dropped and the water cleared it was quite easy to see.'

Frankie said: 'Are you saying that this is the knife that was used on – that this is the weapon?'

'We don't know, ma'am, but the pathologist will be able to tell us. The right knife will fit.' Frankie gasped and turned her head away. 'We have to show it to everyone,' he went on. 'I wonder, would you two ladies care to come with us?'

'What for?' Jerome snapped to attention. 'Where?'

'I was about to say, sir,' Sprague was smooth as butter. 'We're going to Estwick's place and we know Mrs Estwick is rather excitable. I'd like some womenfolk around when we show her husband the knife.'

'You're arresting him?' Frankie was incredulous.

'We have to ask if he recognises the knife.'

'They have to ask everybody,' Jerome said heavily.

'I'll come.' Frankie was fierce. She turned to Miss Pink. 'You, too? See to the dinner!' she flung at Sarah as she stalked away but Sarah did not seem to hear. People had the air of being stunned.

The women were further astonished to find the black and white police car parked outside the front door with Schaffer and Morgan inside, the radio turned low. It had crept up the track without attracting anyone's attention. They got into the back of the detectives' car and no one said a word on the short drive to the Estwicks' cabin. Frankie stared stonily out of the window, Miss Pink regarded the back of the officers' necks and wondered where in these days they had found a barber who would cut their hair that short. Behind them came the second car, more menacing for its silence, the siren off, the lights unlit.

They halted in the Estwicks' yard and each man held a lady's door for her to alight, without a smile. There was nothing amusing about their mission.

Tracy came to the door of the cabin and stood there, her red hair flaming, smiling but effectively barring entrance.

'Where's Sam?' Sprague asked.

Tracy's eyes took in the women and the uniformed police. The smile stayed but her eyes hardened. 'He went towards the ford,' she said.

112

'Is Paula asleep?' Miss Pink asked. The girl nodded. Everyone looked towards the creek. Sam Estwick was approaching the corrals, moving slowly like a man inspecting his land. He came to the gate, unlatched it and closed it behind him. He showed no surprise at the presence of this large party in his yard although his eyes sharpened at sight of the women.

'Before you go any further,' Sprague said without preamble, 'did you see this before?'

Estwick took the knife in its plastic covering. 'It could be mine.'

'Where would yours be?'

His hand went to his hip where an empty sheath was slotted on his belt. 'I mislaid it yesterday sometime,' he said.

'We have some questions to ask you . . . ' Smoothly, they separated in order to flank him, the uniformed men closing in like gross basilisks. The group moved past the women and went to the cars. Frankie whispered: 'They've arrested him?'

'They're taking him in for questioning. It's the knife; it appears to be his.'

'He didn't do it; he couldn't have done.'

'No, I suppose not, but someone did.'

Chapter 9

There was little relief in Salvation Canyon when Sam Estwick was taken in for questioning. Most people felt that he must be guilty but they were distressed and bewildered, although, for the sake of Paula and the children, they put on a show of returning to normality.

The press arrived on Monday but only stragglers; by Sunday evening the focus of attention had shifted to Nebo where both the body and the child's stepfather (the suspect?) were being held. The place where the body had been discovered was marked by yellow tape but there was not much interest in a bank so overgrown that there was not even the chalk outline of a corpse to be seen as there would be on a city pavement. A few still photographs were taken but never used. Pictures were printed showing a general view of the canyon with an 'X' marking the approximate position of Forset's South Forty and these were more dramatic.

Various reporters made the rounds of the residents and got the kind of reception that might have been predicted, some of it meaty copy but none of it, when analysed, containing information not already known about the murder. Bob Duval was taciturn at first, angry when pressed. Alex, who would have been more hospitable, was working cattle somewhere in the high country. In fact, most people who could, had disappeared; they had caught Bob just as he was about to leave. His horse was already saddled – and that could have explained his bad temper.

Jo and her oldest girls were pleasant 'but low on I.Q.', as a female reporter told her editor back in Nebo. (The younger

114

Olsons, and Debbie in particular, had been packed off early for a picnic, with Sarah and Jen in charge.)

The press got short shrift at the Estwick cabin where they were met by Dolly Creed who promptly swung into a spiel to promote her paintings. Literally and metaphorically there was no getting past her and her hard sell. They abandoned any attempt to see Paula, and drove to the Stenbocks' where Art talked about organic husbandry and flatly refused to answer any questions about his neighbours. They put him down as a crank with all a crank's unbreakable obstinacy, and pushed on to the Forset ranch which was deserted except for the Labrador. So they went across the road to Weasel Creek.

Miss Pink was delighted to see them; she gave them coffee and questioned them at length on the workings of the American news media but could give them no information herself because, as she told them, she had been in the canyon only a few days and knew none of her neighbours.

Glen Plummer was vacant, loquacious and equally uninformative. He offered hospitality and the two reporters who stayed with him longest came away with only the vaguest impression of what he was about. One thought he was in real estate, the other that he was writing a book. It was pointed out to them that it was Jerome Gray who was writing the book, then someone remembered that there was a Melinda Pink who wrote gothics. It was all very confusing, and Jerome Gray had been not only confusing but a trifle menacing. He had dropped one or two names inadvertently and they were the names of influential television sponsors. He was extremely polite and called everyone 'Mr' or 'Miss'. No one stayed long with Jerome.

They did not stay willingly at the last cabin, either. A lot of people thought that at first sight this was the goldmine they were looking for: the beautiful, welcoming Maxine, the garrulous and exotic grandmother, the little boy who had actually seen the killer, but after a while a slow disillusionment set in. Shawn, appealed to, cajoled, most delicately threatened, only twined himself about his mother and steadfastly refused to utter a word, gazing at them with the eyes of a fawn as Maxine stroked his hair and Myrtle reiterated that he was in deepest shock.

Myrtle and Maxine talked in counterpoint, Maxine drank steadily and the reporters came to the conclusion that there was nothing to be learned there. They began to feel the effects of the liquor that was pressed on them, and they remembered the rough drive beyond the narrows and they left. The Nebo reporter had a puncture on the way home and discovered that her *spare* tyre had been slashed.

When it seemed that they had all gone, at least from the lower end of the canyon, Miss Pink ate a light lunch and drove to Forset's ranch intending to ride down to the river to examine it at her leisure. She was quite prepared to catch her mount and saddle up herself as Forset had told her to do any time, but his pick-up was in the yard so she went towards the cabin.

At the porch she paused; she could hear him on the telephone. 'Keep him there,' he was saying urgently and she thought he must be referring to an animal. 'Whatever you do— ' He broke off and there was silence. She looked at the Crimson Cliffs, thought how naked they looked in the noonday heat. 'You're wrong!' came his voice. 'They're intelligent; he wouldn't stand a chance— ' She frowned; this didn't equate with a sick animal. She knew she should move away, out of hearing. She sat down on the steps. 'No one,' he said. 'Just you and me, at least in this valley . . . if Gray did know, he wouldn't talk . . . Hell, man, it *had* to be Sam . . . Look, we know that was a put-up job . . . You're right, of course. We can only hope – God, why didn't he keep Mike with him? Yes, I know . . . '

Sudden silence. A deep sigh. Heavy steps approached, and stopped behind her. She stood up and faced him.

'I heard everything,' she said. He looked utterly dispirited. 'I came to ride Yaller; I've decided it's too hot.'

'You heard everything?' His shoulders slumped as he considered, and came to a decision. 'Then you'd better

116

come in and I'll try to explain. Everyone will know shortly anyway. The police know already, in a sense, but maybe Sprague didn't pull it out of the computer yet. The thing is: Alex Duval is almost certainly in there under "Rape" or "Rapist". And the female in the case was a little girl. And Alex has run.' He blinked at her. 'I don't know what we're going to do about this.'

'Let's go inside,' she said comfortably, and piloted him through the junk room. They sat in big chairs by the window. 'Start from the beginning,' she suggested. 'Who were you talking to?'

'Why, Bob, of course; the brother. I'm moving some cows so I called to ask if they'd turn out: him and Alex and young Mike; we all help each other when a number of hands are needed. Bob said Alex couldn't come and he told me why, because I know about Alex. The Duvals and me, we're the oldest residents; it happened only twenty years back anyway. Bob told Alex he had to leave. I'm not so sure it was the right thing to do: send him away; it looks bad.'

'What happened twenty years ago?'

'A young kid – she was twelve – accused Alex of raping her. Her people worked for Old Duval. There were the three men: the old man and the sons: Bob and Alex. Mrs Duval died some years before. They had a housekeeper and her husband worked as a hand. He was the girl's father. I don't think Bob ever had the whole truth of it from Old Duval and it could have been a lot nastier than ever came out in court. What we did know was that the girl was— ' Forset coughed in embarrassment and sought for euphemisms. 'You must have come across youngsters who were older than their years.'

'Sexually precocious, you mean?'

'Exactly. No better than she should be. No one would come forward in court because she was under age, but there were men in the valley told Old Duval afterwards that she'd approached them – er – on a commercial basis – at age twelve! Can you believe that? All the same, the father put her up to it; Old Duval was sure of that. He was

117

a weirdo, the father. Old Duval caught him stealing money from his desk and fired him, and the family went straight to Nebo, to the sheriff, and accused Alex of raping the girl. There was a court case and he got off. The medical evidence showed that the girl had been – that there had been habitual intercourse.' He looked away. 'There was something about it having been going on over a number of years. The father made a very bad witness. And the Duvals are an old and well-respected family in these parts. There'd never been the slightest hint of anything like that connected with Alex: in school, in the canyon, anywhere. But there's the record, you see. He was arrested and charged – and he's a simple soul; says what he thinks. He could well tell the police he was "very fond of Birdie" which they'd figure was highly suspect; they always think the worst. So Bob's sent him into – sent him off until— ' His eyes begged a question. 'Until it's safe to return.'

She was silent. 'What are you thinking?' he asked.

'You make me wish he had an alibi.'

'You don't think he did it!'

'I don't know, John. When they took Sam, Frankie felt the same way about him. No matter how likeable anyone is, the man who killed Birdie must be put away because he's a danger to other children. No matter that he's never shown any hint of sexual violence before; he has done so *now*. That's the crux of the matter. The person who did it is mad; you must see that. But that means he can't be condemned to death.'

'That's a debatable point. You get a certain type of jury and a hanging judge, they're not going to take his state of mind into consideration. You've met the police; what allowances d'you think they'd make for Alex?'

'Did you have any trouble with them, John?'

'If you mean by trouble, were they hostile, no. I'm too old to be browbeat by city dudes less than half my age.' He smiled grimly. 'Particularly when I've got nothing on my mind – except my neighbours' problems.'

'You have no alibi. On the other hand, we heard your

chainsaw when we were on Calamity Mesa and I was back here within the hour. We had to cover a good six or seven miles but we were in a hurry because of the storm. The only time we slowed down was on the descent to the river. An hour. You wouldn't have had time to walk to the Estwicks' place, and if you rode or drove, you would have been seen.'

'I'd not thought of it like that. If they accuse me I'll tell them to work that out for themselves. You have a quick mind, Melinda.'

'I have a criminal mind. Did you see Erik when he came down?'

'Of course; he wouldn't go by without speaking. He said he met you.'

'Were you expecting him down so early?'

'Early? It was Saturday afternoon. He doesn't usually work at all Saturdays but there was a gap in a fence at the head of the canyon, and that had to be fixed.'

'Why is a fence necessary in a box canyon?'

'Because there are old mines and they're supposed to be fenced, stop the cows falling down a shaft. Once Erik finished he had to go home and fix his chicken-house because a skunk was stealing eggs.' He looked hard at her. 'You do know that all the young Olsons were about their buildings within minutes of leaving Birdie?'

'I knew that. And they went to the chicken-house and spoke to their father?'

He wiped his face with his hands. 'I can't keep it up,' he protested. 'You're worse than the police.'

The telephone was ringing when she stopped outside her cabin. It was Lois Stenbock asking her to go across for supper that evening. She accepted politely, reflecting wryly that Lois would have to do some juggling to reconcile events with her theories on raising children. As she put down the receiver her eyes narrowed. A car was turning into her road-end, and over the past thirty hours people in cars had not brought good news.

The visitor was Glen Plummer who was neither bursting with information nor apparently under any compulsion to learn the latest. What Plummer was after was company. They sat in the shade of the *ramada* behind the cabin while he talked and she listened, observing him more closely than had been possible three days ago at the Grays' party. The ensuing events had taken their toll; his pudgy simian face had sagged and he looked haunted. His trousers and sports shirt were clean and his hair was damp from the shower but there was a stale smell about him which suggested that he had indulged in a second drinking bout last night. He was thirsty and asked for water. He drank half a second glass and sighed, and started to sip his coffee.

'I needed that.' He looked at the red cliffs and added absently: 'This place is terrifying.'

'I think the rock is quite stable.'

'I mean, you get the feel of a threat hanging over you. It's psychological. I wish I could get away, but the police won't let us leave.'

'I'm sure they'd let you go to Nebo. You could stay in a motel provided you let them know where you are.'

'I could do that, I suppose.'

'It would be much more comfortable than trying to look after yourself down here.'

'And I'd get some good food.' He was wistful. 'I miss my wife's cooking – my ex-wife, I should say.'

She was confused. 'I understood you lost your wife last year.'

He shot her a glance. 'That was my second wife. Sally Ann was the first.' His eyes twinkled. 'And now there's another wants to be the third Mrs Glen Plummer.'

'You may have that wrong. I know Dolly isn't interested in marriage.'

'Dolly? I'm not talking about her. We're good friends, me and Dolly. In fact,' – he looked thoughtful – 'if I was to marry again I'd like it to be someone like her. She's reliable – and she's clever. She'd be a great help in my business.' He beamed at her. 'You got me thinking there.'

120

'But there is this other lady who has – er – taken a shine to you?'

'I've not given her any encouragement. I just had the odd drink with her but I never even took her out to a meal.' He ruminated, frowning. 'I'm not ready for responsibilities yet – more of them, I mean; I've got enough on my plate as it is. I need a rest from women, and families, and domesticity. Dolly's all right; she's an *artist*. I adore older ladies: her, Frankie, yourself . . . '

'Quite. But otherwise, and so far as business is concerned, you're bored. What is this scheme to flood Gospel Bottom and build a marina?'

'Oh, that. It was Dolly's inspiration. She was talking about titles for pictures one time and said how a name will sell a product, how "Gospel Bottom" was wasted, the name for just a bit of bottom land where the creek meets the river. Said if it was a resort everyone'd flock to it. So I said I'd put a marina in there. She got mad and I fantasised the idea but then I got to considering it seriously. It gives Dolly and me a meeting point, see what I mean? We strike sparks off each other. She's one very special lady.'

'You are not proposing to dam the river?'

'It's just a *talking* point! Dolly's paranoid about the ecology. She's like me that way: always looking for interests, but she found 'em. That's what I admire about her: she's so intense. Me, I've got no motivation. Who am I working for? I lost my family. Sally Ann's got custody of my daughter and that little girl's taken care of for the rest of her life if I drop dead tomorrow. I lost my house and brood mares worth half a million; that's my ex-wife's hobby: breeding Arabians, with my money. Hell, drop in the ocean. I make a million this week, lose two the next; in three weeks' time I make three million. What for? What do I do next? I'm the man who's got it all. Can you suggest a challenge?'

'Now let me think. A bored, rich man. There are some jobs which are tremendously exciting, but closed to the majority of people because the expenses are prohibitive.'

'Such as?'

'I was thinking of the profession of private detective. Finding criminals, missing persons: that's phenomenally expensive; you have to travel all over the world – but it's dangerous. Of course, that could be a stimulus.'

'That's good. I like it. I love it.'

'You could make a sensational start by tracking down Birdie's murderer.'

His jaw dropped. He said carefully, 'I'm not sure I understand what you're getting at.'

'If Sam Estwick didn't do it, then the killer could still be in the canyon.'

'But they arrested Sam.'

'No, they've taken him in for questioning. Even if he had been arrested, he's presumed innocent until found guilty.'

'You don't think he did it?'

'You do?'

'I never thought about it.'

'Oh, come now; I don't believe that.'

He stared at her in consternation. The situation had changed; she was no longer a sympathetic older lady but a hard questioner. 'You're looking at me as if you thought I was guilty of something,' he protested.

'No doubt you are.' He inhaled sharply. 'We all are,' she went on blandly, and he swallowed. 'You have no alibi,' she pointed out, 'but if I thought you were a murderer I wouldn't be discussing the subject with you, alone in an isolated cabin. All the same, I suspect the police gave you a hard time.'

'You can say that again! I wasn't sober either and that didn't help. I don't mean I was drunk. I was earlier, but I went over to the Grays and Frankie filled me up with black coffee – this was after I saw – saw – you know?' She nodded. Now she did look sympathetic. He continued: 'But soon's I came back I started on the bourbon again, and then *they* came: those smoothies with the button-down collars and the sneaky questions. I was tired; God, I was tired! I just told them the truth. I was searching all night, all next morning: wading the creek, right down to the river . . . Rattlers, they're all over the banks, you know; we were slashing through the willows, making as much noise as possible, never knowing whether our lights would show the coils gleaming or – her: drowned, we thought then, at night. We thought she'd fell off the pony and the flood had took her – little kid like that, no weight, she'd have no chance once the creek rose. We come back exhausted, driving up the road, and here's Sarah: "She's found," she says, and Sam says – well, he can't get it out; he wants to ask is she alive, but of course we all knew – him too – if she *was* alive, Sarah'd be jumping up and down: "We found her!" and laughing and shouting, but she says: "She's found," and she just looks at Sam.' He shook his head as if he were Sam denying the truth. He was as lost as his syntax. 'So then we follows them across the field – I don't know why we went, Art and me, but we been searching for so long, I guess we had to finish it, you know, something like that.' He put his head in his hands.

She got up and went to get him a drink.

When he had gone she drove slowly up the canyon. The evening was clear and beautiful. The Grays' entrance was a mile away when she turned down the Stenbocks' track, but every line of the blue roan gelding was distinct as it stood there on the verge, its rider evidently in conversation with a small figure holding something that glinted – a bicycle, of course.

Lois Stenbock's motive for inviting Miss Pink to supper became clear within a few minutes of the guest's arrival. Lois was aware that she should pay lip service to etiquette but basically she had tunnel vision; obsessed by her personal objective, she had little or no regard for the reactions of other people. So although she welcomed Miss Pink with the remark that she thought it best for everyone that life should return to normal as quickly as possible, that having Miss Pink over was part of the programme, it was obvious that she was protesting too much; she had other things on her mind.

Miss Pink agreed that a resumption of normal behaviour

was the wisest course, accepted a glass of apricot juice and regarded her hosts benignly. They were patently uneasy. It was Lois who started the ball rolling, suddenly, without preamble.

'Now we shall all be invoking hindsight,' she began. 'All the same, there was a marked deterioration in Sam Estwick over the past few weeks.'

'He was drinking more,' Stenbock said, as if qualifying his wife's statement.

'His behaviour changed! He was blatant: going up to Maxine Brenner's cabin virtually every night. He didn't even attempt to be discreet— '

'Was he going there as often as that?' Miss Pink asked. 'I had the impression that Maxine found him a nuisance.'

'She did. She couldn't stand the sight of him.'

'Then why should she allow him to visit – and how did you find out about this?'

'He went there to drink, and he paid for it. He was using the place as a bar and Maxine needed the money. It was Shawn who told us.'

'The ubiquitous Shawn.'

Lois said earnestly: 'I don't think you understand about Shawn. He's deprived.' She flashed a look at her husband. 'He distrusts strangers because that's how he's been brought up. I think I managed to make some impression before . . . At least he knows now that not everyone is dangerous.'

'Seems he was right to distrust Sam Estwick,' Stenbock said. 'A pity Birdie didn't.'

'Shawn distrusted Estwick?' Miss Pink repeated.

'He hated him,' Lois said with satisfaction. 'That hatred arose from fear, of course. He was terrified of Estwick, said he liked little boys.'

'What!' Miss Pink was amazed.

'He did say that,' Stenbock assured her. 'I was here when he said it.'

'Did he give – chapter and verse for such an accusation?'

He looked away and it was Lois who answered, sibilant with indignation: 'Estwick kissed him.'

124

Miss Pink shook her head. Stenbock said: 'I never believed that.' She turned to him. 'I thought there was something else, something worse, that he wouldn't talk about,' he said. 'Kissing was a euphemism.'

'It's irrelevant,' Lois snapped. 'Estwick liked little boys.'

'Birdie wasn't a little boy,' Miss Pink said.

'That's irrelevant too. She was a small child, the assault was sexual. That's what matters.'

Miss Pink asked: 'When Shawn told you this, what measures did you take to protect him?'

'The first thing I did was to call his mother.' Lois was virtuous.

'And what was her reaction?'

'She laughed.'

'She said Shawn watched too many movies,' Stenbock put in.

'I told her,' Lois said, 'that she was being criminally irresponsible to rent pornographic videos, and she hung up on me. She's a woman can't face the truth. She's an alcoholic, anyway, and her brain's softening. I wasn't going to let it rest there so I called Paula. Of course, there was no way I could tell her what Shawn was saying, but I hinted, you know, said I didn't think her husband was suitable company for small children. I had to admit that my information came from Shawn and she said that the child needed thrashing within an inch of his life and his mouth scrubbed out with soap. There! With all the feeling there is against that child I'm only astonished that it wasn't his little body that was found on the creek bank.'

'So am I.' Miss Pink was thoughtful. 'Did you know that Shawn told the police he saw a man carrying Birdie, or her body, away from the Estwick place and towards the creek?'

The Stenbocks fidgeted and avoided each other's eyes. 'Yes,' Lois said. 'We heard that.'

'Shawn didn't identify the man.'

'There's the knife,' Stenbock pointed out. 'Evidently it's Estwick's, and he admitted his was missing. He was mending a halter and he put the knife down on the table and went outside because he thought he heard a dog or a coyote upstream. And that reminded him of a deer carcass and he went straight to bury it and forgot the knife. He reckoned it went missing then. Now, that's just his story.'

'It's plausible,' Miss Pink said.

'All child molesters will be plausible,' Lois told her.

'That confounds your theory that children should be brought up to trust strangers.' Miss Pink could not resist that.

'Not at all. For one thing, Estwick is no stranger – and no one can guard against abuse inside the family; for another, he's aberrant. I still maintain that children should trust *normal* people.'

'Did you suggest to Shawn that it might be wiser not to be alone with Sam Estwick?'

'As a matter of fact, he didn't come – he wasn't allowed to come here any more, after I called his mother and told her she had a pervert frequenting her house. But I was satisfied in my own mind that Shawn would be on his guard; he was quite terrified of the man.'

'How curious,' Miss Pink murmured. 'When I arrived here I thought that the canyon housed a peaceful, integrated community, and you're telling me that beneath the surface there was child abuse?'

'It certainly wasn't peaceful,' Lois said, 'nor integrated. There was Birdie running away from home frequently – now, why was that, d'you suppose? Estwick was drinking in another woman's house, waiting his opportunity to corrupt a little boy; there was Glen Plummer— '

'He doesn't come into it,' Stenbock said quickly.

'Everybody's a suspect,' Lois began, then corrected herself. 'Everyone *was* a suspect before they arrested Sam Estwick. Why, even you had to prove your alibi!' She gave him a wry smile.

'You have an alibi?' Miss Pink asked politely, not troubling to inform them that Estwick had not been arrested, at least, not initially.

'I offered them my coveralls,' Stenbock said. 'I'd washed in the creek after I cleaned the flues – that's what I was doing Saturday afternoon: cleaning the cookstove. The soot was still on the coveralls – soot stains, I mean, so I figured that since blood stains can be detected in a laboratory, they'd better have the coveralls to prove my innocence. The police wouldn't take them. I knew I wasn't a suspect then even though I didn't have an alibi.' He looked at his wife with a kind of defiance.

'You still have the coveralls?' Miss Pink asked.

'I've burned them now,' Lois said. 'They were too filthy to keep and no way was I going to wash them. He's got plenty of old clothes he can use cleaning flues. Why, I'd rather go to the Thrift Store, pay a few dollars for old pants and a shirt than wash coveralls every time I have my cookstove cleared of soot.'

Miss Pink nodded agreement, reflecting that murder, that being in the vicinity of a murder, made some people extraordinarily garrulous.

Chapter 10

At eight o'clock in the morning the Forset place was already astir. Saddled horses were tied to rails and Forset was conferring with Bob Duval and Erik Olson. He was surprised to see Miss Pink this early but she pointed out that morning was the best time to ride, that although she planned to stay out all day, she would rest her horse during the hottest hours. He apologised that she should have to catch and saddle Yaller; if he'd known . . . 'It's no trouble,' she assured him. 'Don't let me hold you back.'

'We're bringing some cows out of Gospel Bottom, putting 'em up Mormon Pasture. Now tell me where you're going, eh?'

'I'm going to follow the creek out into the high country above the narrows, parallel with the road.'

'That's right; don't lose sight of the road when you're on your own.' He smiled. 'That way we won't have to come so far to look for you if you don't come back.'

She returned his smile and went into the barn for a halter.

They were gone by the time she had saddled Yaller; they had even taken the dog. As she led the horse to the mounting log she felt as if she had been abandoned. She thought of the route she had sketched to Forset and wished she were taking it: a quiet hack compared with where she proposed going. She had a map but maps were one thing, the terrain another. Maps seldom showed cliffs and never conveyed atmosphere; today she would be in unknown country in more ways than one.

She must have communicated something of her uneasiness to the horse because he turned skittish once they were clear of the corrals. This had the effect of concentrating her mind wonderfully and, since she was in something of a hurry, she was forced to devote all her attention to controlling him at a trot.

She followed the route she had taken with Dolly four days ago. At the creek below the great cove, Forbidden Creek, she slowed down. This was one of the places where the trail came close to the water, and Yaller, although sure-footed on mountain trails, had little regard for where he put his feet when he was in the valley. Edging him away from the eroded bank, she paused at the little side-creek and studied the gouge in the cliffs above.

It was curious how the rock literally encircled the floor of the bay, rising to towers on one side of the lowest point (where water from flash floods had stained the sandstone); even part of the cliff on that side, the Maze side, was hidden, as if the towers were protecting it. She looked around. No houses were visible; all were obscured by their own clumps of cottonwoods or the trees on the banks of Salvation Creek. But the cove was high in the cliff and that part which was invisible from below might be visible from her own cabin, which stood somewhat above the road and at a distance. This evening she might see more with the aid of binoculars. And then she wondered why this was important. It was not because she wanted to get into that place but because no one could. Had other minds worked like hers, wondering if the Anasazi had been there, if the Cave of Hands was against the hidden wall of the great cove?

She came back to the trail and pushed the horse into a lope, slowing to a walk as she passed the Olson place, not wanting to attract attention with the sound of pounding hoofs. She skirted the loop of the creek where it contoured the plinth that supported the Blanket Man. She looked up at the Stone Hawk on her other side and reflected that, if it was in the cove, the Cave of Hands could have nothing to do with the secret way down to the valley from Rustler Park; she was nearly two miles from Forbidden Creek.

Beyond the Olson and Estwick homesteads she resumed a

gentle canter, came to the Duvals' property, which appeared deserted, and left by way of the gate in Horsethief Canyon. She was fastening the gate when she saw a familiar flash of colour at the back of Wind Whistle: brown and white, a pinto pony. It was a poignant moment, mistaking it for Birdie's pony, and then she realised that it could well be the same animal; Paula might have asked the Duvals to look after it. She turned to her own horse, wondering why the pinto was standing at the back door of the house instead of grazing in a meadow. She looked back. It had not moved. She focused her binoculars.

There was a saddle on the animal. Could Alex have been in the house when she passed? No, Alex was much too heavy for the pinto. Of course – one of the Olsons, probably Mike, had borrowed it, and he worked at Wind Whistle, had probably gone indoors for a can of pop or something. The blob of colour changed shape. A figure had emerged from the house, mounted, and was moving fast through the corrals and across a meadow towards the Horsethief trail.

She mounted and rode to the first thick clump of pinyons. She was sitting on the bank watching a turkey vulture when the pinto approached. She lowered the binoculars and turned to the rider. 'Why, good morning, Shawn,' she said, unable to conceal her surprise. 'Isn't that – an Estwick horse?'

'It's Birdie's,' he said. 'Her mom said I could ride him.'

'And where are you going on him?'

'I'm going up Rustler, ma'am. The others were there yesterday but my mom wouldn't let me go, so I'm going today on my own, try and make up for it.'

'Make up for what?'

'Being left out of the picnic.' He bit his lip.

'Do you feel safe on your own?'

'Birdie could do it. She was only six. So's Shelly, and she come up here yesterday too.'

'Shelly was with Sarah and Jen.'

He muttered something and moved his hands. The pinto took a step forward.

'What did you say?'

'I said you're not always safe with other people.'

She saw the fear in his eyes. Was he frightened of her? 'Get down, Shawn,' she said, and patted the earth. 'Sit here and— '

'No, I can't! I have to— '

'Sit down and tell me about Sam Estwick.'

That cut across his protests and he gaped at her, his eyes wide. For long seconds he stared, then pushed his pony up the bank, slid off and tied it in the shade beside Yaller. He came back and sat about six feet from her.

'I told the police all I know,' he said.

About to speak, she changed her mind and watched the vulture come in to land on a tree above the Lower Jump.

'I never said it was Sam,' came the small voice.

'No, that was nice of you.'

'I like Sam. I respect him.' Miss Pink remained silent. 'I wish he was my dad.' He seemed to be thinking between each utterance. 'Sometimes,' he added.

'And is he fond of you?'

Delicately he started to pick the flowers from the stem of a lupin. 'I don't know. Sometimes I think he is, sometimes I don't, but then I don't always like him; when he talks about whipping I hate him.'

'I'm not surprised. So what do you do then?'

'What could I do?'

'I don't know. It takes an ingenious mind; you might, say, put something nasty on his saddle.'

His eyes danced. 'Like super glue?'

'Or make up stories about him.'

'Such as?'

'Stories that would make other people despise him.'

'Such as?'

'That he likes little boys.'

He had destroyed the lupin and now his hands were still. He was a beautiful child; in profile the lack of expression was not obvious. He turned to her, and his face was full of expression. 'It was what I wanted!' he said earnestly. 'I

131

wanted him to like me but I didn't – I don't think he does, so I told a lie.'

'You wanted him to kiss you.'

He squirmed on the bank. 'No, that's kid stuff; my mom's always holding me tight and stroking my hair and stuff, I hate that, I'm not a girl. But I never had a dad; I got lots of uncles, they're *her* boy friends, so it's not the same thing. I want a dad. Mr Plummer'd do, I s'pose. I get a bit mixed up with all of them, don't know which is for the best.' He looked very small and helpless.

'Let's get this straight; when you told Mr and Mrs Stenbock that Sam kissed you, it was a lie?'

'Right.'

'And that he liked little boys?'

'I want him to like me!'

'Who told you that some men liked little boys?'

'It were in a movie.'

'So you were getting your own back at Sam because he didn't like you enough, is that it?' He nodded miserably. 'And when you said you saw a man carrying Birdie towards the creek, that was a lie too?'

'No, no, no! That were true!'

'Who was it?'

He was still as a rock, even holding his breath, then he glanced at her and spoke jerkily as he had done at the start of the encounter: 'I don't know. I were too far off. It were dark, and raining. There were no way of knowing.'

'So it could have been Sam.'

He looked away, squeezing his hands between his knees, the picture of misery. There was no lack of expression now. There was too much.

'I'm sorry,' she said. 'You've had a hard time. You'd better go on now. And enjoy your ride.'

'Yes, ma'am.' It was a whisper.

He untied the pinto and rode away up the trail.

The yellow horse had a longer stride than the pony and would have overtaken him had she not held back. From below she caught glimpses of the pinto climbing the ledges towards the Barrier and when she could see him no longer and knew that they had entered the Twist she pushed forward, past the fork in the trail.

The way to Rustler bore the tracks of a number of horses, but the path that continued up Horsethief had seen little traffic since the rain. A few yards beyond the fork there were marks of deer and, speculating on their sudden appearance, she realised that the trail had been joined by a narrow path coming up from the bottom of the canyon. Below her now was the Upper Jump, the sun shining on a pool under the waterfall. The path did not end at the pool but climbed the opposite side of the canyon by way of an obvious break: a steep gully, sparsely vegetated, that cut through the crags to emerge on the rim about half a mile away. She considered, and then dismissed the route. She might explore it in company but not alone; it was too steep.

Her trail continued to climb; there were no hairpins, only a steady rise for a mile or so, and she saw that she was approaching a corner of the headwall. At that point the outer rank of the needles was close to the canyon but in the corner, between headwall and cliffs, there was a dip in the rock, more scoop than saddle, and on the skyline stood a small cairn.

She rode through the notch and the trail dropped easily to a narrow valley that was long and straight, and dead flat. The bottom was green with new grass except for the pale sand of the wash and the threads of game trails. The far side of the valley was craggy, and when she descended to the wash and looked back she saw a long reef clumped with ragged buttes, which had an air of familiarity. Light showed through holes. She was looking at the back of the reef that formed one side of Rustler Park.

People had said that there was no way to the park except by the Twist and yet, looking at that reef from this side, the slickrock appeared to be no more than a scramble for a tolerably agile person on foot. Tracing a line carefully with her eye, retracing it downwards, she saw that trees at the

133

base of the rock were bright green, not the bottle shades of pinyon and juniper but the green of hardwoods. That must be the spring in Sheep Canyon.

She studied her map. There were three ways out of this canyon, if you were mounted: north, following the wash to the river, eight miles distant and a dead-end because you could not cross the Colorado. You could go south into the empty country or, less than half a mile away, take a low pass that led to the next straight canyon.

She folded the map and headed for the pass, noting with satisfaction that it was marked by the prints of a horse coming towards her, into Sheep Canyon. Shortly she joined a wide track coming in from the left, and then she reached a rocky defile through which she rode for several hundred yards until she could look across another rift of a valley parallel to the one she had just left. This was Antelope; beyond it was Ringtail Canyon.

The country seemed deserted and there was very little sound. Small brown birds rose from the sage with a twittering like that of pipits. Occasionally a speck in the sky marked the presence of some large raptor, but generally speaking the Straight Canyons seemed as empty of wildlife as they were of people. The day was hot and no doubt the animals would emerge from cracks and burrows as the sun sank. Now, at noon, it seemed wise, like them, to seek shade. She turned back to Sheep Canyon and rode across the flats to the spring.

Two hundred yards from the cottonwoods, Yaller, already stepping out as he smelled water, threw up his head and whinnied. There was an answering neigh from the shadows. Miss Pink rode forward, a look of bright enquiry on her face. Alex Duval was standing, brushing leaves from his hair, smiling diffidently. A horse was tied close by, a rifle in the saddle scabbard.

'How do, ma'am.' He nodded and blinked at her. 'Nice day.'

She enthused about the weather as he led her to the spring: a scummy place of water-weed and tadpoles. The horse did not seem to mind but she was glad that she had brought water with her. She chatted about springs and wild-life as Yaller drank, then she removed the bridle and tied him to a tree by the halter. She loosened the cinch, aware that Alex was watching her with mounting uneasiness. Taking her saddle bags she moved away from the horses, talking, drawing him with her.

On a red-checked cloth she set rolls oozing with butter and ham and breasts of chicken, lettuce – limp but green – brownies, bright red apples, cans of beer. Alex stared, and grinned with delight. He said wonderingly: 'Bob told you I was here?'

'I didn't know you were here.'

He laughed. 'You always eat this much on your own?'

'Not at all. I thought I'd meet someone, lovely day like this. And I did, but he wasn't coming this way. Shawn was at Wind Whistle.'

'You mean he was at the house? What was he doing there?'

'I didn't ask him. Bob is helping John Forset get his cows out of Gospel Bottom. No doubt Shawn called to see if anyone was home.'

'That would be it.'

'And then he came up Horsethief and we had a long talk.'

'You and Shawn?' Alex was surprised, his ingenuous eyes studying her face. 'He talked to *you*?'

'I'm used to children.'

He shook his head. 'You must be good with 'em. I can handle animals and I love kids but I don't know how to handle Shawn.' He thought about that. 'He's not at all like the Olsons.'

'In what way?'

'One,' he ticked his fingers, 'they're happy. Two, they're polite. Three, they're workers – but that don't count; Shawn's too young to work. And that's not true neither; Mike was working cattle at his age. The twins can ride good as a man, too. 'Course,' he turned those disconcert-ingly innocent eyes on her, 'kids always ride better than men

135

because they got no fear, so really they're not so good. Can you understand that?'

'No fear means no respect. That's dangerous.'

'They learn it quick, though. Young Mike is careful. He knows if his pony breaks a leg that animal's gonna have to be shot. By the time they're Mike's age they've grown up some.'

'And he has respect for people too – Mike?'

'Mike's a good kid. He's around the age our boys would be if we'd been married. 'Fact, he sorta takes the place of our own kids, the ones we didn't have. We're the last of the family, Bob and me, so there's no one for the old place to go to.' He stopped short and looked away, smoothing his face.

'Something wrong?' she asked.

'Can you forget I said that?'

'I can, if you tell me why I should.'

'That's fair. It's family stuff; I forgot I shouldn't talk about family and such.'

'Let's talk about something else then. Cattle? When are you going to bring the cows up here?'

He peered through the trees, calculating. 'Soon's there's enough grass; pretty soon, when Bob gives the word.'

'You bring them up Horsethief?'

'Yes. Not the way you came, but the other side of the canyon, back of the rim. There's an old stock driveway, musta been in use since the Mormons started putting their cattle in the Straights.'

'There's a little trail that crosses the creek at the Upper Jump.'

'That trace comes up the steep draw south of the Jump and joins the stock driveway on top. That's where I should be fencing— ' He hesitated, and began again: 'I was pulling fence there last Saturday.'

'A nasty place to be in a storm.'

'I wasn't. I left, went on home with the tractor. There was thunder and lightning and stuff but it didn't bother me, not on four rubber wheels.'

136

'But Mike was on a horse.'

'He left early.' Alex grinned. 'It was Saturday afternoon, that's holiday time for young boys; he shouldn't have been working. I told him: I could get that old fence finished on my own, and I sent him off middle of the afternoon. Had his fishing rod with him, see. Off he went, down that old draw, but slow like, dainty, you could say; he takes care of his pony.'

'Well, you did have your eye on him.'

'All the way – oh, I see what you mean: he went careful because I was watching. No, Mike's a good kid anyways.'

She started to pack things away, talking as if for the sake of being polite. 'He couldn't have caught many trout with the storm coming and all.'

'Storm didn't come till later. He had an hour or so there and then the thunder started getting close, I hollered down to him and pointed to the sky, and he packed up and went home.' His eyes sparkled. 'Went fast too – good thing he's got a pony like a goat. By the time I got home, he'd been and gone.'

'Been in to Wind Whistle?'

'Of course! It was baking day, and Tracy and Sandy cook like angels.'

She sighed and sat back on her heels.

'You wanta rest a whiles? Old Yaller'll be all right.'

'I am resting, but thank you all the same. Were you upset at what happened to Birdie?'

He was startled. 'I'd forgotten it.'

'That's the best thing to do.'

He didn't seem to hear that. 'Now I've remembered. It was dreadful.' He shook his head. 'Cruel, cruel. Sam wasn't her father, you know that? Paula was her mother but one of our hands was her father. I hope he never learns what happened. She was a lovely little girl.'

'Do you know what happened?'

'Bob told me as she was hit and thrown in the creek, but the police said terrible things; Sam Estwick couldn't have done that, what they were saying. He might hit her p'raps, in anger, not meaning to hit so hard, but the knifing – no!'

'It was almost certainly done after she was dead.'

'Why would anyone do that? Once a body's dead, there's no *reason*. A deer gets shot once, even twice, by a poor marksman and someone goes and finishes it off, but you don't keep stabbing a dead body. I don't understand it.'

'Where were you searching, Alex? You and Bob?'

'We were upstream of Estwicks', clear back to Horsethief.'

She got to her feet. 'Is there a way up to Rustler from this side, up the slickrock?'

'You want to see it? I'll take you.' She hesitated at such eagerness and then realised it could be due to the change of subject. 'It'll only take five minutes.' He was pleading, like a small boy, anxious to show the visitor a favoured place.

'Five minutes?'

'It's steep,' he admitted, regarding her doubtfully now, and without embarrassment.

'You've done it?'

'Oh yes. You can see the whole of Rustler from the top. We used to put cows in the park in the old days, and when we gathered, I'd often run up the rock from this spring, see what was happening in Rustler.'

He was not young any longer and it was some time since she had scrambled up steep rock, moreover they were both wearing smooth-soled boots with high heels; not the footgear for rock climbing, she thought wryly as she heaved herself up incipient chimneys and toiled up sloping slabs in his wake. All the same, it was quite a reasonable route for a person on foot, and it was ridiculous to suggest that Rustler Park was inaccessible except by way of Horsethief and the Twist.

Alex had stopped. She reached him and found that they were on one of those long ledges characteristic of the country. Above them was the wall of a butte. He grinned and led the way along the foot of the wall. He stopped again and watched her approach. She looked at him, then at the wall. She saw light in the rock and stepped forward.

138

'Wait,' he said. 'I'll go first.'

He walked into a kind of short tunnel with a kink in it. She stumbled after him for a few yards and again found him waiting.

'There,' he said.

They looked out, as if from a doorway, over the sunlit expanse of Rustler Park. She could see all of it except for that strip which lay immediately below. There was the solitary reef, more or less in the centre of the huge meadow, the Barrier with all its needles to left and right, and straight ahead; and there, less than a mile away, was the Pale Hunter above the Maze.

Downwards, her view was obstructed and she went to step forward. His hand was on her arm. 'Careful, ma'am; that's a hundred-foot drop.'

'Oh! There's no way down?'

'No, just up one side is all. It's like being rimrocked.'

'Rimrocked?'

'You get into the bad canyons, go past a place where you can't go back – like you jump down, or something? Can't jump back. So you go on, 'cause that's all you can do, and you come to a place like this. That's being rimrocked. Of course, we're not rimrocked, we can go back.'

'How do people escape from a situation like that?'

'They don't, not alive. They get a fever from the sun and thirst and then the cold nights and they walk off the edge.'

She shuddered. 'Like sheep stuck on a ledge, and when they get weak enough the ravens knock them off.' She turned back to the park. 'Do you know the other way down to the valley, that goes through the Maze?'

'There isn't one.'

'And the Cave of Hands?'

'You been talking to Dolly.' He was smiling but then his face changed. 'Or little Birdie.'

She sighed and looked away from the sad eyes. 'Oh, there's Shawn,' she said brightly. 'I hope that child doesn't go near the old cabin; there's a rattler— '

139

'Rattler won't hurt him, cabin's the other end of the reef; you can pick out the old corrals. I see the pinto but I can't see the boy, can you?'

She was focusing the binoculars. 'I didn't see him either, just the pony. There it is, and it's tied. He is a careless boy, tying it in the sun. So where is he? Ah.'

'You found him?'

'Yes. He's sitting in the rocks at this end of the reef.'

'What's he doing?'

'Nothing. Just sitting and watching.'

The glasses moved fractionally as she looked beyond Shawn. He was in line with the Pale Hunter. So he had thoughts about the Maze? It must be an open secret – but why should he remain half a mile from the start of that mysterious (and cairned) trail and just stare at it? Through the glasses she studied the base of the Hunter, working through the little trees, and then she caught a glimpse of an alien colour. The rock was pink and grey, the grass was sage and green, the pinyons almost black, but this short strip of colour was yellow, too bright and high for flowers. It seemed to be on a boulder of blueish grey – and then the yellow moved with the rock. She inhaled sharply.

'What is it?' Alex asked.

She turned slowly. 'It occurred to me: could Shawn have heard the story about the Cave of Hands and the secret way down? Would he be silly enough to go and look?'

'Shawn isn't silly. Is he going? The pony hasn't moved.'

She handed him the glasses and watched his face. He tried to focus. 'I'm not very good with these things. I've altered the focus for you.'

'Never mind.' She held out her hand. 'You can probably see better without them.'

'I think I can.' He squinted towards the reef. 'I can still see the pinto so Shawn won't be far away.'

She focused again, not on Shawn but on the object of his interest: a blue roan horse in the shade (the yellow slicker revealing its presence) at the top of the slope leading to the Maze. She wasn't sure why she didn't tell Alex that Sarah

140

was down there. She may have remained silent because he denied knowledge of the area, an area which seemed to fascinate Shawn. These three people had secrets, shared or unshared; it might be better to keep quiet about the curious tableau below.

They returned to the horses and she made leisurely preparations for departure. Her going seemed to revive his anxiety.

'Does Bob know you're here?' he asked.

'No. I told no one I was coming to the Straights.'

'Are you going to tell people you met me?'

'Not if you don't want me to.'

'I'd rather you didn't.'

'Then I won't.'

'Good. Because Bob said—'

'I'll say nothing about meeting you, Alex. I promise.'

She rode up the canyon without looking back. She was fairly certain that he would leave the spring. There had been no sign of a camp; that must be in one of the other canyons, or back in the really wild country to the south. She wondered if he had ridden over here to meet Bob, and then thought that she would prefer not to meet him herself. So instead of taking the trail by which she had come she rode on until she intercepted what must be the stock driveway. Turning east, she broke into a canter.

The rift of Horsethief appeared on her left but the trail ran some distance back from what would be dangerous crags for cows. When she came to a pile of old fence posts and wire she rode out to the rim and found herself looking down the steep draw above the Upper Jump.

On the far side of the canyon the slickrock plunged in sweeping slabs from the needles to the gorge of the inner canyon. She was amazed to think that she had climbed that slope on a horse, on this horse, she remembered, patting his damp neck – and then she tensed. A patch of colour was moving down the slickrock: the pinto.

Looking more closely she saw that Shawn was not alone, and once again it was the yellow slicker that alerted her. The

141

roan was ahead; Shawn was coming down in company with Sarah. All the same, he was not in her company in Rustler Park – but Sarah had found him, so that was all right. Whatever mischief he might have been up to, in a position that suggested he was spying, he had been discovered: an anti-climax really, but at least Miss Pink no longer had to make the decision whether to tell Sarah that she was being watched.

At home that evening she remembered that she had meant to try to look into the back of the great cove, but even with binoculars she could see nothing. All that side of the valley was in deep shadow, the cove showing merely as something darker than the cliffs.

Chapter 11

'Shawn was at Wind Whistle?' It was next morning. Myrtle paused in her sweeping and regarded Miss Pink blankly. 'Are you sure?'

'He was riding Birdie's pony.'

'That's right.' Myrtle put the broom behind the door and removed the piece of chiffon that was protecting her immaculate coiffure. 'Paula said he could ride it.' She stepped out to the porch and looked across the valley. 'Who was at Wind Whistle?' she asked sharply.

'I don't know.'

'So how d'you know he was there?'

'I saw the pony tied outside, then he came out of the house and rode up Horsethief Canyon. He caught me up and we had a long talk.'

Myrtle stiffened and her hand went to her lips. She bit her knuckles. Miss Pink observed her without expression.

'Which brother was there?' Myrtle asked.

'I'm not sure that I understand you.'

'Who was in the house: Alex or Bob, or was it both of them?'

'Neither. The house was empty.'

'So what did he tell you?'

'Well,' Miss Pink seemed embarrassed. 'He was eager to talk— '

'About— ?' Myrtle was tense as a spring.

'Young children find it easier to unburden themselves to strangers . . . He spoke about men.'

'Which one? Men, not a man?'

143

'He concentrated on Sam Estwick but he also mentioned Glen Plummer.'

'Glen! Why?'

'You're forcing me to tell you things which may well have been confidential,' Miss Pink said gently. 'A little boy's secrets?'

Myrtle was very still. 'Why are you smiling?' she asked. 'Is something funny?'

'I'm not amused, I'm embarrassed.'

Myrtle looked away. 'I *am* the boy's grandmother.' She was trying to keep her voice even. 'I have a right to know what he's saying. It can't be confidential from his family.'

'Perhaps not, but – you're right. He was comparing their merits, d'you see? He could well feel that to discuss such a matter within his own family might imply criticism of his mother. He's terribly concerned that he doesn't have a father. A normal attitude in the circumstances.'

Myrtle seemed to have lost control of her head. She turned it slowly towards the visitor, jerked away, swivelled to the creek and then, as if aware of eccentric behaviour, she started to roll her skull deliberately, doing neck exercises.

'I came to look at your jewellery,' Miss Pink said.

The old woman retreated inside the store, automatically taking up a stance behind the display counter. Miss Pink stood back and surveyed the cluttered shelves. 'Did you see any strange cars or hikers on Saturday?' she asked.

Myrtle's eyes showed the effort involved in adjusting to the change of subject. 'We came home late – later than we'd intended. We stopped – we'd been to town, and Maxine saw a friend's car outside – some place, and we stayed there a while.'

'That's important?'

Myrtle gaped. 'Well, we wouldn't see anyone, would we? We were too late. I mean, it happened much earlier, didn't it? He'd have been gone, time we turned off the highway – and of course, no one'd notice a strange car on the highway.'

'What time did you reach home?'

'About seven, eight, some time around there.'

144

'Shawn was alone for quite a while.'

'He watched a video. He knows how to work the set. He's old for his years. He'd got himself some supper, and changed his clothes. He was drenched, out in that storm. We shouldn't never have stopped, but there, no harm done, and he didn't even catch cold.'

'A very self-sufficient little boy, but, I think, lonely too. He's so conscious of not having a father.'

'Everything's going to be fine.' Myrtle was relaxed now, even a trifle smug. 'When Maxine re-marries we shall be a complete family.'

'And he's fond of Glen.'

'Well, Glen's easy-going, promised him an Arabian horse – pure-bred; I don't mean Glen would try to *buy* Shawn's affections, but it is kind, isn't it, give a little boy a pony?' Her expression changed, became censorious. 'But he shouldn't never have talked about his mother's business outside the family.'

Miss Pink ignored this. 'Nevertheless, he seems to favour Sam Estwick,' she murmured.

Myrtle gave a snort of derision. 'He can't stand Sam Estwick! None of us can. Just because my daughter be-friended him once, felt sorry for him married to a Mormon, what passes for Mormon, and him a drinking man, now he comes up here trading on a friendly gesture. It looks bad. One thing, I'm here, and little Shawn, but he's so thick-skinned he can't see where he's not wanted. No, no one in this house has a good word to say for Sam Estwick. Besides, he's in jail.'

'He was taken in for questioning— '

'Shawn saw— ' She stopped, her eyes wide behind the gaudy spectacles. She gripped the square of black velvet on the counter and started to knead and stretch it. Miss Pink watched the thin, arthritic hands and waited for the cloth to tear. 'It was Sam?' she asked softly. Myrtle's head twitched sideways. 'It was Glen?'

'No, no! Not Glen! He told you that? Shawn said it was Glen?'

'It wasn't Sam,' Miss Pink said, making a statement of it this time. Myrtle stared at her as if she were a snake. 'Who was it?' Miss Pink asked. 'Alex Duval?'

'I shouldn't think so.' It was a whisper.

'Shawn was at Wind Whistle yesterday morning.'

'So you say. It's worrying.'

'Aren't you worried that he should ride alone up to Rustler Park?'

'Is that where he went?' The voice was listless now. 'He's a good little rider.' But she wasn't thinking about his horsemanship.

'Isn't Maxine worried?'

'About what?'

'That Shawn knows who the murderer is.'

'He told *you*!'

'Not the identity of the man.'

'No more he told me. Maxine isn't well; she's very highly strung. She's sick in bed so she doesn't know about any of this.' She made a gesture of indecision. 'Don't you think he should tell us?'

'Definitely. Perhaps we could impress on him the need. How about now? The sooner the better.'

'When he gets back.'

'Back – from where?'

'He's with the Olsons today. He'll be home this evening. I'll make him talk then. And if he won't, I'll send for that detective, the fatherly one – Sprague? It was him got Shawn to admit he'd seen the killer taking Birdie to the creek.'

Shawn was not at the Olson place. No one had seen him that day, in fact, none of the children had seen him since he left them just before the storm on Saturday.

The Olson family was busy. Mike was working at Wind Whistle, the big girls were out in the alfalfa, irrigating, the twins were in the kitchen, drawing maps of Alaska: geography lesson, Jo explained. The baby was stumbling round the kitchen followed by the solicitous collie. Debbie tapped Miss Pink's arm. 'I've got time to talk if you don't mind me working at the same time.'

They went round the back of the cabin to the vegetable garden.

'I'm running late,' Debbie said, bustling along the rows. 'I have to get these old peas weeded before dinner, and I should be out helping with the irrigating— ' She sighed heavily and Miss Pink accepted the broad hint and started to work on a parallel row.

'How did the picnic go?' she asked.

'Oh, it was fun!' Immediately Debbie forgot the urgency and straightened her back. 'We went up Rustler. Why didn't you come?'

'I had to talk to people. I would have liked to come. Tell me about it. Did Sarah photograph the rattler at the line camp?'

'No, we didn't go near the rocks. Sarah says there are rattlers all round that reef, not just at the old cabin. We had the picnic in the trees.'

'Near the Pale Hunter?'

'Across from there. We rode past the Hunter; we rode right round the park after we'd eaten.'

'Dolly and I picnicked above the Maze.'

Debbie stood up again, gave an ostentatious sigh and pointed past the Stone Hawk. 'That's the Maze.'

'True, but Rustler Park's up there too. Isn't there a way down to here from Rustler through the Maze?'

'Heavens, no!' She rolled her eyes. 'There's only one way to Rustler: up Horsethief.'

'Why didn't Shawn go with you?'

Debbie turned back to the peas. 'I don't know.'

'He felt left out.' Debbie struggled with a dandelion root. 'I saw him in Horsethief yesterday,' Miss Pink went on idly. 'He went up Rustler on his own.'

The child stood up, staring. '*Walking?*'

'No, on Birdie's pinto.'

'He stole it?'

'Mrs Estwick is letting him ride it.'

'I don't believe it.'

Miss Pink was untwining a convolvulus stem. 'She's not thinking straight,' Debbie amended. 'My dad's gone over there, see if he can help. He'll sort that one out.'

'Why shouldn't he ride the pinto? He's good enough. I watched him on the trail yesterday; he doesn't ride as well as some, but he's not *bad*.' Debbie said nothing. Miss Pink straightened her back. 'I'm going to call on Mrs Estwick. Is there any message for your father?'

'Tell him what you just told me – in case Mrs Estwick didn't tell him yet.'

'I'll do that. You're worried about Shawn. I can understand that. People shouldn't go riding in these canyons on their own. It's too easy for a horse to put a foot wrong and go over the edge.'

The child looked at her, and deep in those clear blue eyes something moved that was not at all childish, something that made Miss Pink distinctly uneasy.

Paula and Olson were in the corrals when she drove into the Estwicks' yard, Paula smearing ointment on the back of a horse while Olson held its head. They came out of the corral and greeted her without enthusiasm. Paula, as might be expected, appeared dull and incurious, but an unwonted belligerence on Olson's part contrasted sharply with the attitude of the rest of his family. He might be in pain; he was limping, having been kicked by a cow. Forset had said that Olson was careless. When Paula went indoors Miss Pink asked him if he knew that Shawn had ridden the pinto yesterday. No, he hadn't known.

'Is he safe, d'you think?'

He shrugged. 'I'm not bothered about Shawn.'

Annoyed, she said tartly: 'You don't have to bother about Mike's alibi either.'

'What's that got to do with— What's that supposed to mean?' He was more frightened than wantonly rude.

'Mike was fishing in the pool below the Upper Jump. Didn't he tell you?'

'That's what he— What *are* you talking about?'

'You gave him a false alibi, and he didn't need it. Alex Duval was watching him all the time. And then Mike called at Wind Whistle so that must have been just before Jo arrived. You only have to ask Tracy and Sandy what time he was there, or how long before Jo got there that he left – and you know what time he reached your place, so you can work out that he didn't have enough time to come over here and do everything that was done, and to wash. Was he wet when he came in?'

'Not like he'd been in the creek. How did you work it all out?'

'Once Alex said he was fishing in the pool I realised why Mike was so surprised when you said he was with you around three on Saturday. You thought if he told the police he was fishing, that wouldn't be good enough. Didn't he tell you he was within sight of Alex? And that he called at Wind Whistle?'

'I didn't think. I just thought the more people had been with Mike around the time that Birdie went home the better.'

'And saying Mike was with you gives you an alibi.'

'I don't need one.'

A car could be heard approaching and Dolly's white Volkswagen nosed into the yard. She got out carrying a casserole.

'Hi, you guys!' Her smile suggested that she was trying to behave as if nothing had happened, but her eyes were wary. She raised her brows and nodded towards the cabin. 'She O.K.?'

'She's all right,' Olson said. 'I got her to come out. We've been doctoring Sam's horse.'

'I looked in to give her this casserole, see if there's anything she needs. Then we can have a talk.' (This to Miss Pink.) 'You staying a while, Erik?'

'We're going to go and look at the cattle.' He lowered his voice. 'Just to get her out, get her moving about the place.'

'Good. Put her up on a horse – best thing you can do.'

'It would be, but there's only one horse. Sam's has got a nasty saddle sore.'

'Hm, you're both too heavy for the pinto. You'll have— '

'Shawn's out on the pinto.'

'What?' Both women exclaimed together. 'He's taken it today as well?' Miss Pink asked. 'Where did he go?'

'I don't know and I don't care,' Olson said flatly. 'If that old pony bucks him off, all's I can say is it's no more'n he deserves.'

'Do you know what that boy's saying?' Dolly hissed.

'Shawn? No. What?'

'He says he does know who the killer is.'

'So?'

'Jesus, Erik! Don't you realise— '

'Shut your car door!' Miss Pink interrupted loudly, seeing Paula emerge from the cabin. 'You're wasting your batteries.'

'Hi, Paula!' Dolly turned, almost smoothly. 'I brought you a casserole . . . '

'Who told you?' Miss Pink asked as, their having driven in convoy to Dolly's cabin, the younger woman came hurrying back to the jeep.

'Myrtle called me asking what she should do.'

'And what did you suggest?'

'I told her to hang on till he comes home and then she must make him tell her. Then I started looking for you. Jo told me you were at the Estwicks'. The casserole was a blind: my dinner for the next few days. But it does mean it can't be Sam, doesn't it?'

'It would seem so. Since all the indications were that it was him, Shawn seems to be implying now that it was someone else.'

'But this is wild! Shawn's saying it's one of us? I mean, one of those left? Where is that kid? He didn't tell Paula where he was going but someone must have seen him. Do we call people, or what?' Miss Pink was deep in thought. 'I

150

'mean,' Dolly pressed, 'he's in a terribly dangerous position, don't you think? Should we call the police?'

'He could be lying.'

'There is that. Shawn will say whatever suits his convenience at the moment.'

'But someone may not take that into account, may decide to be on the safe side.'

Dolly twisted an ear-ring. 'Surely it's up to his family to take the initiative?'

'I don't think anybody's capable. Maxine is "sick" which is probably a euphemism for drunk, and Myrtle's a broken reed.'

'Oh, hell. So what do we do?'

'Let's try to discover if anyone's seen him. Start with Wind Whistle.'

There was no reply from the Duvals' number, nor from John Forset, nor Glen Plummer. Lois was at home and asked why Dolly should think that she had seen Shawn when his mother had forbidden him to visit with the Stenbocks. 'Why's that?' Dolly asked, replacing the receiver. 'Why doesn't Maxine let Shawn visit with Lois?'

'Because— ' Miss Pink checked.

'Oh, come on! I can find out from Lois easily enough.'

'And she'll tell you.' Miss Pink was grim. 'Shawn told her that Sam Estwick was too fond of small boys, so Lois told Maxine what she thought of her as a mother.'

'Shawn said that! The little bugger.'

'But I met him yesterday and he retracted, admitted he was lying; it seems he was getting his own back on Sam for some slight or other. Maybe Sam did whip him at one time. On the other hand he said he'd like Sam for a father.'

'This gets even more weird. He was having you on.'

Miss Pink studied Dolly's face. 'He was very plausible.'

'He is. Now I come to think of it, he's so plausible, and such a little bastard – particularly when I remember what he did to my painting – I'm not all that keen to find him after all. Let him take his chance, is how I feel.'

151

'I'm going to call the Grays' cabin. They might have seen him at a distance; no one can miss the pinto.'

Sarah answered the telephone. She had not seen Shawn or the pinto; was something wrong? Miss Pink hesitated and Frankie came on the line.

'Something happened?'

Miss Pink explained that Shawn was dropping hints that he knew the identity of the killer.

'It's not Sam then!' Frankie exclaimed. 'That's a relief— '

'Then it's someone else.'

There was silence on the line. Sarah came back. 'What's Frankie so upset about?'

Cornered, Miss Pink had to explain, despite Sarah's tender age, but then Sarah was not all that tender. 'Did Shawn say anything to you?' she asked. 'When you went to see him Sunday afternoon. You talked to him just before the police did and he told them he'd seen a man carrying Birdie's body. Surely he told you?'

'I knew he was concealing something but he wouldn't talk. The police must have brought pressure to bear. I couldn't.'

'Have you any idea where he would be now?'

'None. I'll tell you what, though; Shawn's quite safe as long as you know where everyone else is.'

'I don't see – oh.'

Frankie came back on the line, hard and triumphant. 'She means there are eight suspects. One of them's sitting out by our pool at this moment, and this time I'm not asleep.'

'I appreciate that,' Miss Pink said. 'And after all, the child isn't missing.

'Exactly.' There was a long pause. 'When do we assume he is?'

'What would Shawn be doing inside Wind Whistle when the house was empty?'

'Helping himself to a Coke?' Jerome ventured.

'Stealing,' Sarah said.

Miss Pink and Dolly had lunched with the Grays: an

alfresco meal beside the pool. Somnolent after two glasses of wine, Miss Pink had put her question generally to the company.

'Do you have evidence to back that up?' she asked.

'The criminal mind,' Frankie murmured.

'You mean, proof that he steals, not just that he was stealing at Wind Whistle?' Sarah asked. 'The Olsons could answer that one better than me. He cheats at games and he tells lies. He's basically dishonest.'

'He's anti-social,' Frankie said. 'What he said about Sam was amoral.'

'Immoral,' Sarah corrected. 'He knew what he was doing.'

Jerome cocked an interested eye at his daughter. 'How d'you know that, miss?'

'He was deliberately slandering Sam.'

'He knew what he was doing all right,' Dolly put in grimly.

'I'm not so sure,' Jerome said. 'He may have seen or heard some reference to child abuse and repeated it without being fully aware of the consequences.'

'Like a psychopath?' Sarah asked. 'Daddy, you're being naive.'

'And you're another one.' Jerome was not in the least put out.

'A psychopath?'

'Not fully aware of the meaning of terms.'

'So he's a fledgling psychopath. His wings aren't grown.'

'Perhaps they should be clipped.' Dolly leaned back in her *chaise longue*. 'Perhaps someone's done that,' she added lazily.

'Don't, Dolly,' Frankie said.

'Sorry, my subconscious is coming to the surface. I'm hot; I'm going in the pool.' She got up and went to the house.

'We have plenty of swimsuits, Melinda,' Frankie said.

'Thank you. Later, perhaps.' She looked at Sarah. 'How many ways could Shawn have taken when he left Paula's place this morning?'

'Up or down the canyon, and on either side of the creek.'

'This side of the creek he'd be on the road,' Jerome pointed out, seeing what was in her mind. 'Someone would have seen him. It's more likely that he crossed the creek and went up – or down – the trail on the far bank.'

'Then John Forset would have to see him, or Bob – or Alex.' She had kept her promise and told no one that she had met Alex in Sheep Canyon. 'At either end of the trail on the other side of the creek he had to pass one of those ranches.'

'But you called John and the Duvals and no one was home,' Frankie said. 'If they all left early, before Shawn set out, no one need have seen him go except Paula.'

'When did he leave Estwicks'?' Jerome asked, but no one knew.

'Shall we call Paula?' Frankie asked.

'I wouldn't do that,' Sarah said. 'It's a bit casual, a telephone call. I'll run down there, take some cookies and stuff.'

'You won't run down there, in this heat.'

'I'll take my bike.'

Jerome said: 'Are you sure— '

'It'll save Frankie the trip, and Paula will talk to me. Frankie goes down every day.'

They went indoors, passing Dolly, plump and tanned in a blue swimsuit. She plunged in the deep end of the pool and started a slow crawl.

'Oh, bliss,' she gasped, coming to the side. 'The others coming in?'

'Frankie's putting up some cookies for Sarah to take to Paula. We want to know what time Shawn left there this morning.'

'You still bothered about him? Come in the water and cool off. It's super.'

Jerome smiled politely and turned to Miss Pink. 'How do you feel about Shawn?' he asked. 'Are you worried?'

'Not yet. I'm intrigued. I keep wondering why he was in Rustler Park yesterday. Has he gone up there again, and if so, why?'

'You must ask Sarah that. She was there too. They came down together.'

'What did he tell her?'

'Just that he wanted to go to Rustler because he wasn't invited to the picnic. It sounds reasonable. It's considered quite an adventure by the children to ride up Horsethief and through the Twist. A paranoid child would feel he hadn't been invited because he wasn't considered a good enough rider, so he'd do it alone, to prove that he was. Would Shawn be paranoid? Dear me, this is infectious: psychopath, paranoid. What next?'

Sarah returned within the hour to say that Shawn had left the Estwicks' place some time after nine o'clock and Paula had not noticed which way he had gone. Paula had been quite chatty, Sarah said, turning to Miss Pink. 'You thought Shawn was trying to get his own back on Sam because Sam threatened to whip him. It was a bit more . . . significant than that. After Shawn threw the stone at your horse Sam took him aside and told him that if *he* was his father he'd send him away to a special school where people knew how to deal with spoiled kids. Shawn said he wasn't his father and never would be, and Sam said no, but he'd have a word with Glen Plummer and put him straight on the subject. Plummer had enough money to have Shawn put away in a very secure special school.'

'Paula told you this?' Frankie said in amazement. 'And Sam told Paula all that?'

'Maybe he told her more than we know – but he certainly told her about this rather nasty exchange with Shawn. Sam was worried afterwards about what the kid might do.'

'What could he do?' Jerome asked. 'He's only ten, for Heavens' sake! You mean slashing tyres, that kind of mischief?'

'Or torching his cabin,' Dolly said.

Frankie gasped, then turned on Sarah. 'Did Sam think Shawn was that bad?'

'I'm just telling you what Paula told me.'

'But she lets him have the pony—' Frankie stared at

155

them. They looked at each other in amazement.

'Deliberately?' Dolly breathed. 'Hoping . . . expecting the animal to throw him?'

'I wonder if he did speak to Glen Plummer,' Miss Pink said. 'Glen seems ambivalent about Maxine.'

'What makes you say that?' Frankie asked.

'He was talking to me about women, and he was concerned about someone who had set her cap at him.'

Dolly clapped her hands in delight. 'Is that what they say in England? That's neat. I'd put it a bit heavier myself. Maxine's got her talons in and won't let go. But if Sam did warn Glen he was taking on a subnormal stepson, you wouldn't see Glen's dust.'

'Shawn's not subnormal,' Jerome said. 'He's highly intelligent.'

'Glen hasn't gone,' Miss Pink pointed out. 'And I suspect he knows all about young Shawn. It occurs to me, however, that the story Shawn told Lois couldn't have been in retaliation for the threat about a special school. If Sam uttered that on Friday, the sequence is wrong. I got the impression from Lois that Shawn told her his nasty little story some time ago.'

'Immaterial,' Dolly said. 'Shawn would always be in a state of retaliation for something someone said. You don't need a time sequence with that piece of bad news. Incidentally, was there any good news, Sarah, like he hasn't come back yet?'

'I hope he does come back, for your sake,' Frankie said with only a trace of amusement. 'Still, we're all friends here; your indiscretions will go no further.'

The telephone was ringing. Sarah got up to answer it, came back and told Miss Pink that John Forset wanted to speak to her. She approached the instrument warily.

'We took some of Bob's cows up Sheep Canyon,' he told her. 'Alex said he met you yesterday.'

'That's so. I changed my mind and went up Horsethief.'

'You wouldn't have been looking for Alex?'

'You didn't tell me where he was.'

'Have you told anyone?'

'No one. I promised him I wouldn't.'

'Are you going to keep quiet?'

'Of course. John, did you see Shawn Brenner today?'

'Yes, we did. Why?'

'Oh, good. We thought – well, he's been out alone for two days running and it seems, it doesn't seem safe for a little boy who—'

'Don't concern yourself with that young rip. Alex says he was up to Rustler yesterday. Today he was at the Upper Jump, fishing at the pool below the waterfall.'

'What time was that?'

'When we came down from the Straights, getting on for three.'

'Where are you calling from now?'

'From home.'

'Yesterday Shawn was inside Wind Whistle when it was empty. Bob was with you. I saw the boy come out of the back of the house.'

'So Alex said. Bob isn't missing anything.'

She returned to her hosts and told them Shawn had been seen. Four faces were turned towards her: Frankie relieved, Dolly mock-resigned, the Grays, father and daughter, non-committal.

'Where did John see him?' Frankie asked.

'Fishing the pool at the Upper Jump.'

'I never knew Shawn to fish,' Sarah said.

Dolly grinned. 'He probably stole a rod when he was in Wind Whistle yesterday.'

'He didn't have a rod when he caught me up in Horse-thief,' Miss Pink said. 'Not even a telescopic one on the saddle.'

'Anyway, he's found,' Dolly said. 'Now we can all revert to normal, wondering what his next trick will be.'

They laughed, not quite naturally; their relief was tinged with hysteria. And they were less relieved that a small boy had been found than because everyone had been wondering what had happened to him. He was the second child missing, thought to be missing, in four days, and no one could forget what had happened to the first.

The relief was short-lived, although Miss Pink remained in ignorance until late in the evening when Frankie telephoned to say that people were searching for Shawn, had been doing so since early evening but in a desultory fashion then because no one had been much concerned. They were more bothered about the pinto, or Paula was. He had been badly cut by wire and he was extremely nervous but she managed to quieten him and clean the cuts and apply salve. No bones were broken but the point of his shoulder was very tender and swollen, and he was lame. Paula thought he had jumped wire, not cleared the top strand and come down on the shoulder. And since his chest was lacerated she thought he must have crashed through another fence. Bob Duval thought the pony must have broken loose when the boy was fishing and run home, jumping and crashing through weak points in the upper and lower boundaries of the Duval property.

Paula had called Maxine when the pony came home, but it was Myrtle who answered. She telephoned Bob Duval to ask if Shawn were there and he was not, so Bob saddled a horse and rode to the Upper Jump. There was no sign of Shawn anywhere. Duval came back and summoned John Forset and a few others and they concentrated on searching below the Horsethief trail, thinking that the pony must have fallen and thrown the boy, who would have rolled down into the canyon.

'That's where they are now,' Frankie said. 'Sarah's with them.'

Miss Pink said: 'You'd think that a pony going over the edge of a trail would leave tracks; the path would be broken away, plants flattened. Besides,' – she had another thought – 'the creek is within shouting distance of the trail. He can't be far away. He should be able to hear the searchers – if he's there – if he can answer.'

158

Chapter 12

They searched the canyon until nightfall and then they had to give up because, rough as it was in daylight with crags and fallen timber, the gorge was a death-trap in the dark. Besides, by that time they were convinced that he was not there; people had ridden back and forth between the Upper Jump and the boundary of Wind Whistle and no one could see any sign of a horse having gone over the edge. Had it stumbled and the boy fallen off, and rolled, they would expect to see a swath of flattened vegetation, even if he had crawled under a tree and lost consciousness. They saw nothing untoward.

They abandoned the canyon as darkness fell and started to search the Wind Whistle meadows and the rest of the ground as far as Paula's cabin, and across the road towards the boy's home. They discovered where the pony had crashed through the Duvals' upper boundary; there were white hairs sticking to sagging wire on the bank of the creek. They could track the pinto well enough; from the broken wire they back-tracked to the gate. The pony had come down the Horsethief trail, reached the gate and followed the fence line to the creek looking for a weak place. They knew Shawn had not been on the animal at this point because he would have opened the gate. The reason why they searched the meadows was on the chance that the boy, having been thrown from the pinto, perhaps concussed, had wandered down the trail, seen lights, attempted a short-cut towards his home and lost consciousness. That was how they rationalised; the truth was that no one could bring himself to go home while the boy was missing.

The men using Wind Whistle as a base were Bob himself, John Forset, Olson and Stenbock. They had not called on Glen Plummer, nor Jerome, and Alex was still in the Straights. No one remarked his absence, so presumably some kind of explanation had been given for it. In Wind Whistle's kitchen Sarah, and later Miss Pink, brewed coffee and made sandwiches. Myrtle kept telephoning for news. She did not come across because she would not leave Maxine, who had not yet been told that Shawn was missing. Myrtle had given her a sleeping pill. Miss Pink raised her eyebrows at this: sleeping pills on top of alcohol, but at the moment it was far better that Maxine should be comatose in her own bed, rather than drunk at Wind Whistle.

Not long before dawn Miss Pink, who had been dozing in a chair, awoke to a stir in the yard. Dolly appeared in the doorway and glanced round the bright, untidy kitchen.

'Where is everybody?'

Miss Pink rubbed her eyes and reached for her spectacles. 'They're all snatching some sleep. Coffee?'

'Thanks. I'll get it. I rode over. I'll come out today, least I can do. They haven't found anything – no sign?'

Miss Pink shook her head. 'He's vanished. If he's in Horsethief he can't be conscious. The same applies if he's between here and his home.'

'Could it be amnesia?'

'But he could still answer shouts, Dolly. An amnesiac isn't unconscious.'

'A snake. Did anyone think of that: snakebite?'

'I'm sure they did. What difference does it make whether he fell off his horse or got bitten by a rattler? It's not what happened to him that concerns people but where he is.'

'You think he got bitten?' Sarah had entered the kitchen. She went to the sink and dashed cold water on her face. 'Thrown, then bitten?' she hazarded, reaching for a towel.

Miss Pink asked suddenly: 'Sarah! What was he doing in Rustler Park two days ago?'

The girl showed no surprise at the question. 'He said

he should have gone on the picnic but his mother kept him home.'

'Was that all?'

'It was all he said, but the press were with Maxine that morning. Shawn could have found reporters more interesting than a picnic.'

'He told me he wasn't asked.'

'The young Olsons aren't all that mad about Shawn.'

'Your father said he came down with you from Rustler the following day. I wondered if he followed you up there.'

'Maybe he did, but not closely. He went in to Wind Whistle and then he talked to you on the trail.'

'I meant, did he go up there after you, because you went? At what point did you meet him?'

'You mean where, or when?'

'Both.'

Dolly, who had been following this with interest, said: 'You think this has some bearing on what's happened?'

They didn't answer her. 'I met him as I was coming home,' Sarah said. 'He caught me up.'

'What was he doing when he was in the park?'

'I don't know. I didn't see him, but it's a big park with hollows, as you know, and then there's the reef in the middle; you can lose sight of people. That's where I was, by the reef: trying to get pictures of the rattler; I wouldn't have noticed Shawn.'

Dolly said: 'What on earth would a kid of ten find to do in Rustler Park? In any case, that's got nothing to do with what happened yesterday, because he was fishing in Horsethief.'

There were voices and other sounds from the back of the house. The men were getting up. The women started to busy themselves with breakfast.

It was Erik Olson who was to ask the crucial question. He paused as he wiped egg off his plate and turned to Forset. 'I s'pose he *was* fishing when you saw him from the stockway? He wasn't laying down or something?'

Forset blinked at him. 'I assumed he was fishing. There

was the pinto, tied— ' He turned to Duval. 'Wasn't anything wrong with the animal then; remember, he lifted his head when he heard our voices? He looked all right to me. 'Course, we were some way above— '

'He hit the wire after that,' Duval pointed out. 'But he wasn't tied; he was drinking.'

For a moment no one spoke, then Dolly said: 'Shawn couldn't have been fishing at the same time his horse was drinking. He had to be holding it. Although maybe, if he wasn't, that was the moment it got away. So Shawn— '

'He wasn't holding it,' Duval said, and looked at Art Stenbock.

'I never saw anything,' the man said quickly. 'You rode out to the top of that draw, to look at the fencing, where you would put the new fence, and you only glanced down Horsethief. I stayed back on the stockway, with Mike.'

Forset looked at Duval. 'You saw the boy.'

'I didn't. It was you who said: "There's young Shawn." I only saw the pinto. You really saw the boy?'

Forset grimaced. 'No, I didn't. I just assumed – you do that, don't you? There's someone's horse so you think the rider's with it.'

Miss Pink asked curiously: 'What made you connect the pinto with Shawn?'

'Everyone knew he was using the pinto; besides, Alex mentioned it.' He held her eye. 'Alex is up in the Straights, putting out salt and stuff for the cows. He saw Shawn in Rustler on the pinto the day before so he knew the boy had the loan of the pony.'

Sarah said: 'How could Alex be in Rustler if he was in the Straights?'

'I didn't say he was in Rustler. He looked down on the park from the rimrock above Bighorn Spring.'

'I didn't see him.'

'Yes, you were up there too. He didn't say he saw you but your horse don't show up like the pinto. Anyway, is this important?'

Miss Pink said: 'It shows Shawn had an interest in Rustler –

162

and that since you didn't see him fishing, and the pony wasn't tied by the pool, the animal could have been loose at that point: loose and on its own. Shawn could be in Rustler.'

They stared at her. It was Dolly who broke the silence. 'Or points between. No wonder you couldn't find him in Horsethief.'

Everyone who could ride turned out that day, even the Olson twins. Only the younger Olsons were kept at home with Jo. Glen Plummer stayed in the valley, as did Jerome and Frankie. Myrtle telephoned to say she was keeping Maxine 'sedated' and by now no one was in the least concerned how she was doing it: with alcohol or sleeping pills or a combination of both.

Lois Stenbock stayed at home but Paula Estwick came out: quiet and tight-lipped, riding a bony horse, no longer the bereaved mother – or at least, not showing it, but a plain, tough ranch woman.

The column of riders went up the Horsethief trail without a pause but when they reached the fork above the Upper Jump and turned uphill their interest quickened. From this point onwards there had been no search.

They climbed the slickrock slowly, exploring the ledges, looking behind boulders, dismounting to peer into holes where there had been a rockfall. They found no recent falls but they knew that people overtaken by darkness may crawl into shelter, and often they stay there, asleep or unconscious.

'I figure he's dead,' Paula said. Miss Pink was momentarily alone with her, holding the reins while she clambered over a heap of fallen rocks. Coming back, taking the reins, she made no move to mount. 'There's no hurry,' she said. 'He were dead before the pony come home.'

Yaller rested one leg as if they had all the time in the world. Miss Pink looked along the ledge and saw a bright gleam as a horse turned and halted. Someone shouted: 'You find something?'

'No,' she called, and looked down at Paula. 'Why do you say that?'

163

'It's obvious. Shawn knew who killed— ' She would not pronounce the name, but Miss Pink knew. She went on: 'But Sam were in town so he couldn't have nothing to do with this.' She indicated the searchers. 'They let him go coupla days back, did you know that? No. Well, they did, but he stayed in Nebo 'cause he were afraid of me, still is, I reckon. He called me though, said he'd got to stay, the police said so. He can come home now, I reckon he's been punished enough.' Miss Pink looked startled. 'I mean, for going to that woman,' Paula said coldly. 'He didn't have nothing to do with – with any of – the other business, although it were his knife.'

'It was? Definitely?'

'It were his knife they took out of the creek.'

'And you reckon the same man was responsible for both deaths.' Paula regarded her calmly. 'Do you have any idea as to who— ?'

'If the body's in Rustler then it had to be someone who could ride, so that lets out Glen Plummer and Jerome Gray. Mr Gray can ride but I don't see him coming up here yesterday on Sarah's horse— '

'He didn't.'

'So that leaves five men – and young Mike. Four of 'em, and Mike, was herding cattle yesterday, and that leaves just Erik Olson, and he were with me till dinner time.'

'What time do you eat dinner?'

'At noon.'

She mounted and they walked along the ledge towards the black hole of the Twist. There were tracks in the sand but since Shawn had ridden the pinto past here two days ago, and some of the picnic party had been mounted on ponies the day before that, small hoofprints held no special significance. They worked their way through the Twist at a snail's pace, inspecting every hole and crack, and it was midday by the time they collected in Rustler Park. They dismounted in the shade and ate their lunch, and discussed the afternoon's programme.

'He won't be any further than here,' Forset said, 'so

164

this is our last chance to find him. You know the place best, Bob; how should we work it?'

'Sarah knows it better than me; it's years since we put cows up here.'

Sarah said: 'There's the reef in the middle, that's the most likely place if he's been bitten, so watch out for snakes. I'll take the old line camp because I know there's a rattler in the cabin, but I'm used to him. Apart from the reef, there's all the rocks right round the edge, and then there are shallow draws everywhere in the grass.'

'Sweep search,' Miss Pink murmured.

'What's that?' Forset turned to her.

'We form a line, say, fifteen to twenty feet apart, and ride across the park. When we come to the far side the line returns on a parallel course. In theory every inch is covered systematically.'

'Excellent. We'll do that after we've ridden round the edge. And everyone,' – he eyed the youngsters – 'don't forget to make plenty of noise. But when I signal – ride out in front, wave my arms – everyone stops calling and we listen, see if *he's* calling.'

All through the stifling afternoon they searched the park. There was no water apart from that which they had brought themselves, and Forset had made sure that everyone carried a good supply, but the horses suffered.

The central reef and the perimeter cliffs were quickly covered, and then they turned their attention to the park itself. As the afternoon wore on it became obvious that a meticulous sweep search could not be accomplished before nightfall and it was thought that, if Shawn was lying in a hollow or behind a fallen pinyon, he would not survive another night in the open. So Forset told them to spread out, with a greater distance between each rider; that way they could cover more ground more quickly. Some of the mounts, particularly the children's ponies, were flagging and, mindful of the long trail home, the younger riders were told to stop searching, to go into the shade and rest the horses. It was not before time. Even Mike made no protest, and an hour later Art Stenbock and Miss Pink dropped out of the line.

By six o'clock they had covered the whole park and everyone was exhausted. For the past hour there had been infrequent shouts as people thought they glimpsed a recumbent figure, but always it turned out to be a rock or a log. They ended the day even more baffled than they had been at the start. Dismounted in the shade, Forset's eyes rested on the forms of children sprawled like rag dolls and he winced. 'I guess we're finished here,' he said heavily. 'There's nothing else we can do. The horses will be giving out shortly. What does anyone think?'

Duval said: 'The horses are finished. We need a helicopter.'

'Police? Or Search and Rescue?'

'Doesn't matter who provides the chopper so long as they've got someone with good eyesight. But I don't see what anyone can do on the ground other than duplicate what we've done. Besides, by tomorrow he can't be alive.'

'He's not alive now,' Paula said.

'Meaning?' Forset's fatigue made him sound belligerent.

Paula's eyes went round the circle and came to rest on Sarah. 'You tell them,' she said.

Sarah glanced at the children but they appeared to be asleep. All the same, she spoke quietly. 'She means Shawn was murdered.'

Watch it, Miss Pink thought.

After a long silence Forset said: 'I know why you think that, Paula, but the law says the body has to be found— '

'Why bother?'

He took her literally. 'Because it's the *law*, but, I agree, it's pointless killing ourselves— ' he checked, and changed his wording, 'pointless wearing down the horses if he's already – no longer alive.' He glanced at the sleeping twins uneasily.

'It's time we started down,' Duval said. 'We've done all we can here. We'll go down and call the police. A chopper should be here at first light.'

They returned to the valley, Duval leading, Forset bringing up the rear. He had stood at the entrance to the Twist, watching them file past, and Miss Pink guessed that he was counting. He was taking no risks, nor was Bob Duval; on the descent they kept the pace slow and the column orderly.

They reached Wind Whistle without incident and separated, Miss Pink handing Yaller over to Forset who had a horse trailer hitched behind his pick-up. She got in her jeep and drove home, entering the deep shade of the valley with relief. Within a moment she felt cold. She glanced up at the needles. If he was up there, she thought, Bob Duval was right; there was no way he could survive a second cold night after a day when temperatures must have been well over a hundred degrees in the shade – if he was in the shade.

Chapter 13

Something large and white fluttered on a fence post at the start of Weasel Creek's track. It was a message from Frankie: 'Have to see you. Come and eat whatever the time.' Miss Pink turned the jeep and drove back to the Grays' cabin. Frankie met her at the door and took her to the living-room. The shadows were reaching out for the Crimson Cliffs and the room was no more than warm, the windows wide open to the evening air.

She collapsed on a sofa and asked for beer. Jerome and Frankie waited on her solicitously, seeming unsurprised that nothing had been found in Rustler Park, and then she noticed that they, or at least Frankie, were waiting expectantly, waiting for her to get comfortable. That took a few minutes; although she had absorbed pints of water at Wind Whistle she was thirsty again. Even her skin, now that she had stopped sweating, felt parched. She put down her glass and sighed. 'You've had some news,' she said.

'The police called with the results of the autopsy!'

'He's *been* found?'

'Birdie,' Jerome reminded her. 'The autopsy on Birdie.'

'Oh. My brain feels crumbly. What were the results?'

'She wasn't raped.'

'Now, my dear, they didn't say that— '

'Not necessarily raped.'

'How could they tell?' Miss Pink's tone was flat.

'They couldn't,' Jerome admitted. 'I'm wondering just how competent the pathologist is. He's certainly imaginative. He put forward a theory that the body could have been cut to disguise the fact that she *wasn't* raped. Apparently it's been done before. Now what do you make of that?'

Miss Pink was alert, thirst and fatigue forgotten.

'Isn't it odd?' Frankie was saying. 'And now no one can tell whether she was or not, the body was washed so thoroughly by the flood. The blow to the head would have killed her; that was another finding of the autopsy, and the weapon was probably a piece of wood like a branch. And the knife from the creek fits the stab wounds, and those injuries were done after death because there's no bruising. Isn't it diabolical – I mean, cutting a dead body? And what difference does it make anyway?'

'A great deal,' Miss Pink said. 'There was something on similar lines in a Scottish city – Glasgow or Edinburgh. The murderer was a woman who'd been taunted beyond endurance by the victim: a small girl. The purpose behind the mutilations then was to suggest that the killer was male, and a rapist. Sam's been framed.'

'A woman!' Frankie breathed. 'A woman could do that! No, it's impossible.'

'Men don't have a monopoly in cruelty,' Miss Pink said drily. 'And Birdie was dead, so torture wasn't involved. If you forget the knife wounds and concentrate on the blow to the head – done in anger, perhaps? – then a woman could have done that easily enough.'

'My God, that widens the field. How fortunate for Paula that she was coming home with Lois at the time. But then Paula would never have used the knife afterwards?' Her voice rose uncertainly. The others were not paying attention. She went on: 'There's me, Dolly,' – her eyes widened – 'Sarah!'

'Hi,' she said quietly, coming into the living-room, dropping into an easy chair. She looked pale. Jerome stood up and went to the refrigerator.

Frankie said: 'The autopsy reports came through. There's a theory that Birdie wasn't raped at all; the woundings – after she was dead – were a cover. So a woman could have done it. I was listing the ones who had the opportunity.'

'Thanks, Dad.' Sarah took a Coke from her father. 'Why me?'

'You just walked in! I was greeting you!'

'These two are worn out.' Jerome was kindly but firm. 'I suggest we feed them and put them to bed.'

'I've got to go and give my horse more water,' Sarah said.

'You leave the horse tonight. I'll see to everything.'

'His back's sore too, Dad. Will you see what you think? And I didn't check his feet.'

He went out. A strained silence descended on the room. Coyotes were calling on the far side of the valley. Miss Pink and Sarah drank deeply, Frankie looked from one to the other, Miss Pink set down her empty glass and it sounded loud, peremptory. Frankie brought another bottle of beer from the kitchen. Miss Pink said: 'I shan't be able to drive home.'

'You're staying here,' Frankie said.

She slept for twelve hours in a guest room, waking to a sound that was familiar but so much out of context in the surroundings that she failed to identify it until she caught the rhythm of the rotor blades. The helicopter had arrived.

In fact it had arrived shortly after sunrise and had already flown up Horsethief and over Rustler Park: 'Covering all the ground we searched yesterday,' Sarah pointed out as the Grays and their guest drank coffee on the shadowed balcony. Their eyes followed the aircraft now coming up the line of Salvation Creek from Gospel Bottom.

'What's it doing there?' Frankie asked.

'They're covering the whole area,' Jerome said.

'But Shawn has to be somewhere between Rustler and Wind Whistle!'

'We don't know how their minds are working,' he reminded her. 'And don't forget: everything they've been told they'll treat as hearsay; they don't trust any of us.'

Miss Pink went home to find a familiar car in front of her cabin, and Sprague and Pugh coming round the corner of the building.

170

'Have you been waiting long?' she asked icily.

'We thought *you'd* disappeared,' Sprague said, 'so we were looking to see if you'd left any indication as to where you'd gone.' He regarded her mildly. 'Or to see if there'd been a break-in, foul play, something like that.'

'My car wasn't here.'

'That could have been stolen.'

'But you're here,' Pugh said brightly. 'You been out searching, ma'am?'

'I need a bath badly. Perhaps you would postpone your questions for half an hour.' She moved towards the porch.

'It can't wait,' Sprague said. 'This is a murder investigation.'

'If you'll come round the back,' – Pugh was playing polite boy to Sprague's heavy – 'it's cooler in the shade.'

There was no way that they could inveigle her 'round the back' – a loaded phrase – and out of sight of the valley. She was becoming paranoid; they would be out of sight in the cabin too. They were watching her closely. 'We'll go indoors,' she said, and produced her key.

'You lock your door, ma'am?'

'Since the murder, Mr Pugh.'

She opened the windows in the cabin and they sat and regarded each other expectantly. Sprague produced a sheet of paper.

'This is a list of all local people over the age of sixteen. I want you to tell us where everyone was on Wednesday.'

'Wednesday? Today's Friday. Ah, you mean the day that Shawn disappeared.' She was amazed. 'I have no idea where everyone was.'

'Just the ones you can remember,' Pugh said kindly. 'We'll fill in the gaps later. Everyone is being asked the same questions, of course.'

She didn't miss his use of the present tense. People were being asked at this moment; there must be a swarm of police in the valley. There was no opportunity to compare notes in advance.

'Let me see that paper.' Her own name was at the top

of the list. 'Wednesday,' she murmured. 'Everyone was very active: visiting and discussing events. I called on Myrtle Holman in the morning, then I went to see Mrs Olson, across to Mrs Estwick – do you really want all this?'

Sprague said: 'If everyone tells the truth – or everyone except the killer – one person's not going to check out.'

Pugh was making notes. She raised her eyebrows. No tape recorders?

'Now, as to times,' Sprague prompted.

'I can't help you there. Time's of little consequence down here.' She didn't add that the only time that could interest them in this context was the time it took a person on horseback to go up to, and return from, Rustler Park. Sprague sighed. She counted the names on the list. There were nineteen. 'You can eliminate many of these straight away,' she said, and waited, but no one contradicted her. 'So Lois Stenbock is out because she can't ride, and probably Glen Plummer for the same reason; in any case neither owns a horse. You do realise someone had to ride up Horsethief and probably as far as Rustler Park in order to intercept him?' They nodded, their eyes intent. She went on: 'Myrtle Holman and Maxine. This is bizarre, but you seem to be listing everyone in the canyon. They don't own a horse and I doubt if either can ride. Now, four men are eliminated straight away; Forset, Stenbock and the Duvals were working cattle together; it was they who saw the loose pony on the way down, so the – accident – had happened by that time. The Gray family? I spent most of the day with them, and so did Dolly Creed. It was an extremely hot day, too hot to move away from the pool; if anyone had taken a horse out in that heat it would have been noticed and remarked on— '

'If they'd been seen,' Sprague interrupted.

She looked up the valley through the open door. 'It appears wooded but that's deceptive. There are gaps in the cottonwoods where a horse and rider would be visible. People gleam in this brilliant sunshine – well, not the riders, but the horses' coats reflect the light. However – how many does that leave?'

'Seven,' Pugh said.

'Erik Olson?' Sprague asked.

'He was with Paula Estwick before lunch.'

'And afterwards?'

'I don't know.'

'And Paula Estwick?'

'She was home in the afternoon because Sarah Gray took her some cakes or something.'

'She went on a horse?'

'No. I said: it was much too hot. She went on her bicycle.'

'And came back?' Sprague sounded tired.

'She was gone less than an hour.'

'That leaves us with the pretty Olson girls and their mother,' Pugh said, smiling. 'Although I understand the older "Olsons" are really Warmans.'

'If that was the first husband's name. The older children were irrigating that day.' She was looking at the list. 'You've got Sam Estwick down here.'

'That's a mistake,' Pugh said, adding gallantly: 'The same as regards your own name, ma'am.'

'Why are you treating Shawn's disappearance as murder?'

Sprague appeared astonished. 'Why? He could identify the person who killed Birdie.'

'I'm not so sure of that. Shawn wasn't the soul of honesty.'

'You're using the past tense,' Pugh said.

'If he fell off his pony, he couldn't survive two nights, in addition to a whole day without water. He must have been unconscious because he never responded to our shouts, so he had to be injured, and probably seriously – a head injury; that would make him even more vulnerable to hypothermia *and* dehydration. I'm afraid he's no longer alive.'

'I agree,' Sprague said. 'But it wasn't a fall from his pony killed him. He wasn't alone up in that park – or in Horsethief Canyon.'

Miss Pink was expressionless. 'It couldn't have been Sam Estwick. He was in Nebo.'

'That's right; Sam didn't kill young Shawn. In fact, Sam's back home right now.'

'Good.'

The silence was loaded. Dust motes flicked through the sunbeams. 'The one we want now,' Sprague said, 'is Alex Duval.'

'Why him?'

'He's got a record— ' Sprague checked as his colleague cleared his throat. He started again: 'Alex Duval was charged with rape once but never convicted. The victim was a young girl— '

'What were the circumstances?'

'I don't think we need go into those.' She didn't press the point. 'After Birdie's murder,' he went on, 'Alex disappeared, took off for the canyons. And we want him. People in the helicopter are watching out for him as well as for Shawn's body but they've not seen Alex yet. There's a hundred places back in the empty country where a man could hide himself and his horse and live on deer meat, particularly a man as knows the country like these Duvals do. We've told his brother we need to talk to Alex but Bob's not going to go up and warn him in broad daylight while the chopper's about. He'll wait and go up after dark, tell Alex to be sure he stays hid. Bob says he's camped up there looking after cows, but there's no sign of a camp in the Straight Canyons, the chopper pilot says.'

'I understood that the day that Shawn went missing, Alex was with the others working the cattle.'

'So they say.' Pugh smiled benignly.

'This is a difficult case.' Sprague lowered his voice confidingly. 'Here we've got a small community, very close, very loyal folk; they don't care for authority – they don't need it here: very law-abiding place, Salvation Canyon, like it always was with the Mormons – on the surface. If there's any nasty business going on they keep it to themselves, all in the family.'

'What kind of nasty business are you referring to, Mr Sprague?'

He looked at Pugh who said, with an air of diffidence: 'People out here in the sticks go a bit weird sometimes.

174

They don't make a parade of it – but things go on behind closed doors.'

'You're talking about incest?'

Sprague blinked unhappily but Pugh was cool once the word had been pronounced. 'It happens,' he said.

'I don't see how it applies in this case.' She was genuinely puzzled. 'What would it have to do with Shawn?'

'Not so much what was done to him,' Pugh said, 'but what he knew.'

Sprague was nodding. 'You see? And I'll tell you something else: why we won't find him, why you didn't, why no one will. He's buried.'

'It's all speculation,' Jerome said. 'No one can have any idea what happened to Shawn until, and unless, the body is found.'

'He could have been kidnapped,' Sarah said. 'He could be hundreds of miles from here, and still alive.'

Miss Pink looked at the girl thoughtfully. It was lunch time at the Grays': iced soup and open sandwiches by the pool; Miss Pink, Dolly, and Glen Plummer were the guests.

'It's not impossible,' Miss Pink said. 'But that theory comes under the same heading as the one of the hiker or hobo coming into the canyon and murdering Birdie.'

'It could be the same person,' Plummer said, eager to exclude villainy from the local community.

'The same person,' Miss Pink repeated. 'But not a stranger, unfortunately – and I agree with the police: Shawn knew too much. I don't think his body is buried because there isn't enough soil in the canyons, it's all bedrock, but it could have been dropped in a crevice.'

Dolly said: 'Do you know more than you're letting on? Did the police tell you who they suspect, if it's not Sam?'

'Just Alex.' She had told them that already but it had been received without surprise or consternation, except by Plummer, who was astonished. In the past twenty-four hours the story of the old accusation against Alex Duval had permeated the community, but evidently it had not reached Plummer until now. Dolly had explained it to him as if he were an adolescent.

'They'll never break Alex's alibi,' she was saying now. 'Three men and young Mike. Alex couldn't have had anything to do with what happened to Shawn. Going after him is a blind. Who do they really suspect? Who do *you* think did it?' (This to Miss Pink.) 'Obviously it's not one of us; we were all here Wednesday afternoon, since before lunch, in fact – except Glen, and he doesn't ride, and doesn't have access to a horse if he did. No way to get up Rustler except on a horse.'

'Or on foot,' Sarah said, and everyone refrained from looking at Plummer with his large, soft body. It was doubtful if he could walk a mile, let alone do the twenty-mile round trip to Rustler Park.

Frankie said: 'It's comforting to know that there are at least six people who couldn't possibly have been in Rustler on Wednesday. So who do you think is guilty, Melinda?'

She responded with another question: 'How quickly could one get to Rustler and back?'

Sarah said: 'I've never tried to do it fast. On the slickrock you have to be as slow and careful coming down as going up, and the trail in the canyon proper is terribly exposed above that drop. If you did it in less than four hours you'd be living dangerously.'

'Someone is doing just that. Could it be done in, say, three hours?'

'Never. And on the afternoon of that day? You'd kill your horse going uphill. Three and a half hours at the outside.'

'So,' Dolly said, 'who was alone for three and a half hours that afternoon, and can ride well and has access to a horse?'

'That *day*,' Miss Pink corrected. 'He could have gone up there in the morning, waited for Shawn, and come down at any time. It's a matter of *at least* three and a half hours.'

They were silent, all withdrawn except Miss Pink (who

176

had already considered this problem) and Plummer who seemed unable to make the relevant calculations. He might have the facts but he looked bewildered. She watched them and waited. It was over a minute before anyone spoke, then Dolly said, in a high voice: 'There's no one it could have been. They all have alibis.'

'You went down to Paula in the afternoon,' Frankie told Sarah, as if checking a gap.

'And she was there.' Sarah closed it.

'The Olsons were irrigating,' Jerome said. 'We could see them from here.'

'Not from *here*,' Frankie put in. 'You've got to stand up and walk round the pool and peer through the pinyons to see their alfalfa. And people don't irrigate all day; they go and come.'

'Three and a half hours,' Dolly said meaningly. 'He'd have been missed.'

'By his family,' Frankie said, catching her drift. 'Eleven of those, and mostly children. The littluns can't be trusted not to blurt out the truth some time if he was absent all that afternoon.'

'Too many alibis,' murmured Miss Pink. 'And why should Erik Olson's be any more watertight than Alex Duval's?'

'Because,' Jerome said, 'the word of adults is more reliable.'

'Is it? It's more likely to be believed, but that's not the same thing.'

'What you're suggesting is that because everyone had an alibi and yet it has to be one of them, then one alibi is false, but we don't know which one?'

'Either that or we're barking up the wrong tree.'

'The wrong tree?' Sarah looked bemused.

'Yes. We should concentrate on Birdie.'

'You already brought Birdie into it,' Dolly pointed out. 'You'd never have dreamed that Paula Estwick needed an alibi for Shawn's death without you'd heard the results of the autopsy on Birdie. Personally, I think her death was an accident.'

She had all their attention: calculating or astonished or shocked. She went on defiantly: 'An exasperating child finally drives you round the bend and you lash out – maybe not for the first time: a slap, a cuff, but this time you happen to have something heavy in your hands: a hammer, a log, anything. And the child has a thin skull. Afterwards you panic. The child is dead; it can't be hurt any more, it's just a body. So – the other wounds, the ones that were done after death – they're inflicted as a cover, put the blame on some wandering bum. It could be a case of manslaughter.'

They absorbed this in silence, then Miss Pink said: 'And Shawn? What happened there?'

'The pony threw him, he was concussed and crawled or fell into a crevice, got more injuries as he fell in, and died there.'

Miss Pink looked at them all. She knew by the way they avoided each other's eyes, by their silence, that although they would like to believe in this theory, they had doubts. It was too good to be true.

'In any case,' Plummer said suddenly, 'Paula was in Nebo the afternoon that Birdie was killed.'

'She was on her way back with Lois,' Sarah reminded him.

'If Lois is to be believed,' Dolly said. 'And why not? Lois and Paula aren't bosom pals. Art Stenbock is the one with the opportunity to kill Birdie – but then he was working cattle when Shawn— ' She clapped her hand over her mouth.

'But you said Shawn's death was an accident.' Plummer succeeded in calling attention to her indiscretion.

'We need some kind of common denominator,' Miss Pink said firmly. 'One hypothesis is that Shawn has been killed because he saw Birdie's killer. So, disregarding all the so-called alibis, who could have got to Birdie on Saturday afternoon and to Shawn four days later?'

'If Shawn was murdered,' Dolly persisted.

'Would you come up to the Twist with me tomorrow? We'll take flashlights.'

'You think he's in the Twist after all?' Sarah asked.

Jerome said: 'Don't go alone.'

'I'll come with you,' Sarah said. Seeing Frankie was about to protest, she added: 'I'll take Dad's pistol. No one's going to attack three of us – are they?'

'No,' Miss Pink said. 'We'll be perfectly safe.' Sarah regarded her curiously.

Plummer said: 'What happened to the chopper? We haven't heard it for a while.'

'Probably searching the far bank of the river,' Sarah told him drily, 'thinking Alex swam his horse across the Colorado. Wouldn't put it past the police to think it's possible, particularly if they know the cattle rustlers used to do it.'

Later they learned that the helicopter had been called away. A fire was raging in the La Sal forests and all available aircraft were needed to spray trees and transport the fire fighters. It was Myrtle who gave them the news, and more. Myrtle had been in dire need of someone to talk to. Frightened at the amount of sleeping pills she had given Maxine, she stopped, and Maxine had left her bed and learned of Shawn's disappearance. The press had been there at the time but, suffering from the after-effects of the drugs, not to speak of alcohol, Maxine had no energy for raving after she had taken the first shock. She was sullen and vicious with the reporters and after a while she went back to her room, taking a bottle of vodka.

Myrtle said that the police had visited her twice that day, each time their sole concern being to discover if Shawn had told his mother or grandmother the name of Birdie's killer. Myrtle knew nothing and the first time Maxine had been abusive. When the police returned, Maxine was out of bed and they had warned her that if she knew the name of the murderer, if Shawn had told her, she was in danger if she kept it to herself. Myrtle had thought her daughter frightened enough to tell if she did know, but she maintained that she did not, and Sprague and Pugh evidently believed her because they went away.

'I feel sorry for Myrtle,' Frankie said, returning to her

guests after this telephone conversation. 'You can't help but admire the old lady, with an alcoholic slut for a daughter, a delinquent grandson, and now carrying all this on her shoulders.'

'I'm sorry for the Estwicks,' Dolly said. 'And that nice guy, Alex.'

'There are nine – ten households in this canyon,' Jerome mused, 'counting the visitors. Two are bereaved, one houses a murderer, and the police are determined to hang a capital charge on Alex. Over one third of the inhabitants are primarily affected. Statistically that has to be a record.'

'Statistics are a load of bull,' Sarah said. Amazed at Jerome's thinking, they were bewildered by her reaction; normally she had a steady rapport with her father and her contradicting him was out of character. As if aware of this she elaborated. 'Everyone's affected, Dad,' she said gently, and looked past him, over the tops of the pinyons towards Rustler Park. Miss Pink looked too, idly at first and then her gaze sharpened, although no one would have noticed, her eyes hidden behind the thick spectacles. She glanced at the others. Sarah had turned to Dolly and was saying: 'In a small community everyone *must* be affected in some way . . . '

Miss Pink looked across the valley again but it was not until she reached home late that afternoon and got out her binoculars that she was sure.

There were vultures above the Maze.

Chapter 14

Beneath the guise of gallantry John Forset was adamant; there was no way he would allow three ladies to go to Rustler Park without an escort. Miss Pink, aware that she could hardly borrow the horse without agreeing to take the owner along, but not averse to adding a fourth member to the party, acquiesced gracefully.

They left not long after sunrise next morning, at a time that ensured a cool climb to the Twist and early enough to forestall the police and the press, who, unable to obtain accommodation in Salvation Canyon, were forced to return to Nebo for the night. Sarah had brought her father's Colt which looked most incongruous on her hip. At the entrance to the Twist she stopped and turned to Miss Pink. 'What's the plan?'

'We're going to the Maze.'

'But I thought—' Dolly began, and stopped because the others were silent. After a moment Forset said: 'Yes, it's possible. Perhaps that's the answer ... If his pony broke loose while Shawn was still fit – or threw him and he didn't get hurt – the boy would have a ten-mile walk home.' He looked at Sarah. 'And there's that old tale about a way down to the valley through the Maze: only a mile. It would be very tempting.'

Dolly polished her saddle horn. Sarah said slowly: 'He'd know the story. You get the Stone Hawk in line with the Blanket Man ...'

'Everyone knows that bit,' Forset said.

'Even I,' Miss Pink put in. 'So it's the Maze?'

There was no dissent. She had not expected any. They

moved on, the horses picking their way carefully in the bottom of the great rift until they came out into the sunshine of the park. The reef rose ahead of them like a sea stack above swells of grass that dipped and lifted with a soft breeze.

'Nice day,' Forset said, sniffing with appreciation, adding wryly, 'but it won't be in the Maze.'

Miss Pink reflected that most of the joints would be in shadow but all she said was: 'You know the Maze?'

'All in good time,' he told her heavily. 'All in good time.'

Dolly glanced at her. Sarah regarded her horse's ears. The ambiguous answer hung on the air yet the lack of comment was unremarkable. There was a feeling of resignation; this was no ordinary day and if the other world could be termed conventional – police, press, helicopters – convention had been left behind in Salvation Canyon.

They rode round the end of the reef and turned northwards to where the Pale Hunter stood at the break in the Barrier. When they reached the pinyons they dismounted and put the horses in the shade. Miss Pink started to untie her lariat.

'Why are you doing that?' Forset asked.

'We should take all of them.'

Sarah said: 'We don't need ropes.'

'What makes you so sure?'

Sarah gave her a wan smile. 'For where you want to go we don't need ropes.'

They turned their backs on the park and looked over the white caps of towers like lumpy cobblestones to the Stone Hawk, its shoulders hunched, the head inclined, watching the canyon. Beyond it could be glimpsed the outer edge of the Blanket Man.

'Well?' Sarah addressed Forset. She sounded defeated.

He nodded and sighed. 'Lead on.'

They descended the earthy gully to the first cairn and turned left. Their deliberate progress assumed the air of an expedition with a definite end in view; this was not a search.

Miss Pink, more perceptive than she had been the first

time in this place, and watching the shadows (not the sun because for much of the time she could not see it from the bottom of the joints) realised that only a short distance from the start they had turned north-east. They still followed joints that ran south-east, but these passages were shorter and fewer than those running at right angles.

They moved fast, Forset having to work hard to keep up with Sarah. Dolly, agile and anxious not to be left behind, was on his heels. Miss Pink brought up the rear, but she, too, was having difficulty and dreading that she might sprain an ankle. For one moment she was alone as Dolly whisked round a corner, and in that moment she felt the terror of a lonely death and knew a fleeting nightmare: that she would turn the corner and no one would be ahead, nor ever had been.

She came to the corner, saw a joint with sunshine high on its wall and Dolly about ten yards away. Beyond her Forset was looking back, saying something, and Sarah was beyond him, in the open well where the little ash tree spread its diadem of spring foliage against pink rock.

Sarah had waited for them, which was sensible because, as Miss Pink recalled, the cairns ended at the corner where she had lost sight of Dolly. There were no cairns in the well although four ways led from here, and despite the fact that cairns could have been built: there were stones lying around. She glanced along the joint that she had taken when she climbed to the top of the tower, but the party was moving away at right angles, along a passage that Dolly had taken when they were here before, but she had gone only as far as the first corner, refusing to lose sight of the well. Today they went past that corner and turned left.

Ahead of them the big red wall rose for over a hundred feet above the level of the towers, brilliantly lit in the morning sun. They turned left again, then right. The fissure they were in bent in a dog-leg and suddenly they were in the open and the ground dropped away to the tops of trees. A few more yards and they stopped on the lip of sloping slabs.

The slickrock descended for about eighty feet to the bed of the great cove. On the right the slabs were simple and easy; on the left the view was blocked by a massive buttress.

Dolly said: 'We're not going down there!'

'I'll go first,' Sarah said.

They moved in single file down a kind of sloping staircase in the slickrock and as they approached the floor of the cove and the buttress on the left ended, shadows passed across the rock. Forset stopped and looked up and Dolly followed suit. 'Vultures!' she gasped, and turned to Miss Pink. 'How did you guess?'

'I saw them last night.'

'Why didn't you say?' Forset asked.

'It could be a deer, or a bighorn.'

Dolly swallowed and turned back to the descent. They reached the floor of the cove and followed a path that could have been a game trail except that the cove was too small to hold game. They picked up dead branches and moved slowly through the flecked sunlight under the pines and cotton-woods, banging the tree trunks, peering at the shadows, watching for the gleam of coils, listening for the rattle.

'Don't you long for a pair of thick rubber thigh boots?' Dolly asked wistfully.

'Like a fly fisherman,' Forset said.

'A Highland stream seems a world away,' Miss Pink volunteered loudly. They were talking for the sake of the snakes, pleading with them to get out of the way. Only Sarah was silent.

Miss Pink trod on Dolly's heels. The others had stopped. The cove had its own small bay scooped out of the shadowed side between Maze and wall. The last rank of towers formed a wall themselves where they were fused together. The bay was roughly the shape of a half moon. On the right, inside the horn and protected by that gently curving bulge she had seen a week ago, was the scoop that reflected light from sunlit stone. On the wall of the scoop under the gentle bulge were the imprints of innumerable hands.

It was still and very quiet until a canyon wren sang a few notes to end on a dying fall, and then it was quieter still.

'Oh,' Dolly breathed, 'look!'

Miss Pink looked left from the Cave of Hands to see on the wall a huge red form with hunched shoulders and folded wings, watching them with large circular eyes.

'It's the Stone Hawk,' Dolly said.

'She has no feet,' Miss Pink said, and stopped, not because she had attributed sex to the Stone Hawk but because at her feet, or where the feet should have been, was all that the vultures had left of Shawn Brenner.

They were drained of emotion. As they moved forward – all except Dolly, who held back – Miss Pink said, as if remarking on a new flower: 'Here is a skull.'

'There was nowhere to bury it,' Sarah said listlessly.

'No, I suppose not. There's only a skin of sand.'

Miss Pink stood a few yards from the body and the others flanked her like guardians. The sand was scuffled and marked by the vultures. The ragged clothing was pierced by shattered bones. Not much flesh was left.

'There's no doubt?' Miss Pink asked generally.

'No,' Sarah said. 'Those are a child's sneakers. Besides, no one else is missing. Of that size.'

'How long has he been here, John? How long does it take for scavengers to reduce a body to this?'

'Not long. There's not much smell. I'd say not more than twenty-four hours. I mean, he's been dead twenty-four hours.'

'And why did he die here?' She looked back at the wooded cove and added, as if to herself: 'Of course, it isn't murder.'

'He couldn't get down to the valley,' Sarah pointed out. 'There's no way *up* to the cove, only down from Rustler: the way we came.'

'Where is the way down to the valley, then?'

'There isn't one.'

From behind them Dolly said: 'I never thought there was – but I didn't know about *this*.' She was blocking out the presence of the body, staring defiantly at the enigma painted on the wall. 'You kept all this from me, John; I'll never forgive you.'

'I'd have brought you here eventually.'

'So Birdie was right,' Miss Pink said. 'How old do the children have to be before they're shown this place?'

Sarah shrugged. 'Old enough to keep the secret. There's nothing mystical about it.' She was suddenly earnest. 'It was just that, you know what happens when Anasazi relics are found: graffiti, litter, tourists, commercialism? We kept it to ourselves, that's all. But Birdie guessed – and then Shawn.'

'Why was Shawn so eager to find the place?'

'Simply because it was a secret? Because adults knew and children didn't?'

'So he was spying on you that day you met him in Rustler, trying to find out where the cave was?'

'I wouldn't be surprised.'

'How would he know where to start? Or did he follow you through the Maze that day?'

Sarah shook her head. 'I haven't been down here since last spring when I came with Sandy and Tracy. But everyone knew the bit about getting the Stone Hawk and the Blanket Man in line – although that's just for the start of the route – and anyone who's ever been in Rustler has seen that the only gap in the Barrier, apart from the Twist, is the one beside the Pale Hunter. Ride to that point and you've got the start of the trail.'

'Marked with cairns, too.'

'Only so far,' Forset put in. 'Remember that place with the ash tree where we stopped? There are three joints from that place, not counting the one you came in by. There's no cairn marking the right joint, and none afterwards. That's deliberate.'

'So from that point you need a guide.'

'Exactly.'

They stepped back to Dolly who had picked up the old skull and was smoothing it with her hand. 'I know who this is,' she said. 'And I always thought it was a legend! This is the poor guy who went searching for the Cave of Hands and never came back. What d'you think happened to him?'

'The same as the boy,' Forset said. 'Rattlers got him.'

'How appalling.' She turned wide eyes on them. 'Is that why Shawn lasted so long, why he didn't try to get back to Rustler?' She looked through the trees. 'He must have gone across the cove, thinking that was the way out – it's obvious, look: there are the Crimson Cliffs – and then he came to the top of the precipice above Forbidden Creek, and the trail only a short distance below . . . He'd look over the edge and *see* the trail, even the houses, and the lights when it got dark, but he couldn't get down – and too far away from a house for anyone to hear his shouts. So he'd come back to here – meaning to go back to Rustler? – but on the way he trod on a rattler in the dark— '

'All right, my dear; it's all over.' Forset went to take her arm but she recoiled.

'Don't! If we're going back through that lot,' – she motioned to the trees – 'we're going to make so much noise there won't be a rattler within a hundred feet of us.'

'We'll do that.' He turned to Miss Pink. 'What are we going to do about the body?'

'Someone will have to come up with a large bag. I suppose it will have to be the police.'

'Not necessarily; it's obvious it was an accident. However, there's no way we can take it down.'

'Then we'd better do what we can to protect it.'

It took them some time to build a kind of shelter over the body, trying not to drop rocks on it, although that was mere sentimentality for it was in such a state that it must be immaterial if another bone were broken. When they had finished they retreated to the shade of a pinyon.

'Where is the spring?' Miss Pink asked. 'Can we drink the water?'

'No,' Sarah said. 'It'll be dirty this time of year.' But she took them all the same. In different circumstances their progress would have been amusing: noisy and rowdy in that quiet place, but they were taking no chances in an overgrown basin where two people had died.

There was a pool and it was scummy. Water bubbled in the centre but they were not tempted to drink. There was mud but no tracks. The sight of water made them thirsty and there was a concerted movement towards the slickrock. The sun was now in the south and shining straight into their eyes. They pulled their hat brims down and trudged doggedly up the slabs towards the Maze, Miss Pink struggling in the rear, the distance increasing between her and Dolly. The gap closed as the younger woman, not so agile on slickrock, paused for breath.

They retraced their steps through the joints with the terrible sunshine close above them on the glaring walls and the air stagnant as still water. They went slowly; all were accustomed to heat and knew the dangers of speed, however easy the gradient, however tempting the thought of containers full of water back where they had left the horses.

They turned right towards the wall, then left from the ash tree, into the hot depths of a joint, turning into one in deeper shadow, marginally cooler, and—

'Where's Miss Pink?' Sarah asked.

'Shit!' Dolly exclaimed.

They went plunging back, Dolly in the lead now, Forset stumbling behind her.

'Wait,' Sarah shouted. 'Wait!'

They stopped. 'Don't panic,' she said quietly. 'Sit down, John – and Dolly. Sit in the shade and wait. I'll go back.'

Miss Pink was waiting too. She was standing on the edge of the tower above the short jump, the jump that could not be reversed because one cannot leap upwards if there is nothing to grab hold of on the upper tower, the cap of which had been as smooth as a billiard ball. Except that it was no longer smooth. Where she was standing, at the place where the eighty-foot joint might be leapt with ease by an elderly lady, or a ten-year-old boy, was a cairn.

188

Sarah was breathing hard. She stopped a few yards away and looked at the cairn and the tower below and back to Miss Pink. The pistol on her hip no longer looked incongruous. Each waited for the other to speak and Sarah gave in first.

'We thought something had happened to you. Why did you come up here?'

'Because I saw another cairn.'

Sarah looked puzzled. 'You can't see this from below, surely?'

'I saw one in a joint leading out of the well.'

Sarah thought back. 'I didn't.' She moved forward a step.

Miss Pink drew aside. 'Where are the others?'

'Back there. What is this cairn for?'

'This one is to mark the place where you can virtually step across to the next tower.'

'Oh. You've done that?'

'No, because you can't get back.'

'So what are you trying to tell me?'

'That Shawn didn't die of snakebite. Most of his bones were broken. He fell from the top of a tower – that tower.' She pointed to the next. 'He jumped down from here, walked across the lower one and found himself rimrocked. And he couldn't get back. He was stuck on that cap, and no one knew he was there. Eventually, probably delirious from thirst, he walked over the edge.'

'How did you work it out?'

Miss Pink moved towards the way down. 'It was just an educated guess. It may not have happened like that at all.'

There was a rattle of stones behind her and she turned to see Sarah demolishing the cairn, kicking the rocks into the joint. 'We'll make sure no one else makes the same mistake,' she said.

They climbed down the crack and squeezed through the hole behind the jammed boulders. At the foot of the gully they turned left and, at the place where they should turn towards the well, was another cairn.

'I missed that one,' Sarah said, and kicked it to pieces.

'Who built them?'

'I don't know. Ask John. They've been here for decades.'

'I don't understand— ' Dolly began.

'I'm not sure that I do,' Forset interrupted. 'Why would anyone build a cairn in a place that was dangerous?'

Miss Pink's gaze was unfocused but she was looking straight at Dolly who dropped her eyes. They were sitting in the shade under the Pale Hunter, eating a belated lunch.

'I think that's exactly why it was put there,' Miss Pink said. 'Usually people build cairns to mark a trail, but since the basic motivation is to mark *something*, occasionally you'll find one built as a warning; it's still a marker but it denotes danger. There's a big cliff in Wales with an easy way down for walkers, and several hard climbs further along. Some thoughtless people built a cairn at the top of a climb which a hiker might well think marked the start of the easy way down.'

'That's highly irresponsible,' Forset said angrily, visualising it. 'And a hiker got rimrocked?'

'No. Someone demolished the cairn.'

'You should have demolished this one, on top of the tower.'

'I did,' Sarah said. 'There was another, down below, in the joint. Who built them, John?'

Miss Pink's eyes passed casually over Dolly, who concentrated on opening a can of beer.

'There were cairns already when my dad brought me up here,' he told them. 'The kids will have added a few stones down through the years.' He paused, staring in the direction of the Maze. 'You can feel sorry for the boy now; I guess he came to the well with the ash tree, scouted around, found the cairns and ended up on top of the tower – and there, you say, was this crucial one, right at the spot where he shouldn't go?' His voice rose. 'The guy that built that cairn's got a lot to answer for.'

'He must have died long ago,' Dolly pointed out. 'Jesus!' They stared at her. 'I know who built them. It was the guy who died in the cove – remember, the skull? He was building cairns all the way through the Maze so's he could find the way back; that's what— '

'I don't know,' Miss Pink interrupted, apologising immediately, but continuing: 'I'm sorry, but wouldn't the place to put the cairn be after the jump, not before? Oh, he couldn't: there were no stones on the last tower . . . '

'Thanks for stopping me there.' Dolly topped up Miss Pink's glass with lemonade and lowered herself into a wicker chair on her porch. 'I thought I did very well on the whole; there was no way they could have guessed we'd been in the Maze already – but why should we keep quiet with Sarah and John?'

'Because they might talk,' Miss Pink said absently. 'The fewer people who know we were there the better, particularly now . . . You did very well, my dear.'

'I'm not a child.'

'What?'

'You're treating me like a child. You're miles away, Melinda; what's on your mind?' Miss Pink said nothing. Dolly resumed, but more gently: 'It was a terrible shock and, personally, I couldn't bear to look, but, as John said, it's over. I'm sorry for Maxine, though. Do you think she feels things very deeply? Perhaps not. But then there's Myrtle; she adored Shawn – and she'll have Maxine to cope with— '

'Could he have been pushed?'

'Maxine will flip – *what did you say*?'

'He was too bright to go into the Maze with Birdie's killer. Besides, if he was pushed, how would the killer get back? You can't jump back – there's nothing to grab hold of. No, it had to be an accident.'

'Of course it was an accident,' Dolly said, and listened. 'Damn, there's a car coming.' She stood up. 'Who do we know drives a white Porsche? And someone behind him in a green Subaru. This is an invasion.'

'It'll be the police.'

'The Subaru maybe, not the Porsche.'

Neither car held the police. The driver of the Porsche was very large and fat and genial, inclining his head to them but waiting without self-consciousness for the arrival of the other car and the emergence of a copper-haired girl in mirror glasses and hot pants. They approached the porch together and introduced themselves. The girl was Carol Taft from the Nebo *Examiner*; the jolly Porsche driver was Butch Maguire and he was a repossessor. He collected cars when people defaulted on the payments, which was how he came by the Porsche, as he explained to Dolly who admired it; a beautiful automobile but somewhat cramped, he said, and how might he get in touch with her neighbour, Glen Plummer?

There was a charged silence. 'Just go and knock on his door,' Dolly said weakly. 'May I get you all a drink?'

'That would be very welcome,' Maguire said, settling in his chair and stretching his log-like legs.

Carol Taft said brightly: 'He was here yesterday afternoon?' She raised her eyebrows at Miss Pink who smiled, interpreting it as a statement.

Dolly brought bottles of beer and glasses. She stared pointedly at the bulge under Maguire's jacket. 'I'll allow you to remove your jacket, Mr Maguire, provided you also remove your gun.'

'That's most congenial of you, ma'am.' He was not in the least discomfited. He stood up and, watched by the women, draped his jacket over the back of his chair, placed his gun underneath it, and resumed his seat, beaming at them.

'I want Plummer's Volvo,' he said.

Dolly made a strangled sound. 'Are you telling us that Glen Plummer defaulted on payments of a *car*?'

'That's what I'm all about, ma'am, it's what you might call the reason for my existence.'

Dolly looked at Miss Pink. 'But he's a multi-millionaire!'

'Oh, yes?' Maguire smiled politely.

Carol Taft's eyes were sparkling. 'What did he tell you?' she asked in a tone of patronising amusement.

Dolly was furious. 'We take people on trust here!'

Miss Pink studied the outline of Calamity Mesa and tried to hide a smile.

'*You* knew, ma'am.' Maguire didn't miss much for all his appearance of softness.

'I didn't know anything,' she confessed. 'Was someone after him besides yourself?'

'There, you see? It was some people from up north, around Salt Lake. He had a lot of irons in the fire, I suspect, but the scam they want to talk to him about concerns a company building log cabins out in the desert, sub-development, you know? Mr Plummer wouldn't start work without he had a nice little advance and the idea was to collect commissions from a lot of people with more money than sense, and run.'

'How much?' Dolly asked.

'I should think the rake-off there was about ten thousand.'

'Is that all?'

'Well, he wasn't very clever, not at the top of his profession, but that was just one little company and it was mostly profit. All he needed was letterheads and an office and a clerk, but he owes money to printers throughout Utah and Nevada, and he never paid his rent, and his clerk was his wife.'

Miss Pink laughed helplessly but Dolly was livid. 'You're telling us he was just an ordinary con-man!'

'Well, not all that ordinary; he had a modest success.' Maguire seemed concerned that denigration of his quarry might diminish himself.

'What was he doing here?' Miss Pink asked.

'Lying low after the log cabin scam and waiting for his wife to join him. She's on a trip to the coast to see the children. They live with Plummer's in-laws when their parents are working away from home.'

Dolly said spitefully: 'He left here at a bad time. Now the police will be after him.'

'I doubt— ' Miss Pink began, and stopped. Carol Taft was taking a notebook out of her bag.

'You don't think he's a suspect?' she asked Miss Pink.

'How much do you know?'

For a moment the girl was disconcerted. 'Your colleagues will be with the police,' Miss Pink said meaningly.

'Probably. They're a bit slow. I've been with the police and I know that you found the little boy's body and he was thrown over a precipice by the same person killed the Indian kid. That's the gist of it.'

'You know more than we do,' Miss Pink said drily, and turned back to Maguire. 'The police will try to find him simply because he did make a break for it, but he can't be a suspect if they're thinking Shawn was murdered. Plummer can't ride so he was never in Rustler Park. However, your best bet is to work with the police; they'll lead you to him.'

'Perhaps his landlord has an address.'

'For my money, Mr Maguire, his landlord will also have been bilked of his rent.'

'Not John,' Dolly said stoutly. 'He'd have insisted on rent in advance.'

Chapter 15

That evening the news spread like a forest fire and local people reacted nervously, resentfully, as if the finding of Shawn's body was an interruption in their attempts to return to normal after Birdie's death. Maxine was the exception. She went into deep shock and was taken to hospital where she could be supervised as she came out of the stupor engendered by alcohol and drugs to face a reality exacerbated by withdrawal symptoms. Myrtle went with her.

As for Plummer's flight, Sprague and Pugh did not seem interested, nor did the press. Even the most inexperienced reporter thought that professional con-men were too wily to commit murder.

There was no news of Alex Duval who was presumed to be still out in the country beyond the Straight Canyons. Bob Duval had been questioned again. He was suddenly eager to help the police, said he had gone up to Bighorn Spring to tell Alex the police wanted to talk to him, but had found no sign of him, and there was no telling where he was; the only way to find him was with a helicopter. And Bob knew as well as the police did that no one was going to authorise the expense of another chopper to look for a man who knew these canyons like the back of his hand.

The immediate and infuriating problem was that of reaching Shawn's body. Sprague was furious when he learned that it had been touched. When Miss Pink pointed out that it had not been touched so much as protected, his anger did not lessen. She told him coldly that, had they left it exposed, by tomorrow there would have been no flesh on it at all, and the bones would have been scattered, even carried away by the vultures.

Sprague floundered. Having had the great cove pointed out to him, he proposed approaching it from below. A suggestion that this might not be feasible was termed obstructive. With Pugh and a number of uniformed men, trailed by the press, he crossed the valley and followed Forbidden Creek back to the big wall. They walked along its foot unable to believe that there was no place where an agile man could not climb into the cove, only a hundred feet above. Ropes, they said, knowing that ropes were used in rock climbing, but then they realised that someone had to go first to get the rope up there.

They telephoned Nebo in order to try to find a policeman who was a climber but they had no success. Again Sprague tried to get a helicopter, this time to lift them into Rustler Park, but all helicopters were still in the La Sals. Fire-fighting had priority over crime.

None of the police could ride, and by the time they could reach Rustler it would be dark anyway. And it was pointed out to them that although no one had seen rattlers in the Maze in the daytime, even the local people would not go there at night. As for the cove: to go there after sunset was suicide.

The police had to wait until Sunday and daylight. They sent a car back to Nebo for food and persuaded John Forset to let them sleep in the cabin which Glen Plummer had left so precipitately. In theory he was still the tenant, having paid his rent to the end of the month; in practice the police did not think he would be returning to sue them. Despite that, they were meticulous about not touching the odd bottle of spirits he had left behind, although less meticulous about his beer. It was a bad time for them. Holed up in the A-frame with its wide picture window, they stared across the valley at the cove only two miles away and fumed impotently. They were quite sure Shawn had been pushed.

The valley, that Saturday evening, was quiet. No one went visiting. The local people knew Rustler Park and the configuration of the Maze, even those who had not been there. Many of the canyons were lined with the squat capped towers, so they could envisage the ground where Shawn had died. They knew what being rimrocked meant – and that stranded animals: cows, horses, people, usually fall to their death eventually, victims of delirium or apathy. The consensus among the locals was that Shawn had not been pushed but had fallen; he had died by accident. What was worrying people, keeping them watchful while at the same time aware that they were being watched, was that they did not know who had murdered Birdie.

That was the reason why people wanted to believe that Shawn died, if not naturally, at least without foul play; if Birdie had died by accident too – well, nearly by accident, with someone (no one would dream of mentioning a name) hitting harder than he or she intended – then there was no malicious murderer in their midst. But if Shawn had been murdered, the implication was that Birdie had been as well, and since no one knew why that had happened, who knew where the killer would strike next?

No one slept well the night after Miss Pink's party came down from Rustler, their thoughts like birds: sheering away and returning to the Maze and the wall above the cove where the body lay in the dark at the foot of the Stone Hawk's image.

The police left Plummer's cabin before the sun reached the valley and drove south. Miss Pink guessed that they were heading for Wind Whistle. Evidently Sprague and Pugh were going to ride to Rustler. 'We wonder how they're going to manage on the slickrock,' said Frankie, telephoning after breakfast. 'There hasn't been so much activity in these canyons since Indian times. Did you know the press are going to look for Alex today?'

'On horseback?'

'No, they're bringing in a helicopter from Salt Lake. Sarah says they'll never find Alex, and I hope she's right . . . Are you still there?'

'Yes, I was thinking.'

'A pretty desperate exercise. One keeps going round in circles. I was awake most of the night. Come over for lunch and a swim.'

'I thought I might ride— '

'It's going to be much too hot.'

'I have things to do – after yesterday . . . '

'Of course. Come when you can. Any time.'

She drove to the Olson homestead. Steve – the senior of the 'true' Olsons, blond and blue-eyed – was sitting on the porch steps shelling peas. There was a smell of baking bread and someone was playing a recorder in a room off the kitchen. Jo sat at the table feeding cereal to the baby. She smiled a welcome and Miss Pink looked around. There was no child in the room other than the baby.

'The police have gone up to Rustler,' she said quietly.

'Poor guys. It's going to be a hot day.'

'And they have to bring the body down.'

Jo shook her head. 'The silly kid. He was the first one to do that, go up there alone. All the others knew to wait until they were old enough to be taken. It always put me in mind of an initiation ceremony, like in a primitive culture.' She smiled. 'Primitives never hurry things. Maybe Shawn was too civilised.'

'Too civilised?'

'He was out of touch with the earth.'

'Would you expect a small boy to be in touch?'

'He had no respect. And he was very greedy.'

'You're suggesting greed and lack of respect had something to do with his death?'

'In a broad sense, yes. He wanted to see the Cave of Hands, he *had* to see it, he wouldn't wait until he was old enough. When Shawn wanted something he had to have it *now*, this minute, and he was a terribly determined kid. Perhaps he thought the Cave of Hands, the ritual about waiting until you were old enough, was a silly game dreamed up by the older kids – and he was too clever to stick by the rules . . . '

Debbie was coming up the porch steps, wearing an ancient Panama hat and carrying a jam jar. She greeted Miss Pink gravely, went to the sink and filled the jar with water.

'How's it going?' Jo asked.

'It's awful hard trying to do it if I can't copy the picture. Can I take some more cake?'

'You need worms, not cake.'

'It's too dry, Mom! I can't find no worms.'

'Any worms. You can try some cake; they don't like it.'

'What are you doing?' Miss Pink asked.

'Biology. If you'll just carry the cake for me I'll show you – if you want to see.'

'I'm fascinated.'

At the end of the vegetable garden was a log seat on which was a sketch pad, a paint box and a bird book open to the plate of thrushes. They sat down and Debbie opened the pad.

'This is the male robin.' It was, of course, the American robin, which is a thrush. Miss Pink was astonished by Debbie's firm lines.

'You've got a steady hand, and a fine eye for colour. Did Dolly teach you to draw?'

'Some. Not much.' She was drawing with a soft pencil, sneaking glances at the picture but trying a different stance. 'Do you like her pictures?'

'Not all of them.'

'Some are hard. You know: hard and bright? The little one in Mr Forset's cabin is soft, the one of the Grand Canyon, all pale and misty.'

'Ah, yes; that's my favourite.'

Debbie sighed. 'That's a neat painting, but people don't buy that kind. She paints second-rate pictures for second-rate people. Mom says that's sin – sick— '

'Cynical?'

'Yes, so that stuff Mrs Holman sells isn't the best.'

'I suppose Mrs Holman will be selling Dolly's pictures again now.'

199

'I expect so. They'll be safe. Here she is. See the difference?' The female robin pecked at the cake crumbs in a desultory fashion and flew away. 'Damn!' said Debbie. 'She's awful shy.'

Miss Pink sighed. 'It's an odd thing to do: spoil someone's picture, even if you do think it's second-rate. Did he hate all pictures, or just Dolly's? Did he spoil any of yours?'

'Huh! He never got the chance.'

'And you always had your big brothers and sisters around. He'd never dare.'

'He was a coward. Frightened of everything.'

'Not everything. He rode up to Rustler on his own.'

'On a nice day. But he was frightened of the dark and of thunder.' Debbie glanced at the sky. 'We're going to have a storm today; it's too hot. Don't the Stone Hawk look pretty?' The monolith was more impressive than ever in the side-light. Debbie looked at Miss Pink out of the corner of her eye. 'You know about the Stone Hawk, what she does in a storm?'

'No. Tell me.'

'She moves.'

Miss Pink felt the hairs shift on the back of her neck.

'How far?'

'Well, not far but, like if you're here and it thunders, next time you look, she's moved to about the other side of that cottonwood.'

'Have you seen this happen?'

The child's face fell. 'No. And I don't know anyone who has. We used to watch but I don't any more. Maybe I will again today. She used to.'

'Who?'

'Birdie.'

'Used to watch for the Stone Hawk to move?'

'Only in the storms. She wanted to see the Stone Hawk move more than anything 'cept seeing the Cave of Hands.'

Miss Pink was silent for so long that Debbie looked up. 'You don't believe me, do you?'

'Yes, I believe you. I was trying to see it happening: the Stone Hawk moving. Did Birdie say anything about it at the rodeo when your mom shouted that there was a storm coming?'

'I don't remember. But we all knew about the Stone Hawk; she's part of the storm.'

'Sometimes I have the feeling she's watching.' They stared at the hunched figure.

'She looks all ways,' Debbie said. 'She sees everything.'

'Is she guarding people?'

'What do you mean?'

'Watching over you, like protecting?'

'Well, if she is, she's not doing a very good job of it.' It was so unexpected that Miss Pink was shocked.

'That sounds disrespectful.'

'I was thinking of Birdie. The Stone Hawk sort of belonged to her. Birdie was Indian, so's Hawk, so how come she let Birdie be killed? It wasn't fair.'

'If Hawk is good, could there be a bad rock somewhere – could Blanket Man be bad, and he was more powerful, and he slipped past Stone Hawk at that moment?'

'Blanket Man didn't kill Birdie.'

Miss Pink's mouth was dry. She said delicately: 'Could he get a person to do the job for him?'

'It had nothing to do with Blanket Man.'

'I see. He's good too, like the Stone Hawk.'

'They're only rocks.'

The robin alighted on a fence post and sang a snatch of song.

'She's got a white eye ring,' Miss Pink said. 'Is that natural or has she got ringworm?'

Debbie glanced at the book. 'It's natural – but that's the male.'

'So it is. Why were you so worried about Shawn riding the pinto? He didn't come to grief riding. It was after he left the pony that he got lost.'

'The pony left *him*. I expect he beat it. I wasn't worried about Shawn getting hurt; I was worried about the pony.'

'Why did Mrs Estwick let him borrow it if he was cruel to animals?'

Debbie smiled. 'Maybe that was why she let him have it.'

Miss Pink stood up. 'Do you mind if I take a walk?'

'Not at all,' Debbie said politely.

She climbed through the garden fence and crossed a meadow to the creek, emerging at the ford where Birdie must have crossed to reach home after the rodeo. She waded to the far bank, the water coming only to her calves. She looked west and saw that from here the Stone Hawk was obscured by trees. She walked upstream for a few yards and the rock appeared in plain view, beyond the plinth of the Blanket Man. There were no cottonwoods on the near bank for some two hundred yards, and a short distance upstream a stake had been driven into the earth with a yellow ribbon attached. The opposite bank was low and covered with willow scrub.

The Estwicks' cabin, although close at hand, was not visible because she was in that pasture where the steers grazed, the one dotted with trees. She remembered that the Stone Hawk could not be seen from the cabin, so if Birdie wanted to see it during a thunderstorm she would have to come down to the bank of the creek or go up the track towards the road, but in the latter case the Blanket Man would be in the way.

She returned to Debbie. 'Did Shawn hate Birdie?' she asked.

'He was jealous of her.' Debbie stood up and began to put her gear together. 'It's too hot for painting; my sweat's running all over the paper. He were jealous of all of us. We had ponies and nice things to eat.'

'So he didn't hate anybody?'

'No-o. I never thought about it before but Shawn didn't last – I mean, he'd hate you one day 'cause you wouldn't let him ride your pony, and next day he'd forgotten – I think.' She looked doubtful.

'He had a nasty temper?'

'No.'

'What happened, how did he look, when you said he couldn't ride your pony?'

'He went white and he stared at you and then he walked away. Sometimes he went home.'

'How did you feel then?'

'I kept clear of him next time he came. He was bigger'n me. He was ten.'

'But you never thought he hated you.'

'No, I said: it never lasted. Anyway he didn't hate kids. Just Mr Estwick.'

'Why was that?'

'Mr Estwick used to visit with Shawn's mom so he was probably jealous of him too, but I heard *someone* say' – Debbie motioned Miss Pink to come closer, and whispered – 'someone said Mr Estwick told Shawn he ought to be put away.'

'Put away?'

She nodded solemnly. 'With the mad people.'

By two o'clock the heat was stifling, and the party about the Grays' pool drifted back and forth between the hot shade and the limpid water.

'I hate to think of even Mr Sprague in Rustler Park on an afternoon like this,' Dolly murmured, floating with her eyes closed against the glare. 'Although I'm more sorry for his horse.'

'Perhaps they'll get a lift down in the helicopter,' Miss Pink said. 'The men anyway.' She was sitting in the water on the steps of the pool, wearing a regulation swimsuit and a coolie hat. Behind her Sarah and her parents were stretched out under the *ramada*.

Jerome said: 'The press will be occupying every inch of space in the chopper. The pilot won't be able to pick up anyone else. Besides, the press are searching the Straights.'

'I think they're going up and down Limbo,' Sarah said, and everyone smiled except Miss Pink.

'Limbo,' Dolly told her, 'is big and crooked, full of trees and caves. Even if they did spot him there's nothing

203

they could do about it. If they could land on the rim they wouldn't know how to get down. I don't see the press walking anywhere. Alex is safe for as long as he wants to be.'

'But, if he killed Shawn?' Miss Pink ventured.

'That had to be an accident,' Sarah said.

With a swirl and a splash Dolly was at the steps. Miss Pink moved aside, allowing her to emerge, dripping. The younger woman shivered. 'We don't *know* there isn't a double murderer in the canyon,' she said, towelling her hair. 'How are the Olsons taking it, Melinda?'

'Jo thinks it was an accident. I mean, Shawn; she didn't speak about Birdie's death.'

Frankie said miserably: 'Are we going to be wondering for the rest of our lives whether the person we're talking to killed Birdie?'

'If the police don't catch him,' Jerome said.

'Is Alex going to be the scapegoat?' Sarah asked.

'It looks that way,' Miss Pink said. 'The press will be hounding the police, particularly if they do catch a glimpse of him today, in Limbo Canyon. He has an alibi for Birdie's murder but not for Shawn's. If the boy died the day after he went missing, Alex has no alibi. By that time he was missing too.'

Jerome said, as if he hadn't heard her: 'Alex was pulling fence when Birdie was killed, or he was on the tractor coming home.'

'Quite.' Miss Pink was casual. 'I rather favoured Art Stenbock for that.'

'You thought Art killed Birdie!' Dolly was incredulous.

'He had the opportunity.'

'What was his motive?' Sarah asked.

Miss Pink looked confused. 'It could have been some kind of accident.'

Jerome said: 'You can't be suggesting there are two murderers in the canyon?'

'Actually I could, if Alex was the second one. He's simple and loyal; he could have killed Shawn because the boy

204

threatened to expose Art Stenbock. Or he could have killed him just because he was a blackmailer and a psychopath: put him down as he would a dangerous animal.'

'Alex would have shot him,' Sarah said.

'I don't think Alex is so simple that he's unaware of the penalties for killing a human being. If he was responsible for Shawn's death in the Maze, he did it in a manner that can never be brought home to him.'

'Can't it?' Frankie was caught up by this new theory. 'Are you absolutely sure?'

'My dear!' Jerome protested.

'We may learn more when the police get back,' Miss Pink said.

The police returned in the late afternoon. They had gone up to Rustler on Duval horses and guided by Bob. They found Miss Pink on her shaded porch, watching the sky, waiting for the storm to break and clear the air. Sprague and Pugh were pale with fatigue, and Sprague must have been additionally exhausted by anger. Every cairn in the Maze had been demolished.

'Every one?' she repeated blankly.

'All the way from the park,' Pugh told her. 'Duval said there wasn't one left.'

'He did it,' Sprague said, accepting a beer with a grunt of thanks.

'Bob Duval?'

'His brother. Alex Duval. If that guy's in Utah I'm going to find him.'

'What would be his purpose in destroying the cairns?'

'They want to stop tourists seeing the rock pictures,' Pugh informed her. 'And without the cairns no stranger can find his way through the Maze. The press would have been there tomorrow, get the chopper to lift them into the park, and they'd walk down to see where the boy died. Now they can't go without a guide – and who's going to guide them? Duval won't.'

'So demolishing the cairns has no sinister motive?'

205

'We don't know that,' Sprague said. 'What we do know is that Alex Duval can come and go easy as a mountain lion, and no one any the wiser, so if he was up there some time after you were there, ma'am, who's to say when else he was up there?'

'Why should he have killed Shawn?'

'Because the kid knew he killed the Indian girl, that's why!'

'But Alex was fencing in Horsethief— '

'So young Mike says. We'll break that alibi, so-called. He'll crack like an egg, will Mike, once we take him in for questioning.'

'How did Alex kill Shawn?'

Sprague stared at her blankly and she saw that he was too tired for his brain to be working properly. Pugh said: 'We'll find out in due course; pushed him over somewhere else, and carried him to where he was found?'

'He wasn't moved after he'd fell,' Sprague said dully.

'There was a cairn on top of that tower,' Pugh said, his spirits seeming to rise as those of his colleague plummeted. 'Forset says you saw it and that Sarah Gray kicked it down. Who built that?'

'We assumed it was the man who died near where we found Shawn's body, the owner of the skull. You saw the skull? He probably fell in the same place. If you could find the rest of the bones they'd be broken too.'

'The skull wasn't broken.'

'Was the boy's?'

'Yes.'

That train of thought reminded her to ask about the significance of the stake and the yellow ribbon on the bank of the creek.

'That was where we found the knife,' Pugh told her. 'Estwick's knife. It had been thrown out in the middle of the creek and got caught in some stones on the bottom.'

'You must have dusted everything for fingerprints: the pony's saddle, the bridle, even the knife.'

'Nothing on the knife; you couldn't expect it, but it

would have been wiped anyway. The pony's harness had prints on it but they were all the kids'.'

'So Estwick's prints weren't on the saddle?'

'No—'

The telephone was ringing. It was Jerome. 'Melinda, are Mr Sprague and Mr Pugh with you?' The formality of it astounded her. 'Would you be so kind as to ask them to come over? We'd like you to come too.'

'They're about all in.'

'They'll come. Sarah has information for them. She knows who killed Birdie.'

'Does she indeed? I hope she's told you and Frankie.'

'Shawn lied. And Sarah has photographs.'

Chapter 16

Sprague said: 'I don't believe it.'

'She's been holding out on us,' Pugh said. 'You remember: that afternoon she said she was photographing snakes. She had to be near the Estwicks' place. She saw something.'

'So did Shawn.' Sprague did not move from his chair. He turned heavy eyes on Miss Pink. 'That's why he had to be killed, wasn't it?'

'No.'

Sprague's eyes did not change but Pugh was on to this like a terrier pouncing on a rat. 'You mean Shawn didn't know who the killer was?'

'Yes, he knew – but he died by accident.'

'If he knew who the killer was, and he died, logic says he had to – oh, God— ' Sprague was at the end of his tether.

'Who did kill Birdie?' Pugh asked.

'Shawn,' Miss Pink said.

There was silence. At length Pugh said: 'I think we have to go over to the Grays'.' He looked doubtfully at Sprague who started to pull himself to his feet. 'Everyone's gone mad,' he grumbled. 'Their brains have melted in the heat. She's got photographs, the father said? Photographs of what? Snakes? What's that going to prove?'

Miss Pink took her jeep, the others got in the police car, Pugh driving. Lightning rent slate-coloured clouds above the Barrier. Ten seconds later thunder crashed and rolled through the canyon. There was a smear of rain over Wind Whistle and the Stone Hawk stood up livid against the dark side of the cliffs. By the time she turned in at the Grays' road-end the world had darkened and the next flash of lightning made her cringe at the wheel. Then the thunder exploded and she glanced up the canyon to see an opaque wall of rain on the near side of the narrows. She was vividly reminded of that other afternoon, when Birdie had died.

The cars skidded to a halt beside the big cabin and the occupants hurried into shelter, Sprague limping in the rear. In the sitting-room the big windows had been closed and there were splashes of rain on the glass. Lightning struck the needles of the Barrier, and the thunder, echoing through the canyons, was continuous.

Frankie, seeing Sprague's condition, brought coffee immediately; Jerome produced brandy. Sarah sat on a sofa looking resigned, a trifle bored. Miss Pink thought the girl was very tightly controlled. Her parents sat down and looked at the police expectantly.

Sprague's opening remark was a shock all the same. Taking a new lease on energy under the influence of the good brandy, he turned to Sarah.

'So you got pictures of young Shawn killing Birdie?'

Astonished, Jerome and Frankie stared at him. Sarah blinked once before she replied, but that reply, for Sprague, was more shocking than his own facetious question.

'Not quite, but as good as.'

'There they are.' Jerome motioned to the kitchen table. 'They're still damp; we only just finished printing them.'

They were four large black and white prints, very clear and professional. They showed water, and Shawn standing in it, waist-deep. He was washing himself, and he was wearing a T-shirt and jeans. On closer inspection – and the police and Miss Pink were fascinated – they saw that it was not *any* water, but a creek, flowing away from the viewer, and that the far bank was bare of trees.

'You know where this is,' Pugh told Sprague, who nodded. 'The stake is there.' Pugh pointed. 'You took these?' He looked back at Sarah who had not moved from her seat. He returned to her. 'Perhaps you would tell us about it,' he said politely.

It was a week ago, she said: Saturday, the afternoon Birdie died. She had been working her way down the bank of the creek because rattlers like the banks. She had seen the storm coming before she left home so she had taken two cameras, one loaded with colour for the snakes, the other with black and white film, for the storm effects.

She had been in the willows when she heard a splash which she attributed to some large animal, a calf perhaps, so by the time she came to the water and parted the willows whatever had made the splash was gone, and Shawn Brenner was on the opposite bank jabbing repeatedly at the ground. 'It looked as though he was killing something,' she said. 'And when he stood up and threw it in the water it gleamed. It occurred to me he'd killed a snake and thrown it in the creek. I went on watching and then he slid down the bank and started soaking himself and his clothes. I thought it was some kind of revulsion associated with killing the snake, and it looked so odd that I took the pictures. That's all.'

Not quite, Miss Pink thought.

Pugh said: 'Why didn't you tell us before, miss? It's a week since the body was discovered.'

'You wouldn't have believed me.'

'She thought you'd say she was making it up in order to protect Sam Estwick,' Jerome explained.

'But she had the photographs.'

'We only just developed them this afternoon. My daughter doesn't have a criminal mind. What she thought she'd seen was a boy killing a snake and throwing it in the water. It never occurred to her that he'd been cleaning the knife with which he'd mutilated a body, and throwing that knife in the water.'

'The splash she heard was the body, him throwing the body—'

'She wasn't to know—'

'Rolling,' Miss Pink said. 'Rolling the body in. Shawn was only ten.'

The situation changed gear as their attention was transferred from Sarah to Miss Pink.

Sprague said thoughtfully: 'You knew it was Shawn before ever you saw those photographs.'

'I didn't know. I suspected.'

'Why?' Frankie asked. 'How? What on earth gave— Oh, I'm sorry.' She glanced at Pugh. 'You ask the questions.'

'I don't know when I started to suspect him,' Miss Pink confessed. 'Once one came to consider him, there were a number of pointers . . . I don't think it was when he said he saw a man carrying Birdie's body; if I suspected him as early as that, it would have been only of lying. Of course, it became increasingly obvious that he was out to get Sam. But when he seemed to change his tune, having – as he thought – got Sam into jail, or custody, or at least made sure he was the most obvious suspect . . . He changed his tune and implied it was someone else, and at that point I felt that this was something more than a bad boy getting his own back on a man who'd threatened him with a whipping.

'The people down here have been in a turmoil for over a week. It's one thing to have the neighbours suspecting there's a killer amongst themselves, but to have the press – and the police – at a loss, and at loggerheads, impotent: running after Estwick, then looking for someone else . . . Alex Duval forced to flee to the back country: all this on the say-so of one small boy, that was heady stuff. Shawn was manipulating the whole valley – and the visitors; he was cock of the walk but – and this was the strange thing – he was exposing himself to incredible danger, because he wouldn't divulge the identity of the killer. I thought he was lying. So might the murderer, but he couldn't be sure. It appeared that Shawn was stupid and reckless but then he talked to me and he was very polite and sensible, and even gave good reasons for some of his lies. Momentarily I was sorry for him: the confused little boy with too many "uncles" and no father, but when he left me I realised that I'd been manipulated; he'd *made* me feel sorry for him. I also realised that he was neither stupid nor reckless.'

'That didn't have to make him a murderer,' Sprague said. She ignored him. 'I thought him highly intelligent and very prudent. So how could that be reconciled with his claiming to know the identity of the killer? There was only one answer: that he was the killer himself. It was a fantastic answer but it was a theory, and once I'd entertained it, I started looking for facts. I had seen him come out of Wind Whistle when no one was home— '

'Duval never missed anything,' Pugh said. 'We asked him.'

'Probably there was nothing lying around that he could use at that moment and which he could conceal. The point about his entering Wind Whistle is that, when Sam Estwick went out to bury the deer just before Birdie was killed, he left his hunting knife lying on the kitchen table. Shawn was light-fingered. By his own admission he was there. It would be Shawn who unsaddled the pinto – and that was a move which would point to Sam.' She turned to Sarah. 'Birdie couldn't handle a saddle?'

'She might pull it off; I don't think she could lift it onto the buck. Sam or Paula would have unsaddled for her.'

'And how did this boy of ten carry the body of a six-year-old across a field to the creek?' Sprague asked sarcastically.

'He didn't. He told Birdie the Stone Hawk moved.'

Someone gasped. Sarah's eyes narrowed. Her parents were astonished. The police were utterly mystified. Miss Pink explained the tradition, and Sprague snorted his contempt for it.

'Birdie believed it,' she told him calmly.

'They all believe it,' Sarah said. 'At least, the little ones do.'

'So he lured her to the creek,' Miss Pink said. 'He must have slipped the knife inside his jeans, perhaps meaning to steal it originally? He didn't kill her with it. Probably he hit her with a branch and threw that in the creek or just left it to be washed clean by the rain. Before he rolled the body in he mutilated it. He knew that that, most of all, would point to an adult male. No doubt he got that idea from a video too.'

'Too?' Sprague echoed, his eyes glazing.

'He got some of his ideas from movies, and another source would be conversation between Maxine and Myrtle

212

and their visitors when no one paid any attention to a small boy listening in, perhaps after some particularly bad instance of child abuse.'

Pugh said: 'And you figure all this was a deliberate attempt to frame Estwick?'

'Of course it was. Shawn wanted his mother to marry Glen Plummer, who appeared to be very rich and had access to Arab horses, and who had promised him a pony. No doubt Shawn had Plummer weighed up – and the man did give everyone the impression of being a soft touch. But his mother was afraid the attentions of Sam Estwick would frighten Plummer off – and being what she is, Maxine could well have exaggerated Sam's nuisance value. Finally when Sam said he'd advise Plummer to put Shawn in a special school, Sam almost signed his own death warrant. Shawn never hated Birdie. She was the tool that would be used to frame Sam for murder. If Shawn could have done it, he'd have killed Sam himself. As it was, the state would do it for him.'

'He was too devious to do it himself,' Sarah said. 'He preferred to do it the way he did.'

Pugh threw her a glance but he addressed Miss Pink. 'If he was really after Sam, wanted him executed, why, once Sam was taken in for questioning, did he suggest the killer was someone else?'

'I think he was carried away by his own sense of power and this was a way of bringing terror back to the canyon: suggesting the murderer was still among them. But removing Sam was the most important aspect for Shawn and I've no doubt that within a day or two the boy would have said that he'd meant all along that he'd recognised Sam as the man carrying Birdie's body to the creek.'

'But this is monstrous!' Frankie exclaimed. 'He was a little boy!'

'There have been younger murderers. And they were equally good actors after the event.'

'Monsters,' Sprague muttered. His eyes were almost closed.

'You're the one who put it all together, ma'am.' Pugh's tone was gently insinuating. She gave him a thin smile. He returned it and went on: 'Someone might have thought it was doing society a favour to push him off the top of that tower.'

'How would they get back, Mr Pugh? Could you jump back?'

'No one could.'

Jerome said: 'So tomorrow we can go out and try to find Alex and bring him home?'

'Yes, sir, you can do that.' Pugh sighed. Sprague was asleep. 'I guess all we got left now is a mountain of paperwork. We'll start with the photographs. I'll make out a receipt.'

Chapter 17

'The police didn't ask *you* how you came to suspect Shawn,' Miss Pink remarked as she rode with Sarah above Horsethief next morning.

'There was no doubt about it when we saw the prints developing.'

Miss Pink refrained from pointing out that this did not answer the implied question; instead she studied Yaller's mane and considered an alternative gambit.

The morning was not conducive to discussion of murder. The storm had left the world fresh and sparkling with rain-washed colour. Puddles lay along the stockway, and on the pale pink mud were throngs of small butterflies the colour of the sky. Below the riders, in Horsethief, the leaves of the cottonwood canopy shimmered in a breeze, and the Barrier rock was bright and innocent in the sunshine.

Ahead of them the other ponies danced along the track; Miss Pink did not know where they were going except that it was to Limbo Canyon, but, despite unanswered questions, she did not feel insecure. There was no menace abroad today, otherwise why should Debbie and Jen have been allowed to help bring Alex in, with only Miss Pink and Sarah as escort? People's faith was touching – and based on a premise so false as to be contrived: that Shawn had died by accident. Now she said: 'You wouldn't have produced those photographs had the police not been considering Alex as a suspect.'

'Or anyone else. But you were very strong on Alex being the scapegoat.'

'Sprague was losing his sense of proportion: the unrest in

215

the valley forcing him to produce another suspect to replace Sam. And the police never give up on a man who has once been associated with a sex crime even when he was found not guilty. It's the theory of no smoke without fire.'

'Why did you leave me to tell them? You could have told them yourself.'

'It was better coming from you; you were a witness.'

'How could you know that? You didn't know about the photographs until last evening.'

'I kept quiet about one thing: I saw you in Rustler the day that Shawn was spying on you.'

'I know that; you saw me coming down from the Twist with him. There was no secret about it. You must have seen us from somewhere around here.' They looked to their right and saw the Twist above the slickrock.

'I saw you in Rustler,' Miss Pink insisted, and amended it immediately. 'I saw your horse tied below the Pale Hunter.'

'Where were you?'

'On top of the slickrock above Bighorn Spring. Alex showed me the way up; he thought it would amuse me. That's why I kept quiet: because I'd promised Alex that I wouldn't give him away. When we looked into Rustler the pinto was obvious immediately – it was hidden from you but not from us – and, with the glasses, I was able to find Shawn among the rocks of the reef. He was watching you, or rather, your horse.'

'I was after rattlers.'

'You'd been in Rustler the day before, picnicking with the Olson children. Shawn didn't go but he met you when you came down.'

'He did?'

'On the road. I was turning in at the Stenbocks' road-end and you were on your horse below your cabin talking to Shawn. He was on his bicycle.'

'I remember now. Of course I talked to him; he'd been left out of the picnic and was upset.'

'Did he think you'd taken them – or some of them – to the Cave of Hands?'

Sarah hesitated. 'Yes,' she said at length, 'he did. I hadn't, in fact; we had littluns with us and I wouldn't split the party. Shawn didn't believe me; he said I'd taken the older ones into the Maze and left the youngsters with Jen in Rustler. He said he was going to go up there on his own. I wasn't much bothered about that, he didn't have a pony; all the same I made a big thing about the snakes but he said that I didn't get bitten and the other kids didn't. I told him I was used to them, doing the photography and stuff for Dad, and maybe I said I was going up again next day. He must have seen me go, got the pinto from Paula, and followed me.'

'And you didn't know he was there, hiding in the rocks.'

'I had no idea. I'd never expect anyone to lend him a pony to go out on his own in the first place. He ill-treated animals unless you were watching him. I'm amazed that he managed to reach Rustler without the pony throwing him. Evidently he wanted to see the Cave of Hands so much he refrained from hitting it. How I came to know he was in Rustler was that the pinto neighed as I was coming back across the park.'

'What reason did he give for his being there?'

'That he thought, if he followed me, I'd lead him to the cave.'

'He didn't follow you. He just watched.'

'I'm only telling you what he said. I wasn't in the Maze. I was in the park, working.'

'With your horse at the Pale Hunter.'

'There are as many rattlers there as round the reef. We picnic under the Hunter; that brings rodents and so there are snakes.'

'And at that point you had no suspicion that Shawn had anything to do with Birdie's death.'

Sarah did not respond and Miss Pink gave no indication that she was expecting a response. They rode in silence, a companionable silence it might have seemed to a remote observer, someone watching from the far side of Horsethief, and then they came up to Jen and Debbie who had stopped.

217

'How far is it?' Debbie asked.

Sarah looked around like someone waking from sleep. 'About two miles after the Y; we must be coming up to it soon.'

'Then we go left?' Jen asked.

'Left at the Y, and when you reach the canyon, keep back from the edge.'

'Won't you be finished talking by then?' Debbie was wistful. She had been sent ahead with her half-sister while the grown-ups talked.

'How's the saddle?' Miss Pink asked. Debbie had persuaded Sam Estwick to let her use Birdie's old saddle.

'It's funny, like a chair. You can't fall out of it.'

'Be your age, miss,' Sarah said automatically.

Jen grinned and sped away, Debbie squealing with delight as her pony raced to catch up.

'She was the calm in the eye of the storm,' Miss Pink observed as they resumed their sedate progress. 'But I have the feeling that she knew considerably more than she let on.'

'She did.' Sarah was grim. 'At the rodeo Shawn warned her against Sam, said he liked little girls and never to be alone with him.'

'Little *girls*? A lie, of course, as was the one about little boys.'

'Even Debbie knew that, but she couldn't understand its significance. She knew Shawn was lying about Sam being dangerous but she didn't know why he should. Then when Birdie was killed and Sam was taken away (and the children thought he'd been imprisoned) she thought maybe this time Shawn wasn't lying.'

'So she told you about it.'

'She mentioned it, as something that puzzled her.'

'Shawn was preparing the way for Birdie's death. The premeditation is appalling.'

'I don't think he had it worked out to that extent. He was preparing the ground, and once he'd done that he'd wait for an opportunity. He might not have done anything, at least so soon, except that the thunder was right overhead just as he was at the Estwicks' road-end, and he bolted down there for cover.'

'And he found the cabin door open and the knife on the kitchen table. And then Birdie rode into the yard. And Shawn had just come down the track and he told her he'd seen the Stone Hawk move. When did he tell you?'

'He didn't tell me *that*. What he did tell me, on Sunday afternoon, before the police got to him, was that he'd seen a man carrying Birdie's body.'

'So he did talk to you. And at that point everything clicked into place. You remembered the sequence of events when you were in the willows on the bank of the creek: the splash that could have been a calf, and now you realised it was her body. You remembered Shawn cleaning a knife, not stabbing anything, throwing it – and not a snake – into the water; finally he waded in and washed off what had to be blood.'

'That's right,' Sarah said levelly, and waited for Miss Pink to continue.

'So by Sunday you'd guessed Shawn was the killer. In fact, you knew he was. Monday evening you came down from the picnic and met him and – did he demand that you take him up to the Cave of Hands?' A new thought struck Miss Pink. 'Did he say he was going to find the secret way down to the valley? You told him you were going up next day and he followed you. What I don't understand is why he didn't come down into the Maze after you, instead of waiting on the reef.'

'Maybe he was frightened of me . . . Maybe he was going to go down there after I left the park but the pinto gave the game away. It neighed. So I found him and guessed what he was up to and told him it was far too late in the day, that if he went down into the Maze he'd be coming back after sunset.'

'But there were cairns.'

'Snakes too; they come out in the dusk. That did frighten him – so he came down with me to the valley. I never thought he'd go up again next day, and on his own.'

'You were remarkably protective of a murderer.'

Sarah made no rejoinder. They had emerged from pinyons to a white rock rim. A thousand feet below them a creek shone in the bottom of a gulch that was a winding swath of vegetation. The sides of the canyon were layered in pink and puce and ivory.

'With Shawn,' Sarah resumed, 'warnings acted as a come-on. I told him about the dangers of the Maze. I told him not to go there.'

'And you knew he would. There were the cairns, after all.'

'He'd see the first cairn as he dropped down from the Pale Hunter. But they don't go all the way to the great cove – didn't, even before they were knocked down by some benefactor.'

'And Shawn went wrong where the cairns ended? Except that there was that trio of cairns between the well with the ash tree and the top of the tower.'

'Trio? I remember just two. You saw me knock them down.'

'There was a third: in the well itself, or rather at the entrance to the wrong joint. There had to be because otherwise how would Shawn know which joint to take? After he'd gone along the passage for some distance, he'd see the second cairn, at the place where you turn, and then he'd come to the gully and the obvious way up through the hole, and the easy crack to the top of the tower. If he had any doubts as to whether he was on the right track, he'd step out on top of the tower and there was the third and last cairn, at the place where you can so easily jump down. There had to be three cairns.'

'Probably there were, and I knocked the first one down by accident, perhaps just a duck, you'd never notice it. That will be what happened; I kicked it and never noticed.'

'That's what you were doing in the Maze when I saw your horse below the Pale Hunter: you were building three cairns.'

Sarah smiled. 'They've been there for decades.'

'They weren't there ten days ago.'

After a while Sarah asked: 'How many people know that?'

'Unless anyone else went up there after Dolly and me, no one other than myself.'

'Dolly knows?'

'No, she never saw the cairns, even the second time she went up. You must have knocked down the first one, the one in the well, before John Forset and Dolly reached you the day we found Shawn's body.'

'So only you know. That doesn't bother you?'

'Why should it? Even if I did talk, there's no proof as to who placed those cairns; there's no proof that ten days ago there weren't any cairns there. A good defence lawyer would pour scorn on the concept of an elderly lady climbing a sandstone tower and maintaining there was no cairn on the top. The case would never come to trial. The cairns served their purpose and they're gone. Were you never concerned that he was only ten years old?'

Sarah halted and they faced each other. She said: 'When a puppy's born that's deformed, like no back legs or something, you put it down immediately. If a pup with a damaged brain grows up vicious, you shoot it. The only way that age comes in is, you wish you'd known before it did any harm; you could have put down the one with a damaged brain at birth same as the one with no legs. Shawn was ten years old, but you forgot Birdie. She was six.'

'It was a slow way to do it,' Miss Pink pointed out. 'On top of the tower, and all those hours in the sun.'

'Actually not, he'd soon stop hurting, and for the person responsible it was the only safe way to ensure he didn't go to prison.'

'I thought it was the firing squad for first degree murder in this state.'

'Or lethal injection: you're given a choice. But that applies only to adults.'

Jen and Debbie were waiting for them. They had stopped on a prow of rock where there was a ring of stones on the ground and people had lit fires. Sarah nodded to them as she came up and everyone dismounted, tying the horses

221

to pinyons. The girls brought dead wood to the fire-ring while Miss Pink stood on the rimrock and surveyed the great canyon, speculating vaguely on the whereabouts of Alex Duval.

An eagle came floating along the rim, the sun gold on its back. It regarded Miss Pink incuriously and swept slowly on, looking for prey with the same cool detachment as it had looked at her.

There was a crackle of dry wood and she turned to see them placing green juniper on the fire. A pillar of smoke climbed above the rim. Debbie stepped forward and stood beside Miss Pink. 'He won't be long now,' she said. 'Soon as he sees the smoke he knows to come.'

They ate their lunch, and drank lemonade, and lay in the shade, taking turns to keep the smoke rising, to watch the thread of a trail that climbed towards them out of the trees hundreds of feet below. Miss Pink dozed, waking to see Debbie asleep, her hat over her face, her tiny feet in dirty sneakers, wearing a T-shirt with Snoopy the beagle on the chest. She frowned, remembering Birdie in her Mickey Mouse T-shirt. Feeling herself observed she looked up to find that Sarah was watching her. She nodded to the girl and went back to sleep.

Alex appeared about an hour later, coming up the trail at a steady pace. They watched and waited without excitement.

'Must have been the pits,' Debbie said. 'Living on deer meat and water for a week. No bread, no brownies, no baked beans.'

'I expect he brought some bread and stuff,' Jen said.

He waved as he came nearer and they all waved back. Now they could see his horse was labouring, and they heard its heavy breathing. Horse and rider were wet with sweat. They came out on the rim and Alex dismounted with a grunt. He gave the reins to Jen, and Debbie took him by the hand, leading him to the shade where there were sandwiches and beer and cakes. His eyes sparkled as the younger girls waited on him, their voices like the

222

gentle twittering of small birds. Miss Pink watched from a distance, her head cocked, a smile on her lips, thinking that there was something sweet and sexual, yet innocent, about the picture, hearing Sarah say: 'You start back with Debbie when we're ready. Jen and me will ride with Alex and tell him what happened.'

She agreed, appreciating that it could well be easier for him to learn of events from friends and without the presence of a comparative stranger which might be inhibiting, realising as well that information would have to be doctored for his ears.

So she rode back through the pinyons with Debbie, the sun hot on their backs, their hat brims shading their necks. Miss Pink was considering what subject she should broach that was appropriate for a little girl but which did not seem contrived, when Debbie said quietly: 'Sarah is telling Alex what happened. You have to be careful with him because he doesn't like it when people get hurt.'

'No one does,' Miss Pink said weakly.

Debbie threw her a speculative look. 'Most people are kind, but some aren't. Like Shawn. He was wicked, but Alex is so gentle he may get upset about Shawn being hurt, so Sarah has to leave out some of it.'

'Sarah told you that this was how she was going to – work it?'

'No, but I know Alex gets hurt easy and – well, I know; that's all.'

'I believe you do. Tell me, how much do you know?'

'I know about Birdie, and then what happened to Shawn.'

'The – accident?'

'It wasn't an accident.'

The horses' hoofs slopped in the dust below the pinyons. The trail was drying out and the puddles were long scoops of cracked mud.

'Everyone else can say it was an accident,' Debbie went on, 'but we know.' She smiled sweetly at Miss Pink.

'We?'

'You and me.'

'I don't follow.'

"Course you do. It was the Stone Hawk.'

Miss Pink slumped in the saddle. 'What was the Stone Hawk?'

Debbie sighed. 'Look, Shawn thought there was a way down through the Maze, right? And the pinto ran away when Shawn was in Rustler. He couldn't walk home, not without he could find the way down through the Maze – which isn't there, but he thought it was. Maybe someone gave him the idea there was a way down. We all know the real trail, the one to the Cave of Hands, starts when you get the Stone Hawk in line with the Blanket Man. He seems to have got it mixed up: the proper trail and the pretend one. He got the Hawk lined up with Blanket Man and came down through the Maze and walked off the last tower.'

'What's that got to do with the Stone Hawk? She can't be seen from the place where Shawn fell.'

'That's it! The Stone Hawk moved.'

Debbie made no attempt to break the ensuing silence, thinking correctly that her companion was working it out – not, of course, visualising a rock pinnacle moving over two miles (although after a night and a day on the bare cap of the tower Shawn would be hallucinating) but recalling Sarah's unshakeable confidence, and the fact that, whatever the fantasy, Shawn had died at the foot of the painted bird. As if Sarah had built the cairns merely as a pointer, a false guide, and left the rest to the Stone Hawk.